MW01340867

EPSILON ERIDANI

ENFIELD GENESIS – BOOK 4

BY LISA RICHMAN
& M. D. COOPER

SPECIAL THANKS

Just in Time (JIT) & Beta Reads

Gene Bryan
Marti Panikkar
Timothy Van Oosterwyk Bruyn
Scott Reid
Randy Miller

Version 1.0.0

ISBN: 978-1-64365-029-6

Cover Art by Andrew Dobell
Editing by Jen McDonnell, Bird's Eye Books

TABLE OF CONTENTS

FOREWORD

Cast your mind ahead a few years. We've made our first, fledgling steps toward colonization. Perhaps it's a habitat in orbit, or a colony on the moon, maybe even Mars.

For this to succeed, we'll need systems in place to deliver everything our colonists need to survive. One critical component will be medical care and supplies.

Now imagine our colony has in its possession a device. A digital-to-biological converter that can receive a file, transmitted from Earth, that will enable a doctor to reconstruct, on demand, any medicine a patient might need. Vaccines, antivirals, bacteriophages that kill infections. Insulin.

Not having to ship supplies such vast distances, not needing to wait to receive them, would be life-saving. A game changer.

But what would you say if I told you that this technology exists today? It does. It's in its infancy, and it's certainly not the size of a quarter, like the DBC units in *Epsilon Eridani*. But still, it exists.

Tech advances like this are what fire my imagination, and what make me yearn to see the future. And if I can't see it, well, within these pages, I can at least envision it.

I hope that in some small way with these stories, Michael and I are able to fire your imagination as well.

There's one more thing I've been meaning to say, something that's been on my mind for a while now. A recent event had me thinking that now might be a good time to tell you.

A few weeks prior to the publication of this book, the phrase 'like a house afire' took on an entirely new meaning for me. Thanks to a faulty piece of equipment, I found myself surrounded by an alarming blend of flashing red-and-blue lights that shone against the backdrop of a two-story conflagration.

I experienced heroism that night, on both a large and small scale.

As I stood in the snow, surrounded by those whose duty placed them in peril on behalf of others, I knew that, however often we thank them, it isn't nearly enough.

It is this kind of heroism, the drive to stand between the innocent and the profane in all its forms, that draws me to such tales as those found in Aeon 14. Tales where good triumphs over evil, and the weak are defended by the strong.

Idealistic? Tell that to the warrior who flies combat missions into hostile territory while under fire, or who charges forward into a wall of bullets to pull an injured soldier to safety.

Naïve? Tell that to the scientist who refuses to let the most recent batch of failed specimens discourage him from finding the next cure.

Jason, Terrance, and the Phantom Blade team are a disparate group, hailing from three different stars. They are diverse, both in culture and species, and yet they are united in purpose, their shared resolve compelling them to stand repeatedly between the innocent and the profane.

It is my hope that the story told in this book honors those who currently serve, or have served, their country—be it military or civilian. We owe you a debt of gratitude we can never repay. This story is dedicated to you.

The phrase “thank you for your service” is heard often; it is my hope that when you read it here, you know that it is deeply heartfelt.

Lisa
Leawood, 2019

WHAT HAS GONE BEFORE

An unlikely set of circumstances brought Alpha Centauri businessman Terrance Enfield and Proxan pilot-for-hire Jason Andrews together, along with an elite group of humans and AIs, to form Task Force Phantom Blade.

The black ops team, based out of El Dorado, was founded by the planet's prime minister, Lysander, the first AI to be appointed to such a high position throughout the known worlds. Terrance's company, Enfield Holdings, is a legitimate business that also functions as the white-side face of the clandestine organization.

Their first mission found the team going head-to-head against a criminal organization that had taken a ship full of more than two hundred and fifty AI refugees captive. Phantom Blade shut down the Norden Cartel, but not before they had managed to shackle and sell seventeen of the AIs from the *New Saint Louis* into slavery.

Their second mission, directed by an AI commodore in the El Dorado Space Force named Eric, led the team to Proxima Centauri and pitted them against a sociopathic serial killer named Prime.

Phantom Blade's third mission was simple: find and repatriate the final two shackled AIs, sold by the cartel to an unknown entity in Tau Ceti, a star system thirteen light years away. Unbeknownst to the team, Tau Ceti had fallen victim to nanotechnology run amok—and the two shackled AIs had been acquired as a last-ditch effort to save the planet, Galene.

The team ended up joining with Noa, the physicist forced to purchase the shackled AIs. Together, they stopped the phage, overthrowing an opportunistic tyrant bent on keeping the nanophage alive as a way to assure control over Galene.

Their mission parameters now complete, Phantom Blade takes some well-deserved time off en route to Epsilon Eridani. Their ship, the *Avon Vale,* has been commissioned to seed the route with communication buoys to enable a more rapid exchange of information.

While the team mulls over whether to disband or continue on as a covert team-for-hire, Terrance plans to set up a branch for Enfield Holdings to establish trade relations within the system.

The factions within the Epsilon Eridani system, however, might have something to say about that....

KEY CHARACTERS REJOINING US

Beck – One of the first cats to have been fully uplifted by Jason's mother, Jane Sykes Andrews, Beck (short for Bequerel, so named by Jason's physicist father) bonded with Terrance as a kitten. Beck became an unplanned yet fortuitous member of Phantom Blade during his heroic actions on Galene in *Tau Ceti*, where he aided in the takedown of a band of marauders.

Calista Rhinehart – Former ESF top gun, Calista was hired by Terrance to fill the role of Chief Pilot for Enfield Aerospace. Calista was recruited to Phantom Blade in the first *Enfield Genesis* book, *Alpha Centauri.* During their third mission, Calista was appointed captain of the Enfield Space Ship, ESS *Avon Vale*.

Jason Andrews – Son of Jane Sykes Andrews, grandson of Cara Sykes, Jason is a pilot and a bit of an adrenaline junkie. He is also one of the first few humans to exhibit the natural L2 mutation, which means that the axons—neural pathways—in his brain have a significantly higher number of nodes than a normal L0 human. They function as signal boosters, which allow him to process information at lightning speeds, and give him much faster reflexes than unaugmented humans have.

Jonesy – Calling him the 'best assistant this side of Sol,' Calista hired Jonesy for Enfield Aerospace as soon as his tour of duty was up. Jonesy followed Calista to Phantom Blade during their second mission, where he fell under the control of Prime, and was forced to try to kill Jason. During the long journey to Tau Ceti, Jonesy earned his engineering degree under Shannon's tutelage.

Khela Sakai – A former Captain of Marines in the Galene Space Force, Khela led a fourteen-person special operations team instrumental in the overthrow of a corrupt government. Her efforts put her in harm's way in more than the traditional sense: during *Tau Ceti*, Khela and Hana, the AI embedded with her, fell victim to the nanophage. Hana perished while embedded within Khela during Phantom Blade's third mission.

Kodi – An AI soldier on loan from the ESF to aid in the team's second mission, Kodi embedded with Terrance Enfield during the team's third operation, in Tau Ceti.

Landon – One of five AIs asked to join the original Phantom Blade team, he was illegally twinned prior to the events in *Alpha Centauri*, for a black op that went south. Landon is the more outgoing and garrulous brother; he fell in the line of duty, defending Jason's sister, Judith Andrews, from Prime in book 2, *Proxima Centauri*. In *Tau Ceti*, his twin, Logan, restored him, but Prime's brutal attack still haunts Landon.

Logan – Former ESF Military Intelligence profiler and AI-hunter, Logan was appointed by Senator Lysander to Phantom Blade. He has always been the more taciturn twin. Logan was instrumental in the team's bid to wrest possession of Galene's Main Elevator from hostile forces in the team's third mission to Tau Ceti.

Noa Sakai – As a young man, Noa had rejected his ties to the Sakai family's ancient underworld crime Family, the Matsu-kai. Events in *Tau Ceti* force him to reluctantly embrace them one final time, in order to save the star system from the Phage. He joined Phantom Blade, along with his daughter, Khela, for their mission to Epsilon Eridani.

Shannon – Former chief engineer for Enfield Aerospace's TechDev Division, Shannon is one of the original five AIs recruited to Task Force Phantom Blade. She is currently embedded in the ESS *Avon Vale,* and harbors a secret longing to experience humanoid life.

Terrance Enfield – Grandson of Sophia Enfield, and the former CEO of Enfield Aerospace, Terrance now runs Enfield Holdings, the shell corporation under which Phantom Blade operates. He is the first Enfield in Alpha Centauri to partner with an AI, a former El Dorado Space Force lieutenant named Kodi.

Tobi – One of the uplifted cats bred by Jane Sykes Andrews as companion pets for families living in habitats and on ships. Tobi helped Tobias accompany Jason, carrying his core around in her harness, since AIs cannot embed inside an L2 human.

Tobias – A **Weapon Born AI**, Tobias left Sol after the Sentience Wars to settle in Proxima. There, he formed a close friendship with the Sykes-Andrews family. Along with Lysander—another Weapon Born—he was influential in Jason's early life as a friend, tutor, and mentor, often worn in a harness by a partially uplifted Proxima cat who accompanies the human.

Weapon Born AIs – These are powerful creatures, among the first non-organic sentients in existence. They first appeared in Sol two centuries ago, the product of an illicit experiment involving the imaged minds of human children—a blank canvas upon which nation-states could forge the perfect, obedient soldier. What they got instead were intelligent, self-aware beings who fought for the right to exist in freedom. Tobias—and AIs of his ilk—are practically living legends to other AIs.

THE TECH OF ENFIELD GENESIS

Colloid Nano – Colloids are extremely tiny insoluble particles that are so light, they remain suspended in air. When grafted onto nano, colloid nano clouds can be released.

Thanks to brownian motion, the force of the particles in the air around them is greater than the force of gravity attempting to pull them down, and so they float, and are susceptible to the activity of air currents.

In the thirty-third century, colloid nanobots themselves aren't capable of independent motion; production is not yet capable of creating any form of propulsion small enough to apply to nano.

Colloidene Nano— A colloidene is made from a colloid particle but formed just like single-layer graphene. Patterned in a honeycomb lattice, it employs some of the click-assembly techniques used in chemistry.

Pre-loaded common codes, or 'bricks', give nano creation a jump-start. The result is a nanobot programmed to rapidly alter existing nano to whatever the person controlling it needs it to be.

E-SCAR – Electron-beam Special Combat Assault Rifle

Elastene– A material made using electrospinning techniques on graphene. As its name implies, Elastene has shape-memory properties that allow it to store and release an unprecedented amount of mechanical energy. That means a ship clad in the substance can dissipate heat much faster than any other spacecraft in existence.

Engines built from Elastene can run for longer periods, at up to twenty percent higher speeds than prior output allowed.

Engineering Elastene into a metal foam creates a surface with an elasticity far more successful at deflecting micrometeorites and other impacts than current materials. Its shape-memory properties absorb the kinetic energy of the impact, spreading it across a much greater surface area.

Wearable Elastene – During the fifty-plus-year journey to Tau Ceti, the engineers aboard the *Avon Vale* learned to extrude Elastene as a stretchy fabric.

Most commonly used in military operations, Elastene can function as a deflector for weapons fire. In addition, certain Elastene weaves function as ultra-black Faraday cages, allowing for covert operatives to more easily obscure breaching nano from active scan.

MFRs – Matchbook Fusion Reactors, a new power source invented by Enfield Aerospace on El Dorado in the late thirty-second century by then-chief engineer Shannon. It made use of a Localized Micro-Plasma, and was portable and interchangeable. Taking less than half the volume of current reactors, the new energy source allowed Phantom Blade to replace the original engines on their ship, the *Avon Vale*, with eight reactors where there had originally been only two.

Snowflake Nano – Phantom Blade's own personal, electronic breadcrumb trail. Each snowflake, like its namesake, has a unique geometric signature. That signature is contained in the database of a Phantom Blade app. The app registers the negative space created by each snowflake on whatever surface it resides. Once a snowflake is tagged as 'in use', the search app would keep track of the void that particular snowflake made, pinpointing its location while it remains in range. Also applied to micro drones.

True Stasis – True stasis employs the cessation of all atomic motion, as opposed to its predecessor, cryo-stasis. With true stasis, there is no risk of cellular damage brought about by freezing. An individual in stasis could emerge decades—even centuries—later, essentially unchanged.

MAPS & DIAGRAMS

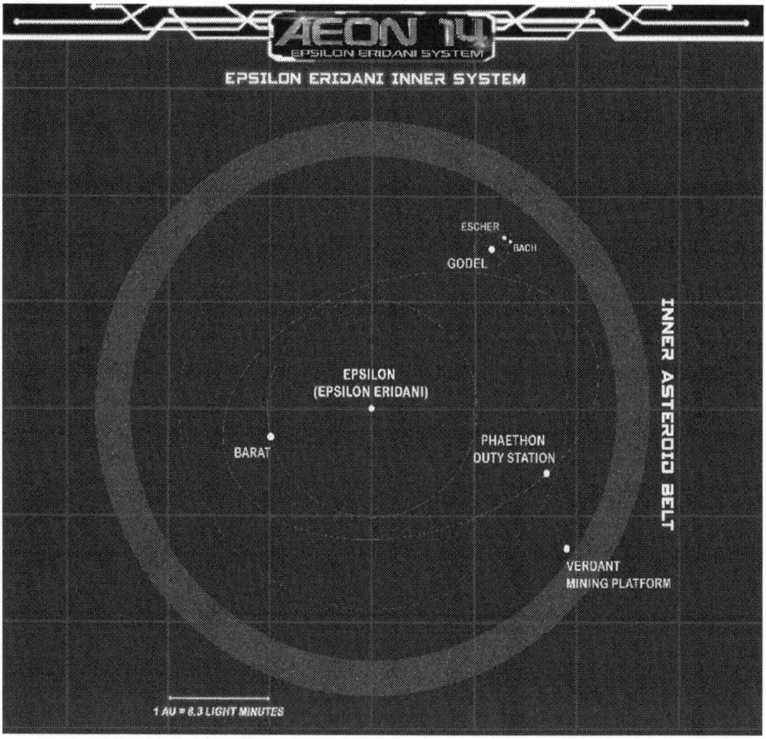

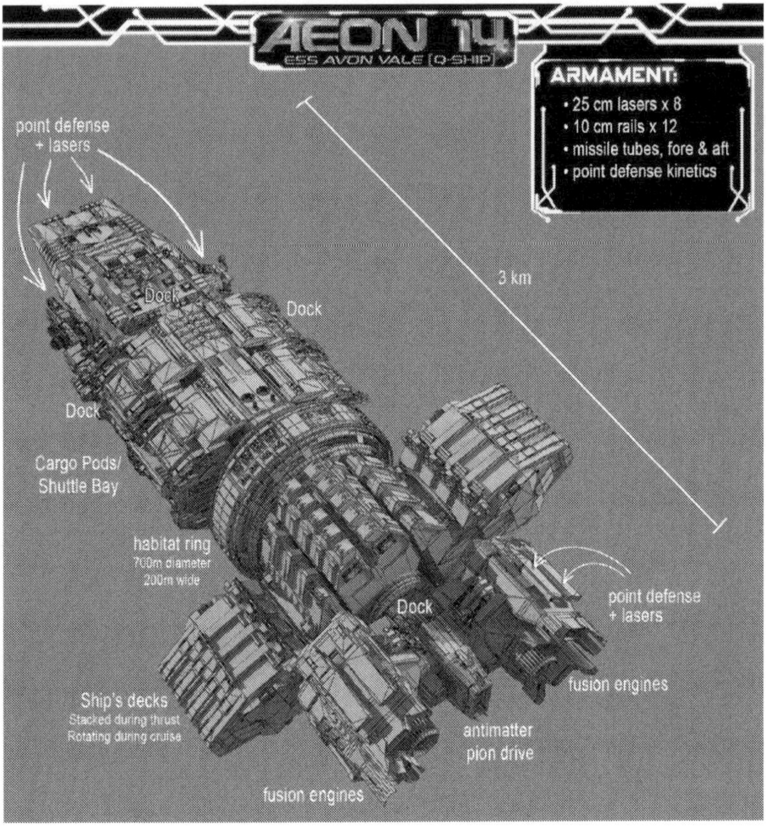
AEON 14
ESS AVON VALE [Q-SHIP]
ARMAMENT:
• 25 cm lasers x 8
• 10 cm rails x 12
• missile tubes, fore & aft
• point defense kinetics
point defense + lasers
3 km
Dock
Dock
Dock
Cargo Pods/ Shuttle Bay
habitat ring
700m diameter
200m wide
Dock
point defense + lasers
fusion engines
Ship's decks
Stacked during thrust
Rotating during cruise
antimatter pion drive
fusion engines

PART ONE: THE SNARE

WEB OF DECEIT

STELLAR DATE: 03.05.3272 (Adjusted Gregorian)
LOCATION: Presidium Offices, Humans' Republic
REGION: Hauptstadt, Barat, Little River (Epsilon Eridani system)

"It's confirmed," Giovanni Perelman informed the Citizens' Council. "Our operatives have successfully infiltrated the Verdant Mining platform."

He allowed the news to sink in as his gaze rested momentarily on Premier Rachelle Feretti before moving to the other two in the secured room, deep inside Barat's Presidium. Citizen Coletti was Barat's Director of Commerce, while Citizen Savin led the planet's Republican Guard.

Both women held their expressions carefully in check as they awaited the premier's response to his pronouncement.

Feretti was by far the most dangerous person in the room, though Giovanni knew his own reputation was a bit disingenuous. He was the Citizen Director of Public Safety and Information, but there was nothing safe about the Human Republic's top spy, although he did deal in information.

As he awaited Peretti's judgement, a part of his mind noted that, of the four, only the premier allowed herself a splash of color among an otherwise muted palette. None of the rest—including Giovanni—would dare.

The severe lines and somber colors of their dress faithfully reflected the ruthless nature of the organization that had founded the colony almost two hundred years ago.

Ironic, given that the most ruthless among them was the

premier.

It would have come as no surprise to anyone familiar with the Sol-based corporation, EpiGen, to learn it had spawned a totalitarian regime. Nor that this regime was primed to expand its territory in Little River.

The aforementioned mining platform was attached to an asteroid in Little River's Inner Asteroid Belt. NaWai was its name, and it had been claimed by their sister planet, Godel, decades before.

None on Barat had known at the time the riches the frozen rock had secreted in its depths. Had they known, they surely would have contested Godel's claim. It was far too late now. That meant Barat would have to resort to other, more devious methods.

This didn't worry Giovanni. The Humans' Republic of Barat was a proven master in the art of being devious.

"These operatives of yours." The premier slanted a glance his way. "Have they managed to sow discord among the employees living on Verdant, as promised?"

Giovanni smiled in smug satisfaction as he gave a brief nod. The discord she'd inquired about had been no mean feat to pull off, considering the platform housed close to five thousand miners, their families, and ancillary support staff.

"Our agents have gained access to the environmental systems," he assured her. "We instructed them to engineer small failures at first, and to leak information suggesting mismanagement and lax safety protocols."

His smile was one of carefully contrived confidence. "The first stirrings of unrest have already begun. Our final act of sabotage will look like a structural failure. We've planted evidence that points to company neglect, purposely hidden from its people. Panic should spread quickly. With a little encouragement, it'll escalate to rioting once the platform is compromised."

"Very good," Premier Feretti's normally expressionless face thawed into a brief smile. She turned expectantly to the head of the

Republican Guard. "And you have a Guard ship ready to render aid?"

Willa Savin nodded. "We do. We have a cruiser with a company of Marines conveniently testing out an engine refit in that sector. They will be ready to provide relief and humanitarian assistance—and of course take over, should the company's treatment of its employees be deemed insufficient."

"Excellent. How soon, then, before we can claim Verdant as a protectorate of Barat?" The avarice in Natasha Coletti's eyes told Giovanni that the Director of Commerce had big plans for Verdant's profits. He'd be willing to bet a significant cut ended up lining her own coffers.

"We need to give it a few days," he cautioned, eyes flicking briefly to the premier to gauge her reaction to his words. "We want to be very sure there is no possible way they can prevent the riot before we commit to any action. That way, Godel cannot protest our very legitimate offer of humanitarian relief. Nor our actions, when we discover the 'deplorable conditions' there."

Giovanni knew he was hedging, not committing to an actual start time, but it was the only way to be certain of success.

"Well, it can't come soon enough." Coletti frowned, arms crossed and with a look of clear disapproval on her face. "Those fools on Godel will no doubt levy sanctions against us for this, just like they did over the shipping lanes. But if our intel is correct—" she shot Giovanni an unreadable look, which somehow managed to question his competence, "and the vein of crystal that Verdant found inside Na Wei truly is pure, unrefined silica, then it's worth the risk."

"And that's where the second stage of our operation comes into play," Giovanni rebutted in a mild tone, refusing to show weakness in front of Feretti. "Should they decide to come to the defense of Verdant, they will quickly find themselves too busy managing crises at home to burden themselves with a mining concern half an AU away. I daresay you won't need to concern yourself over repercussions on that front."

Premier Feretti tilted her head to one side, one tastefully shod leg crossed over the other, foot gently rocking back and forth in thought. "Expand on that," she ordered Giovanni.

He nodded and rose, striding to the controls embedded in the room's encrypted and segmented console. As his fingers danced over the unit, a holotank sprang to life, displaying the blue-and-green orb that was Godel.

"We've managed to smuggle several Digital-to-Biological Converters to our agents on Godel," he informed them as the globe rotated and three glowing icons appeared. "We've identified these critical locations as major planetary food distribution warehouses. Our assets are working on infiltrating the targets now; the DBCs will be operational by the time we're ready to activate our saboteurs on Verdant."

As he spoke, Giovanni slipped a hand inside his pocket, fingers encountering the smooth, centimeter-thick disc hidden there. *Such a small thing to wield such destructive power,* he marveled.

The DBC converters were biological printers. Each one was able to reproduce high fidelity, complex synthetic DNA from files sent to them via encrypted transmission. Each unit could print, on demand, any biological material, from vaccines to weaponized pathogens. Depending on the need at the time, it could preserve life—or take it.

"All we need to do," he said, "is send the DBCs the design for the disease that we'll introduce to Godel's food supply."

Giovanni triggered the holoanimation of the projected outcome. "The mycelia spores we've chosen have been engineered to spread at a rate of sixty percent per day, and at under twenty microns, the spores are such fine particulates that they easily remain in suspension, in the air."

The holoimage morphed from diseased plant life to a blackened cloud, drifting over a field of crops. "The resulting spore cloud will drift along on air currents, dispersing rapidly. It has the added benefit of being highly flammable, so we've equipped the DBC units with the ability to generate a spark, once enough of the biological agent has been printed and distributed. The resulting explosion will depend on the conditions within the warehouses and food production facilities."

He spared the table a glance. "We believe that a single outbreak will serve to capture the attention of the people; three such outbreaks within a few days' time will cause a public outcry and a demand that Godel's government take action."

Natasha lifted her head, eyes narrowing in thought. "Yes, this should keep their hands full," the woman murmured. "And if Godel decides to divide their resources?"

Willa's expression turned speculative. "Godel's leadership might be soft and undisciplined compared to our own, but they're not stupid. Any attempt by those in power to spend time and energy on a police action on a faraway platform will certainly be frowned upon."

"Indeed," Giovanni hastened to agree, with a quick glance at his premier.

"Mmm, yes." The premier's voice took on a mocking tone, her expression cold. "It would be highly irresponsible of those in power to expend resources on a relatively small, privately-held mining company when they have such serious domestic issues at hand. Should they be foolish enough to consider such a move, I'm certain a suggestion can be made to the opposition party."

She smiled, a predator toying with her prey. Giovanni saw the cold calculation in her eyes, and something deep within warned him that he would do well to avoid placing himself within her sights.

SPYCRAFT

STELLAR DATE: 03.05.3272 (Adjusted Gregorian)
LOCATION: State House, New Kells
REGION: Godel, Little River (Epsilon Eridani system)

At the same time, almost a full AU rimward of Barat....

Simone could just make out the soft patter of raindrops from where she waited at the far end of the room. They were striking the panes of real glass before which Edouard Zola stood, looking out. The sound would provide a welcome backdrop to the presidential briefing, if the rain held.

It made the intelligence officer uneasy to see her president in such a vulnerable spot, standing before the large expanse with the Director of Intelligence beside him, admiring the view.

They seemed so open, so…exposed.

She knew the glass was reinforced by an ES field and threaded with countless carbon nanotube strands—just a few of the security measures emplaced to prevent unknown enemies from waging an attack against the leadership of the planet the AI called home.

It was a bit of cognitive dissonance the intelligence analyst admitted privately to herself, for Simone knew that the president and Director Mastai were standing in one of the most zealously guarded locations on the planet.

Wherever President Zola was in residence became a bastion of security. She knew this. And yet, the disturbing sensation that they were in danger refused to be banished from her mind as she took in the vista on the other side of the glass.

Carefully-tended gardens, gently rolling hills whose valleys stubbornly clung to pillowed brumes. Overlaying it all was a blanket of indigo-hued clouds, the rain spilling forth, lending the landscape a watercolor smoothness.

It was a day tailor-made for the cozy fire that crackled a welcoming greeting along an adjacent wall.

At times like this, Simone almost wished for a real, organic frame so that she might better experience what Zola liked to call the 'creature comforts'.

Loath to interrupt the precious few moments her superiors had free between meetings, Simone had politely refused the invitation to join them at the window. She heard their voices quietly discussing the single-page daily brief the presidential cabinet had prepared for their review, as she settled comfortably into a resting stance.

Her position was strategically situated just inside the room's entrance, at the edge of the plush rug that covered the reinforced faux-tile flooring. Any attackers would have to get through her before harm came to her superiors.

Unless they came from above or below.

She forced herself to dismiss such possibilities, focusing on what she could control, which was the doorway. She spent a few minutes reviewing the section of today's brief that warranted her inclusion in the president's meeting instead.

She'd been invited to such briefings before, but could count on one hand—the five-fingered variety—the number of times it had happened.

Simone's job at the Directorate was to study and analyze Barat's economic and political climate. A report by a junior analyst had recently caught her attention. The analyst's brother worked on Verdant's mining platform—a privately held entity situated in the inner asteroid belt—and was growing uneasy about the talk he'd been hearing lately.

Given the crystal the company was mining, the Directorate had felt that someone should bring this to the attention of the State House. It was this intel that had brought Simone here today.

A noise behind her alerted her to the presence of another; that same person's entrance also garnered the attention of the two at the window.

"Nico," Edouard greeted the man who had just entered.

As Nico stepped in behind her, Simone saw the presidential security detail send a sweeping glance through the room before keying it shut behind the man.

Nico was the Assistant Director of Intelligence and Simone's immediate superior. He gave Simone a brief, assessing nod as he responded to his commander-in-chief.

"Sir," he greeted, "I'm sorry to keep you waiting, but the Directorate received a report out of Barat just as I was leaving. Given what Simone's here to brief you on," he nodded toward the AI, "we felt it was best to confirm the information before I came over."

Celia Mastai's gaze momentarily unfocused, indicating she was scanning the electronic missive her assistant director had forwarded. Her eyes snapped to Nico's and then over to Simone before sending the two a curt nod.

"Good call, Nico. It fits with Simone's report," she commended, turning to the president. "Sir, we—"

Zola held up his hand, causing Celia to pause.

"Elie," Zola called out, addressing the pickups that would ping his assistant the moment the man uttered her name, "would you mind sending in a servitor with fresh coffee for us, please?"

"Happy to, sir."

At Elie's response, he gestured to the collection of comfortable chairs and sofas arranged into a small conversational group by the fire. "If Nico's going to be the bearer of bad news, as I suspect from your expressions he is," he said with a genuine smile as they each chose a seat, "then the least I can do is fortify you first with a decent cup of java."

Once the servitor had arrived, Zola waved for Nico to begin as the president began pouring coffee for the two humans.

Nico, in turn, shot Simone a look, nudging his head toward the president. "Let's start with what you learned from one of your analysts."

Zola shifted in his seat, and Simone found herself under her president's intense regard. As he handed Nico his cup of coffee, she said simply, "It's Verdant Mining, sir."

Edouard Zola raised a brow at Simone as he sat back in his seat, looking from her to Nico. "The company that just discovered the vein of HPQ on NaWei?" he queried, mentioning the crystal-rich asteroid.

Nico nodded, pausing to take a sip. He swallowed, then added, "One and the same."

Zola shook his head as he reached across and handed Celia her cup. The woman took it silently, her expression contemplative.

Silicon dioxide—more commonly known as silica—was one of the more plentiful compounds in the universe. High purity quartz silica, on the other hand, was not.

Most silicas were structurally bound to elements such as lithium, titanium or aluminum. While it wasn't impossible for thirty-third century nanotechnology to unbind such contaminants, the process was time-consuming and expensive.

Which made the discovery of high-grade silicon dioxide by a Godel-based mining company a newsworthy event.

"One of our junior analysts has family on Verdant," Simone explained. "He contacted her this morning. Said he wanted to send his kids back to Godel; it didn't feel safe there any longer."

Edouard Zola raised an eyebrow. "Did he say why?"

Simone nodded. "He mentioned there has been talk that the company is cutting corners on the platform's safety, although he told our analyst that the rumors circulating about imminent environmental failure are completely untrue."

"Our analyst told us her brother works on those systems," Nico added, "and that, while they aren't state-of-the-art by any means, the company isn't cutting corners, like the stories the dissenters are spreading."

Celia grimaced and shook her head. "Verdant's never going to make the Top One Hundred list of best places to work, but they're far from the worst," she observed.

"Agreed."

"You think Barat's behind this unrest," Edouard guessed, and Simone nodded.

"Given what they're mining out there, it's possible, yes," she qualified.

Godel itself was a planet gifted with a rich supply of the crystalline substance; Barat, however, was not. Their sister planet purchased much of their HPQ silica from Godel. This had been a sore point for the Humans' Republic ever since the crystal's discovery by Godel, shortly after the planet had been handed over to the colonists by the FGT.

"Okay, we've hurt them recently by placing trade sanctions on any HPQ they buy from us," Zola mused, one trouser-clad leg crossed over the other, elbow resting on the upholstered arm of his chair. One finger tapped his chin, the other was cupped around his half-forgotten coffee as his eyes slitted in thought.

"True," Celia admitted, "but that was only after they had stepped up their harassment in the shipping lanes."

Edouard looked up sharply. "And in response to the deplorable conditions we found on Barat's Hadera Station last month, when we rescued those poor workers," the president reminded her.

She nodded her agreement as Nico straightened. "That brings us to the reason why I was late to this meeting," he said, leaning forward, resting his elbows on the arms of his chair, hands clasped loosely. "We just got word that Barat's premier has ordered their silica distillation plants to ramp up. They're to triple their output by year's end."

"That report you just received says that Barat is dangerously low on pure silica crystal," Celia noted, setting her cup down onto the table next to her. "Given the impact our tariffs have had on the price of the HPQ silica they buy from us, finding an alternative source of pure silicon dioxide could prove to be an irresistible lure."

Edouard Zola sat perfectly still, eyes narrowed in contemplation as he rubbed his thumb along his jawline.

"So," he said after a moment, drawing out the word on a slow exhale, his eyes landing first on Celia, then Nico, and finally Simone. "You're suggesting the rumors are some sort of first step toward gaining access to that vein of HPQ?"

Simone glanced at Nico and then back. "It's just speculation, mind you, but given the rise in complaints about the condition on the platform, they could try to throw the Hadera incident in our faces."

"Make us out to be hypocrites, given the conditions reported on Verdant?"

Simone nodded at Zola's response. "Take it over, under the guise of a benevolent humanitarian intervention. They might even go so far as to sabotage the platform themselves, creating an emergency at a time when they're conveniently nearby to stage a rescue."

Edouard glanced sharply at them. "You think Barat's orchestrating a takeover, don't you?"

His comment was more statement than speculation; they all knew it, for they all believed the same.

Nico nodded. "Not enough evidence yet to prove it, but my gut's screaming at me, sir."

His gaze shifted from Nico to Simone for a few weighted moments as the man contemplated the situation.

"You know," the president said slowly, "you might want to find a reason to visit Phaethon soon."

Simone knew her expression must reflect her startlement at the non sequitur the man had just made. Phaethon was a converted transfer station built by the FGT to ship cargo between the two planets as they were being terraformed.

A standard spoke-and-wheel configuration, the station followed an elliptical path whose orbit crossed that of both Barat and Godel in a carefully-calculated dance.

But what does the duty station have to do with—ohhhh, she interrupted herself mentally as she caught the expectant look on Edouard Zola's face just as she recalled where Phaethon's orbit currently placed it in relation to the NaWai asteroid and its mining platform. "Sir," she said with a smile, "that's a very good idea. I've not been out there to visit in a while. I'll leave this afternoon."

Zola sat back, a satisfied expression on his face. "Good. Interesting that your flight path will pass so close by Verdant, isn't it?"

Simone smiled slyly at her commander-in-chief. "Complete coincidence, sir."

As she rose and took her leave of the three, she overheard Zola ask after a missive the Directorate had received yesterday morning, an encrypted transmission from the prime minister of a neighboring system: Alpha Centauri.

"Isn't that where the Enfield Corporation relocated its headquarters to?" Simone heard Nico ask, just as the door slid shut behind her.

* * * * *

Simone hitched a ride to Phaethon Duty Station on the diplomatic courier ship *CSS Charade*. The ship, crewed by a small complement of Commonwealth Navy and Marines, was carrying a packet of hyfilms for the Trade Commission office as well as a single diplomatic passenger.

The attaché, who was stationed at Phaethon but had been vacationing on Godel, was an old friend of Simone's and the one who had suggested she join her on the courier ship. Simone had been assured that the slight detour a close pass by NaWai and Verdant would necessitate wasn't an issue, and she had readily accepted.

Once on board, Simone learned that Barat seemed to be turning up the heat everywhere, not just around the inner asteroids and shipping lanes. The courier ship had just received word that a Godel agent had been arrested by Barat in the duty station, on spurious charges that were clearly falsified.

They would use this transit time to formulate a plan to get her back, if Barat refused to yield to the political pressures the station's diplomatic attaché would bring to bear.

As they approached Verdant, Simone directed the ship's AI, Charlotte, to request a brief stopover. The station controller who responded cautioned that the platform was closed to visitors at the moment. Simone replied that they were here at the request of a friend to pick up two children for passage to Godel.

Reluctantly, the controller allowed them to dock.

<*I'll be back shortly,*> Simone assured Charlotte. <*Just need enough time to see for myself what conditions are like, and get a feel for the emotional state of the platform's residents.*>

<*Are we really picking up the kids?*> Charlotte asked curiously.

<*If Barbara's brother still wants them off Verdant, then yes,*> Simone confirmed. <*And not just because it makes for a good cover. If they were my children and they were in danger, I'd want someone to do the same for me.*>

<*We can't return directly to Godel,*> Charlotte's voice was troubled.

<*I know, it adds another few days to their trip to come along with us to Phaethon,*> Simone admitted, <*but it's better than the alternative. Could I send them with you, when you're ready to make the return trip?*>

<*Of course,*> Charlotte assured Simone, sending the analyst a warm surge of reassurance.

Three hours later, a very troubled Simone boarded the *Charade,* two children in tow. The junior analyst's brother had not overstated the situation. A brief conversation with the AIs on the platform confirmed the Directorate's suspicions: someone was stirring up trouble on Verdant.

PART TWO: THE STING

TARGET: ACQUIRED

STELLAR DATE: 03.08.3272 (Adjusted Gregorian)
LOCATION: Phaethon Duty Station
REGION: Little River, Inner System

The day after the *CSS Charade* departed Verdant, a small team of citizen soldiers moved stealthily among the merchant's bazaar that was one of Phaethon Duty Station's main attractions.

The operation was carefully staged; booths filled with colorful bolts of cloth, handmade ceramics, and batches of aged lagers masked their presence. Their ability to maintain stealth was rather impressive, considering their uniforms were required to pull off this charade. The stiff greys and blacks of their duty fatigues stood in stark contrast to the colorful atmosphere exuded by the bazaar.

<Heads up! Target is preparing to move.>

The words came softly over Sergei's citizen's implant, galvanizing him into action. Abandoning caution in favor of speed, Sergei skipped his way through the network he'd been hacking, seeking the backdoor their mole inside Godel's Trade Commission had promised.

There.

Sergei heaved a sigh as the system subverted to his control. He spared a glance at his surroundings to reassure himself that they remained hidden from public view, tucked behind the canvas of a vendor's booth.

He returned his attention to his HUD.

<I'm in,> he announced as he inserted his version of the duty station's map and forced an auto-update to the public feed. He'd

barely made it in time.

The feed coming from the spotter showed their targets, two crew of the Centauri ship the *Avon Vale,* seated at a café on the border of Phaethon's retail district. As he watched, one of them called a servitor to the table to close out their tab. They seemed unaware that their movements were being observed with keen interest by six Citizen Soldiers of the Humans' Republic of Barat.

Sergei was pleased to note the Centauri hadn't appeared to notice the auto update either, nor the change to the duty station's map. The map, available to all visitors over Phaethon's public net, was a key element of this subterfuge. It wasn't impossible to entice their victims into Barat Territory without it, but the map made their jobs just that much easier.

The subterfuge was carefully reinforced by the appearance of the merchants' booths just inside Barat; the shopkeepers there had been instructed to closely mimic the look and feel of nearby booths run by Godel shopkeepers, in order to blur the lines between the two territories as much as possible within the bazaar. This was by design, as it helped maintain the illusion of safety.

He knew from experience that these shops were much nicer than the ones outside the bazaar, those that were closer in to the center of Barat's on-station presence.

It wasn't that the Citizen Guard cared one whit about their merchants' financial success, nor did they care all that much about appearances, except where it could further their goals. This fiction was simply a useful tool, one that helped the Citizen's Guard ensnare the occasional high-value target for the Republic.

Today's ruse was one Sergei had performed more than once; as soon as their victims crossed over into the Barat-run side of the bazaar, he and his fellow soldiers could stop them for unauthorized entry. A routine search would then reveal stolen merchandise, conveniently planted on the trespassers. A citizen's arrest would follow.

This man and woman were of particular interest, as they hailed from another star—a rarity here in the system its inhabitants had named Little River. Their ship had been tagged by Barat's Public Safety and Information Office as an object of interest shortly after the *Avon Vale* had entered the heliopause and transmitted their intent to establish peaceful trade.

Those working Godel's Trade Marina had issued an invitation to the vessel and assigned it a docking slip before the visitors had even had a chance to respond to the Republic's initial overtures.

Typical of Godel.

The moment the Centauri ship had accepted Godel's offer, plans had been set in motion to acquire some of the ship's personnel as leverage. They would be held in exchange for whatever tech Godel received, ensuring Barat received the same advantages.

As luck would have it, the two targets Sergei's team had identified were both high-value: the ship's captain and its executive officer.

"Sssst!" The sibilant whisper cut through the tense silence that permeated the small group of Citizen Soldiers seconded to this mission. It was followed by a sharp jab, as an elbow connected with his ribs. "The Citizen Lieutenant just ordered us to relocate. We're to move three rows closer to the target. Come on!"

Sergei frowned, but didn't allow his fellow soldier's demand to interfere with his concentration as he manipulated the interface he was using to monitor their targets.

<You're breaking protocol. Use your implant,> he warned her as he gathered his kit and stood.

Stepping out from behind a colorful wall of fabrics, he shot a cursory glance down the row of wares before he crossed over and followed the woman across the next two aisles. Securing his gear, he reached for his weapon, then watched as the servitor approached the targets as they rose from their table....

* * * * *

Jason Andrews, executive officer of the ESS *Avon Vale*, pushed his empty plate aside and signaled the café's servitor to close their account as he glanced across the table at his captain.

Seeing that her attention was caught by something within Phaethon's merchant bazaar, he reached over to snag the last pineberry off Calista's plate. He grinned unrepentantly and deftly evaded her hand, popping the fruit into his mouth as she swatted at him for his poaching.

"Gotta introduce Jonesy to these babies," he observed from around the bite of sweet, white fruit. "See if he can't find a way to add them to the *Avon Vale*'s gardens."

Growing exotic fruits was one of the ship's engineer's favorite hobbies, and Jason knew this oddly-colored, mildly pineapple-flavored version of a strawberry was something that would intrigue Jonesy.

"Never ceases to amaze me," Calista murmured, and he shifted his gaze from the colorfully-swathed people milling about to study the woman who sat across from him: captain, lover, and friend.

"What, Jonesy's considerable assets?" he asked with a waggle of his eyebrows and a sardonic grin, but she just shot him a look and made a vague gesture to their surroundings.

"All this," she explained, chin resting in the palm of one hand, her expression contemplative. "When you think about it, there's very little difference between this station and any random one in Alpha Centauri—or Tau Ceti, for that matter." She nodded in the direction of the buttressed support beams that formed the clearspan space above their heads. "A bulkhead is pretty universal, you know."

"You mean galactic. We have no idea what kind of station some aliens out in the Andromeda galaxy or the LMC might design," he pointed out, then ducked as she threw a roll at him, a reluctant smile teasing the edge of her mouth.

"You know what I mean, flyboy. A bulkhead's a bulkhead, but

all this," she gestured around at the merchant's bazaar that surrounded them, "somehow has its own unique flavor, distinct from anything I've ever experienced."

Jason cocked his head as they rose to leave, considering her words. "Well, we are almost thirteen light years away from Centauri. Not like we can call back to ask about the latest recipes or fashion styles."

"I know that, Andrews." He twisted to avoid the punch she threw at his shoulder and then scowled over at her, massaging his arm as they walked toward the café's exit.

She looped her hand through his arm in a conciliatory gesture that made him smile. "I didn't say it surprised me, just that it amazed me," she responded. "Listen to the way the people of Little River sound: there's lingual drift, too. The accents, the colloquialisms. It's all so fascinating."

Jason shrugged, settling into an easy stride, his hand covering hers as they exited and began a casual stroll among the colorful booths that lined the boardwalk at the bazaar's edge.

"Humans gotta human, as Tobias always says," he replied.

Just then, as if conjured by his mention of the Weapon Born's name, the AI pinged him. As he accepted the connection, Tobias's avatar appeared.

<*Just had a wee chat with the lads on the dock about the* Vale's *banjaxed docking ring,*> Tobias informed them both, <*the one up at its bow. They'll have a repair estimate for us by end of day.*>

<*Nice,*> Jason replied, sending a wave of relief. <*It's not terribly urgent, since it's our least-used dock, but it'll be good to have it in working order again.*>

He felt a thread of agreement emanate from the AI at his words. <*Aye, that it will, boyo. Oh, and Kodi just pinged me,*> Tobias added, mentioning the AI embedded with Terrance, the *Vale*'s owner. <*Those two are wrapping things up now at the Trade Commission. I'm headed back to the ship. Are you and the lass returning soon?*>

<*I just want to make a quick sweep through the bazaar and then we'll head on back,*> Calista chimed in as Jason shot her a questioning look, and he saw Tobias's avatar nod in response.

<*Don't forget to stay within Godel's borders,*> was the AI's rejoinder.

<*Yes, Mother.*> Jason's jibe was met with a rude sound and a gesture from Tobias that had Calista laughing out loud.

<Don't worry,> the woman assured the Weapon Born. <*We're connected to the public feed. According to the map, we're still several rows away from the bazaar's boundary line. I'll make sure our boy doesn't do anything stupid.*>

<*Why is it always me everyone's so worried about?*> Jason complained, sliding a sideways grin toward Calista.

She responded with a mock frown and a raised brow. <*Maybe because you're the one always getting into trouble?*>

He snorted at her words but let them pass, as a pattern his subconscious mind had picked up on began to solidify. <*Speaking of trouble…*> he began, dropping her arm to free both their hands. He shifted closer to Calista as three figures wearing unfamiliar uniforms materialized from out of the colorful throng. <*Tobias, stand by. I hope I'm wrong, but I get the feeling we've caught someone's eye….*>

<*Dammit,*> Calista cursed softly. <*Just once, I'd like to enter a star system without having guns pointed at me within a week of arrival. Is that too much to ask?*>

Jason sent her a chuckle as he tested their connection to the *Avon Vale*'s shipnet. As he suspected, it was being blocked by a jamming field he felt certain was caused by their new friends. He sensed movement behind him, and the sensor feed woven into his base layer confirmed that the three to the front had brought reinforcements.

<*Two, behind,*> he cautioned, and Calista cursed once more. <*And we're cut off from the* Vale. *Shouldn't be a problem to evade—*>

<*Too many innocent people around,*> Calista warned, and Jason

knew she had sensed him tense, readying himself for action. *<Don't try anything just yet. Maybe we can talk our way out of this.>*

<And if we can't?>

<Take a look around; they have reinforcements closing from all sides. The bazaar's just too crowded, with too many civilians around to risk it. If it comes down to it, you're quicker. You know one of us has to make it back to let the team know what's happened.>

Jason remained stubbornly silent.

<Jason. You know I'm right.> Calista's mental tone was both cajoling and exasperated. He sensed her emotions shift, a steely resolve now emanating from her, and he knew she had donned the mantle of captain once again.

<You escape while I stall them. That's an order, Jason,> Calista added, silencing his nascent protest. *<One more thing. I want you to mask your L2 abilities.>*

He hated when she put limitations on him like that.

Jason's abilities weren't all that special when pitted against the kind of modifications most militaries offered their soldiers, such as augmented strength, stamina, and speed—even expanded mental capacities.

But where the average soldier depended upon artificial means to supply these added capabilities, and SC batteries to power them, Jason—as an L2 human—came by his naturally.

He understood also what Calista had left unsaid. If their opponent threw a suppression net over them, she might well become incapacitated. He, on the other hand, would not.

<Okay, but in case you were wondering, this command structure sucks. I'll hold back, but I'm not too happy about that.>

<Just make it look as if they were having a bad day. You know—poor luck, aim slightly off. Just enough to allow an escape,> she advised.

<Fine,> he muttered. *<But I'm tagging you with a snowflake.>* No amount of arguing would keep him from planting one of their trackers on her.

Calista sent her assent just as the soldiers made their move.

*****

Sergei flattened himself behind the flimsy plascrete wall of a vendor displaying caps and scarves as the two from the *Avon Vale* strolled by. After they passed, he and his partner fell into the flow of shoppers, following at a distance as he sent a countdown to the soldiers up ahead. As the countdown reached zero, three Humans' Republic Soldiers stepped out of the shadows, into the path of the two they'd been sent to retrieve.

This was Sergei's cue. As the man and woman from the *Avon Vale* passed, he and his partner closed from behind, cutting off their retreat. Sergei's HUD indicated that the jamming system had been engaged; this would prevent them from calling in reinforcements.

"Halt," Maritz, the Citizen lieutenant commanding their team, called out as she and the two soldiers flanking her closed on the two. "Stand and be inspected."

He saw the two exchange wary glances. The man moved closer to the woman, his movements striking Sergei as almost unnaturally smooth.

"What's the problem, officer?" the man asked as he shifted into a slouch, one hand slung carelessly around the woman's neck. He began toying idly with her hair as Citizen Maritz trained her weapon on them.

"We received a call from one of the merchants. Two people matching your description were seen shoplifting." With an exaggerated frown, Maritz added, "It may not be the same where you come from, but the Republic has stringent laws about theft."

She gestured to the citizen soldier on her left, and the woman stepped forward, gesturing with her flechette.

"Stand apart and keep your hands where we can see them."

The man stiffened. Before Sergei quite realized the man's intent, he declared, "Sorry, babe. You know I've never been very good at following rules."

With that, the man shoved his companion hard, sending the woman sprawling headlong into the nearest soldier as he bolted back the way they'd come.

The woman must have been less graceful than most, for as she careened into the first soldier, she cartwheeled her arms in a mad effort to right herself. This sent the packages in her hands smashing into the face of the second soldier.

Just as the third member of Sergei's team took off after the man, the woman's feet slipped out from under her, tripping the soldier mid-stride. All four went down in a heap, but by then, Sergei had his hands full, endeavoring to intercept the man before he made it back into Godel territory.

Sergei reached for his own weapon, but Jason Andrews jostled his arm as he passed, and the weapon somehow went flying. Cursing to himself, he made a grab for the man's arm, but he twisted out of the way at the last moment.

* * * * *

Jason was running hot. He'd dipped just far enough into his enhanced abilities to weave adroitly among the crowd, the faces of startled buyers barely registering as they looked up at him in shock when he raced past. He sprinted between vendors, upending tables to slow his pursuers, and sent silent apologies to merchants as their wares went flying.

He despised leaving Calista behind. It was a fine bit of irony that he'd actually meant the words he'd flung at the Barat soldiers. He *didn't* handle authority all that well; it was why he'd never served in any military. Being a member of Task Force Phantom Blade didn't count.... To his mind, the team's structure was much more casual, its missions more straightforward.

He hated being given orders he fundamentally disagreed with, and he sure as hell disagreed with abandoning a fellow team member. The fact that it was Calista made things just that much worse.

But he couldn't disagree with her argument that someone needed to make it back to the *Avon Vale* with the news that they'd been attacked. He just hated that he'd been the one to draw that assignment.

<*Talk to me, Tobe.*>

Jason pinged the Weapon Born as soon as he saw his Link handshake with the ship's net and reestablish its connection. He knew, in his L2 state, his words tumbled out too rapidly for a non-augmented human to understand; he also knew the AI would have no trouble parsing it.

<*They've got Calista. I tagged her with a snowflake and dropped a passel of colloid nano breadcrumbs in her hair. Tell me you've got a lock on her.*>

He charted an erratic course that kept his pursuers from getting the drop on him, sliding under displays and around tent flaps. The very randomness of his flight made him an impossible target for the soldiers pursuing him.

Or so he thought.

He swore as a flurry of flechettes went zinging past his head, ripping through the canvas of a nearby tent. His newly upgraded tactical combat mods immediately analyzed the trajectory, tagged the target, and plotted a firing solution—which might actually have been useful if he'd been carrying any kind of weapon.

As it was, the cry of pain that arose as one of the small darts hit an unintended victim unleashed a flare of fury inside him, directed at those intent on his capture to the exclusion of all else.

<*Sonofabitch! Tobe, where are you?*>

The Weapon Born came across the net, his voice steady and welcome. <*I'm here, lad, and telemetry's fine. We're using the trail of colloids you're shedding to get past their jamming,*> Tobias assured him. <*You're doing a fine job of it, too. We have an unbroken chain leading straight back to her. You even managed to get a nice little batch of nano inside that one soldier who made a grab for you. He inhaled a whole slew of them just as you passed.*>

The sounds of pursuit faded the deeper Jason went into Godel's section of the bazaar, but he didn't slow his pace. He was impressed by how effectively Calista had managed to gum up the works. The five soldiers had them dead to rights, their weapons trained unerringly upon them both, and yet she'd managed with little effort to take down the three in front of them long enough for him to make his escape. The other two had proven easy enough to evade—despite the casual loosing of firearms amongst a crowd of innocents.

Glancing behind him as he cleared the bazaar, he sized up his surroundings and made a break for a nearby alleyway he hoped might provide him rooftop access. Luck was with him, as he spotted a support spar that ran vertically up into the station's dome. He twisted the cuff of his sleeve as he ran, releasing a puff of colloid jamming nano that clung to his shirt and should prevent station sensors from seeing what he was about to do.

Gathering himself, he dug deep into his enhanced state and poured on the speed, using the plascrete wall across from the spar as a pivot point to launch himself up much higher than any unaugmented human could. Just before he planted his foot, he shot a glance up at his objective, the seam that joined the spar to the roof's flange.

The rapid mental calculation that allowed him to know exactly where to place his foot and how much force was required to achieve his goal was also thanks to his L2 abilities. He pushed off, propelled by the momentum transferred from his burst of speed, and his hand hit the exact spot he'd aimed for with a satisfying slap. Moments later, he'd swung himself onto the roof and was crouched over the far edge, checking for signs of pursuit.

<*Lost them,*> he sent tersely. <*I'm doubling back to pick her up now. Send me the feed from the* Vale, *will ya, Tobe? The ship's signal will be able to boost it better than I can.*>

There was a beat of silence, and then the Weapon Born's avatar slowly shook his head. <*Sorry, boyo. No can do. You need to get your ass back to the ship.*>

<*Oh hell no. Not without Calista.*>

The next moment, a feed came across the net, showing Calista surrounded by almost two dozen soldiers that formed a phalanx three meters deep. As he watched, they pushed her head down, forcing her into a maglev car. The soldiers jumped on, weapons raised and pointed outward, ready for any attack.

<*Stars! What in the hell just happened here?*>

<*That's why we need you back on the* Vale, *to help us piece this together.*>

<*Any idea what these jokers wanted with us?*> Jason sat back against a pipe protruding from the roof he was on. With a breath, he released his enhanced state, and the world snapped from a fluid slow-motion back to its normal speed. <*And how the hell did they know where we were? And why did our map show that we were still within Godel territory?*>

<*Best bet is a Barat mole within the organization that governs this station, since they supplied you with the public feed.*> Tobias's tone was grim. <*As to why, I suspect we'll find out shortly.*>

Jason grimaced as he dragged himself into a standing position. <*Yeah…that's what I'm afraid of, Tobe. Headed back now.*>

He stepped to the roof's edge and glanced down three stories to the alleyway below, then swung a leg around the spar and began to slide down to the first level. Tobias's parting comment reached him just as he hit the street and began a steady jog back to the marina.

<*I'll update Terrence on the situation. See you back on the* Vale.>

SLEEPING BLADE WAKES

STELLAR DATE: 03.08.3272 (Adjusted Gregorian)
LOCATION: ESS *Avon Vale*, Slip 512, Godel Trade Marina
REGION: Phaethon Duty Station, Little River

Landon paced the dimly-lit perimeter of the *Avon Vale*'s bridge, the hands of his humanoid frame clasped behind him. His measured stride was meant to convey assurance, his separation from his crew a confidence in their abilities. Accessible, should they need him, yet removed from their day-to-day activities.

And then his brother promptly disabused him of that notion.

<Quit hovering. You're making them nervous.>

Landon pivoted, shooting a glare at the back of his twin's head.

Without missing a beat, Logan added, *<And quit shooting daggers at me.>*

Landon sent his brother a flare of annoyance. *<This is a new bridge detail. It won't hurt them to have a superior officer breathing down their necks for a few hours,>* he countered. Then, before his brother could point out the obvious, added, *<and don't try to derail me by saying I don't breathe. You know that was a figure of speech.>*

Logan responded with a thread of exasperation, but then the team's profiler let the matter drop. Landon went back to his stroll, his optics sweeping the bridge, assessing each station individually.

The human, Hailey—one of Terrance's Enfield employees, who had volunteered for bridge duty back in Tau Ceti—was the only veteran on today's detail.

The over-large Proxima cat, stretched out languorously at her feet, didn't count. Tobi was intelligent—uplifted, in fact—but her position on the ship's bridge was more as a morale booster. Not having opposable thumbs was a bit limiting, as the feline reminded them all frequently.

Florence, the AI running the navigation station, had recently rotated in for third shift duty after expressing an interest in learning to be a navigator. The senior staff had decided to allow her to spend some time on the boards running simulations while the *Vale* was docked on Phaethon.

Another AI was shadowing Hailey at communications, and a human from Proxima who had opted to stay aboard at Tau Ceti and continue on to Epsilon Eridani was on scan.

Landon adjusted his path and began to angle toward his brother, seated at the security station in the back of the bridge near the exit. The moment he did so, he noticed the tension leave the shoulders of the woman at scan. He paused, dismayed that he had been its cause. Then he sensed a glimmer of amusement from his brother and realized Logan had caught him noticing.

<*Okay, fine, dammit. You were right.*> Landon sent a simulated sigh over their connection. <*Have I ever told you how much I hate it when you're right?*>

<*Only thirty-seven-point-two million times since we were freed from Montoya's experiment,*> came the dry response. <*You're worried about Jason, Calista and Terrance.*>

Landon shot his brother a glare that Jason had coined his 'no shit Sherlock' look.

<*You're the one who's been sending me data on the state of affairs between Godel and Barat. How long do* **you** *think it's going to be before things erupt?*> he demanded of his twin.

Logan toyed with something on the security console and shortly, a link to a data file hovered over the connection between them.

Landon swept through the file, assimilating the data in an instant.

<*Do you see the pattern?*>

Landon sent him a shrug. <*I see a governmental system that is totalitarian in everything but its name. Terrance made the right call when he chose to trade with Godel instead of Barat, but he'll need to ward Enfield Holdings against industrial espionage.*>

Logan sent his assent. <*What Barat cannot acquire by legal means, they will steal, yes. But there's more going on here than corporate theft.*>

The AI highlighted a string of data, information Landon knew his brother could not possibly have been able to access from the duty station's public net. His brother had managed to insinuate himself behind the firewalls of one or both of the nations within the Epsilon system.

<*You do realize that's illegal,*> he reminded his twin.

<*They will never know, and our people will be better protected.*> The feeling Logan sent him was both shrewd and pointed. <*That's what you really want, yes?*>

Landon sent resigned assent. <*It's just that—*>

<*They left you in charge, and you feel responsible for the reputation of the* Avon Vale.>

<*Stop doing that!*>

<*Doing what?*>

<*Profiling me.*>

Logan didn't respond, and Landon let the silence between them build.

In the silence that fell between them, he saw Tobi rise up on her haunches, then reach first one and then another massive paw out in a stretch, her two-centimeter-long claws clicking on the sole of the deck with a tinny snicking sound.

Shaking herself thoroughly, she stood and padded back toward the twins.

<*Could smell you bickering again,*> she sent to the two privately as she settled on her haunches next to Landon, her head reaching the top of his frame's thigh. She reached out with her nose and nudged his hand, seeking attention. Obligingly, he turned his hand over and began rubbing her under her chin.

<*You're going to have to tell me someday what my tell is, little warrior,*> he said, not believing for a moment that the Proxima cat could truly scent anything about an AI.

Tobi chuffed and sent him a scoffing sound over the Link as she turned to rub up against Logan. The big cat was always careful to divide her attention equally between the twins, something Landon had always found amusing.

<*I'm not so sure about that, brother,*> Logan sent, his tone musing. <*There have been times when she couldn't possibly have known—*>

<*I **know**.*> Tobi's mental voice was smug. <*I smelled Prime. I smelled the thing he put inside his humans. I can smell you arguing.*>

<*I know that you're a predator, and in your own way as much a profiler as Logan is,*> Landon conceded, and sent her a laugh in response to the disdainful glare she shot at him.

He'd had no idea prior to meeting Tobi—and later, Beck, the Proxima cat who had bonded with Terrance—how expressive cats could be. He saw a wealth of opinion in that look, none of it flattering.

Before he had a chance to compose a suitable response, his connection with the ship's sensors alerted him to a communication coming from the station. He turned to Hailey expectantly and awaited the human's slower response.

He only had a few agonizingly slow seconds to wait.

"Sir!" Hailey gasped, and Landon abandoned politeness—and protocol—to access the missive directly. Tossing the message to Logan, he began rifling through his brother's hacked access to Godel's servers as the human on comm declared to the bridge, "Captain Rhinehart's been arrested!"

Logan shot Landon a query, and at his nod, shunted the feed of Jason's progress to the bridge's main holo. The bridge was deathly still, except for Hailey, whose fingers moved feverishly over her board, as she tried to break through Barat's jamming and reacquire their connection with Calista.

The bridge doors slid open to admit a slight, raven-haired man who approached Scan. A quiet hand placed on the shoulder of the seat's occupant caused the station to be relinquished with a grateful nod. Moments later, he spoke.

"They're on the move."

The words were delivered in an almost inhumanly calm tone. That they were conveyed by a human made it even more incongruous to Landon. Noa Sakai's materialization on the bridge not long after Hailey's panicked announcement didn't surprise the AI; the human had a knack for being where he was most needed at just the right time—as the people of Tau Ceti knew quite well.

Landon had seen firsthand how the man's composure, courage, and brilliant mind had enabled Noa to find a cure that saved the nanophage-ravaged planet of Galene—and quite possibly the entire star system—from utter destruction. He turned now to face the physicist, waiting for him to elaborate.

"We're picking up the colloids Jason placed in her hair. They're floating off—and outside the jamming radius—as she moves. The trail is thinning...." Noa paused, his voice trailing off in thought as he worked the board.

Landon knew the man wasn't as dispassionate as he sounded; Sakai simply imbued a zen-like calm to everything he did. But, stars.... Landon had to force himself to rein in the impulse to prod the nanophysicist for more information.

Thinning did not sound good.

Landon wasn't the only one to think so. At Noa's words, he saw Tobi's ears flatten and heard her soft hiss, just as the avatar for Shannon, the ship's AI, sprang into life next to the bridge's front holotank.

<*What do you mean it's thinning?*> she demanded, silver eyes flashing as she fisted her hands and planted them on her hips. As always happened when Shannon was agitated, her long, silvery-white hair snapped wildly in a nonexistent breeze.

Noa looked up suddenly as if he had only just realized how his words might have been construed. Before he could speak, Shannon laid into him.

<*Noa, don't you* ***dare*** *lose her trail. We have to get her back—you understand? We need her back* ***now***.>

Landon held up a restraining hand, but before he could

intercede, Noa's voice reached her, strong and assured.

"We haven't lost her trail, Shannon—and we won't." The physicist's eyes held hers, a quiet confidence in their depths.

"Thinning merely indicates that the rate at which her captors are walking has increased. While they were standing still, a clump of colloids collected, but now that they are on the move, they are farther apart. Our breadcrumb trail is still quite intact," he assured her.

Landon sent the physicist a nod of thanks and then shunted a duplicate of Noa's feed to the ship's main holo for them all to see.

Shannon hesitated, and then nodded.

Of all Phantom Blade's members, Shannon was the one least accustomed to combat. To top it off, Calista was one of her closest friends. A situation like this one had to be difficult for her to handle, Landon knew.

"Give it some time. The duty station is five hundred kilometers in diameter, and they're taking her deeper into it," Landon pointed out, gesturing to the glittering line of dots floating in the holotank that indicated the colloid trail. "I don't think we need to worry about them spiriting her off-station any time soon."

Shannon glanced from Noa to Landon and then over to Logan. Landon could just make out the faint nod his twin sent before Shannon gave a dramatic sigh, crossed her virtual arms and shot him a pointed look.

"Fine. But don't make me go find a humanoid frame to wear in order to drag her back myself. Because I'll do it," she threatened. "Don't think I won't." And with that, her avatar winked out.

Although she was out of sight, Landon knew she hadn't stopped her own private monitoring of Phaethon.

He turned and spared his brother an amused glance.

<So why is it again that my words didn't reassure her, yet all you have to do is nod and everything's all right?>

Ever the taciturn one, Logan just sat there, and blinked.

<Fine.> Switching from their private channel to audible speech,

Landon asked, "Jason's status?"

"En route to the *Vale*. Shots fired, but he's evading." Logan's words were clipped. "Tobias is headed his way in case he needs an assist. Terrance and Kodi are in transit as well."

<*Let me go. I will hunt them down,*> Tobi's mental voice was mostly growl as the big cat paced restlessly along the back of the bridge, her long, tawny tail lashing from side to side in her agitation.

Jason was her human, the one she'd bonded to as a kit, and the cat was not taking the news of his pursuit well.

"Can't let you do that. You know this system has no uplifted animals. They would tranq you on sight the moment you stepped off the ship," Landon reminded her quietly. "Trust Tobias to help, if he needs it. And we both know he won't."

Tobi bared her teeth at him once and thumped her tail hard onto the sole of the deck in agitation, but then subsided.

"Okay, then." Landon shifted gears. "What do we know about station command structure? Let's send this through official channels while we work up our own solution. How do we lodge a complaint and begin the process of extracting her from Barat's clutches?"

<*Done that.*>

<*Of course you have.*> He shot his brother some side-eye. "Then can you work with Tobias and Charley," he asked, mentioning the AI who had joined their team in Tau Ceti with Noa, "to come up with an extraction plan we can share with Terrance when he arrives?"

The profiler sent his assent, and Landon felt the anxious knot inside him ease the smallest bit at the thought of the three AIs and the havoc they were capable of, should the situation call for it.

First, his brother was one of the finest warriors he knew. Then there was Tobias; the Weapon Born's prowess was legendary. As for Charley, his heritage had yet to be truly tested, but as the scion of a Weapon Born and a multi-nodal AI, the Tau Ceti native was truly formidable. Combined, Landon would pit those three against all comers. If anyone could find a way to get Calista back, it would be them.

Losing a team member was Landon's biggest fear, his one weakness. It had happened to him before—and it had, quite literally, killed him.

He quashed the urge to begin prowling the ship to assure himself that the *Avon Vale*'s offensive and defensive systems were running at peak efficiency. It was unnecessary; he knew they were.

For, unknown to their hosts, the *Vale* was a commercial vessel with teeth; a predator, lying placidly in its berth, playing at being a lamb.

TRADE RELATIONS

STELLAR DATE: 03.08.3272 (Adjusted Gregorian)
LOCATION: Godel Trade Commission
REGION: Phaethon Duty Station, Little River

30 minutes earlier....

Deb Weir glanced up from the holosheet Terrance Enfield had handed her and gave him a pleased smile. Enfield had requested a meeting with Godel's Trade Commission when his ship had entered Little River's heliopause, and she had accepted with alacrity once she'd heard his initial overture.

He returned her look with a smile of his own as he leant back, leg crossed and ankle resting on the knee of his other leg. She set the holosheet down carefully, smoothing it and giving it a little pat as her smile turned into a dimpled grin.

"I think I can say with a high degree of confidence that Enfield Holdings will be welcome on Godel," she began, but paused politely as she saw his expression take on a distant stare—sure indication he was being contacted by someone.

The man's gaze refocused briefly on hers and he shot her a grimace of apology, which she waved away.

<*So sorry for the interruption,*> Kodi sent to her. <*We'll just be a moment.*>

<*Take your time.*> Smiling, she lifted her coffee mug with a pointed look of inquiry, gesturing to the man's own empty cup and he nodded, a grateful expression crossing his face.

She snagged it and rose to afford him a bit of privacy while she went to fulfill the errand. She was more than a bit excited about the new technologies Enfield Holdings would bring to Little River, pleased that Terrance had agreed to open a branch of the company on Godel.

Stars, true stasis! Not cryogenic, but honest-to-stars cessation of atomic movement. Deb's mind boggled at the thought, and she considered once again the impact this kind of advancement might have on the star system.

The potential it had to save lives, by giving medical personnel the time they needed to respond. Transportation benefits, as proven by those on the *Avon Vale,* who'd made use of it themselves en route to Godel.

And the impact on industry! To be able to deliver foods as fresh as the day they were harvested…. With her back to her two guests, Deb indulged in a wide grin as she envisioned all the possibilities.

"Stars!"

Terrance's exclamation caused her hand to jerk in surprise, and she blew out a short breath of annoyance as she reached for a napkin to mop up the coffee she had just spilled. Turning, she retraced her steps, one brow raised in query as she set Terrance's coffee before him.

The expression on his face caused her to check her own feed. She'd placed a 'do not disturb' suppression on her Link for this meeting. Releasing it, she caught her breath as data flooded in with reports of the skirmish in the bazaar moments ago.

Stars, I'm such a fool!

Deb had seen Barat make this kind of move before, but in the past, the few times the Humans' Republic had made such a play, it had always been against a political or business target visiting from Godel. Why had it not occurred to her that they might consider a visitor from outside Little River just as high-value?

She shot a terse message to the duty station's security chief, instructing him to make the recovery of the *Avon Vale*'s captain his top priority. Her stomach knotted as she turned to face her guest.

"Mister Enfield, Kodi. I am so sorry. We'll do everything in our power to help recover your captain," she began, but was interrupted by a hand from Terrance as he leapt to his feet, uttered a hasty apology, turned on his heel, and exited the Trade Commission.

* * * * *

Sergei was stationed toward the front of the maglev car alongside his fellow Citizen soldiers, his weapon trained outward. He stood with one hand wrapped around a support pole, legs braced to offset the sway of the car as it curved inward toward the station's center and the Barat compound. He grimaced as he mentally replayed the escape of target number two.

Citizen Lieutenant Maritz was not pleased with the loss of their second bargaining chip, and he suspected he was on her shit list right now because of it.

As if his thoughts had conjured her, the Citizen Lieutenant's voice cut in sharply over his implant.

<Sergei! Get back here.>

Reluctantly, he turned and began to trot past the citizen soldiers lining each side, weapons trained outward.

For all the good those weapons will do, he thought sardonically. *We're traveling so fast, we'll be well past anyone who decides to take a shot at us, with no way to return fire.*

He skirted the occasional soldier's pack littering the center aisle, and ducked under a protruding elbow, bent back to accommodate the length of a pulse rifle held by a greenie.

He shook his head mentally at that one. *Overcompensating, are we?*

He reached the back of the car where the mag-cuffed woman was being held. Maritz nodded toward the prisoner as he ground to a halt.

<Scan her. Grab whatever information you can while we're en route. I want to know everything there is to know, short of cutting into that brain of hers. Got it?>

<Yes, Citizen Lieutenant.>

He waved toward the seats set against the far side of the maglev car. Motioning for the two soldiers flanking the woman to relocate her, he took one of the seats and rifled through his kit, while they forced her into the one facing him.

He could scan her with his own internal mods, but Sergei opted to use the more powerful external unit connected to his implant. Flipping it open with one hand, he trained the unit on the woman in front of him who was busy staring stonily out into space just past his left ear.

As the unit moved up her body, it revealed pilots' mods, typical of those found in any space navy. Carbon nanotube reinforcements were woven into bone and lay dormant in vital organs, filaments awaiting the command to weave their protective reinforcement throughout soft tissue. The unit reached her head, and it identified high-caliber, military-grade optical implants.

But then….

Elitist trash.

He could see by the folds in her brain that she was one of the privileged, her augmentation determined before she'd even been born. Data matrices, the likes of which the common citizen would never see, and which those born of a lesser caste could never hope to afford. These were interleaved throughout the gyri and sulci—the complex peaks and valleys—that were uniquely hers.

Every Republican child had learned of Sol's shameful past—the Era of the Haves and the Have Nots, when only the wealthy had access to implants. In the Humans' Republic, every child was chipped at birth; that chip was then traded for an implant upon neural maturity.

It was a guarantee given every citizen of Barat, and the Republic's preeminent tenet of 'equality for all humanity' one of the first things taught in school.

He snapped his unit shut and rose, nodding to indicate to the two soldiers guarding her that he was done. As he stepped away to report his findings to the citizen lieutenant, he caught the target's condemning stare.

How dare she.

*****

The station map on the *Avon Vale*'s bridge holo updated as Noa zoomed in. He dropped an icon to highlight a location, and then turned to address Landon.

"It looks like their destination is here, the Republican Central Compound. From what I can tell," Noa cautioned, "their headquarters is shielded, and we will most likely lose the signal once she's inside."

"But we should pick her up again if she's moved?"

Noa hesitated. "So long as she's not hit with an EMP that would kill all her trackers," he qualified, "then yes."

Landon nodded his understanding. "Then we'll just have to make sure we don't give them time to relocate her before we can get her back."

He turned toward Hailey as he reached out to manipulate the smaller holodisplay from the Enfield woman's feed. Highlighting the notification about Calista's kidnapping, he asked, "Where did this information on Barat detaining the captain originate from, Hailey? Did you hear it first from Terrance?"

Hailey shook her head. "No, sir, it came from the Barat Precinct House. The system sent an automated notice that the captain had been detained without bail on three counts of robbery and suspected corporate espionage," she added, her mouth grimacing in distaste. "According to Barat, they have witnesses that corroborate the accusation, and the merchants from whom she allegedly stole the merchandise have filed affidavits against her."

Shannon's avatar sprang into view again. "That is a crock of shit and you know it, Landon! Calista would never steal anything, she's a former Space Force top gun, for star's sake!"

Landon raised his hands in an effort to calm the AI embedded with the *Vale*. "We all know that, Shannon. But we need to gather every bit of information we have. It's possible that in their attempt to frame the captain, they may have made an error we can exploit.

In the meantime, can you touch base with Khela and see what you can do to help her get the Marines ready for insertion, in case we need to make a quick snatch-and-grab?"

As he'd hoped, the mention of possible action that could be taken to retrieve her friend had Shannon responding with alacrity, and once more, her avatar winked out, leaving Landon to the task of sussing out the best way to recover his missing teammate.

* * * * *

Terrance breathed a sigh of relief as they approached the *Vale* and he saw Jason weaving adroitly through the crowd, closing fast on the umbilical that led to the ship's cargo bay. Tobias's humanoid frame was standing guard at the entrance; next to him was a petite, raven-haired woman, a younger version of Noa Sakai.

<*Just be thankful she didn't bring an entire unit of Marines to bring you back,*> Kodi's mental voice was tinged with amusement as the AI sensed Terrance's chagrin at finding Marine Captain Khela Sakai coiled and ready to spring into action.

She shot him a sharp-eyed, measuring glance, assuring herself he had come to no harm, before her gaze returned to scanning their environs. One hand rested by her thigh, ready to draw her laser-dagger at the first sign of danger to him.

He knew better than to restrict Khela's motion when she was working, so he made no move to touch her. Instead, he clapped Jason on the shoulder as the Proxan silently transitioned into the ship. By unspoken agreement, both the Marine and the Weapon Born brought up the rear.

As they entered the bridge, Logan spoke, indicating the holotank in the bridge's fore section.

"While you were in transit, I talked with the officers in charge at Godel's station precinct. I tried to reach an actual person over at the Barat precinct; no answer."

<*Think they're avoiding us?*> Kodi sent, and Terrance saw

Landon spread his hands in a "who knows" gesture.

"The officer I spoke with over at Godel recommended we get in touch with Barat's embassy for advice on how best to get the captain back," Logan continued. "But the NSAI taking calls over at their embassy is now denying that anything ever happened. It questioned where I got my information, and informed me that no patrol routes were scheduled at the bazaar today."

<*I stand corrected. That's outright obfuscation.*> Kodi's acidic comment caused Terrance to scowl, but he didn't disagree with the assessment.

"The database I managed to…lift…from the duty station shows a pattern of this kind of behavior, yes," Logan confirmed. Terrance noted the slight hesitation and used a private connection to send the profiler his approval.

Logan swiveled his frame toward Jason. "I take it that the map you were using to guide you never indicated you had trespassed into Barat territory?"

Jason shook his head. "No. I had it up on my HUD the entire time, and according to the map coming over the public feed, we were still within Godel's borders when they struck."

Landon shook his head. "No, actually, you weren't."

The main holo displayed the station's bazaar. The AI dropped two pins to indicate Jason and Calista's location at the time of the interception. Overlaid was the boundary where Godel gave way to Barat.

"Well, shit." Jason's voice was laden with disgust. He glanced over at Tobias. "Someone hacked the public feed in order to send us a spoofed map."

He angled his head toward Noa. "Any chance we have a solid lock on her location inside the compound yet?"

Noa shook his head. "No, and it doesn't look as if we'll get anything that specific with just the colloids—at least, not inside their headquarters, not with the security measures they have in place." He glanced over at Logan. "Any additional information you can get from our friends on the Godel side of the station would be helpful."

Terrance's head shot up at that, and he snapped his fingers. "Almost forgot. Just as we got back to the ship, Commissioner Weir contacted me privately. Asked if we could discuss the situation in a more secure setting."

<*I got the impression she suspects someone in her organization is feeding info to Barat, as well,*> Kodi added, and Terrance nodded his agreement. "We need to reach out to her to set up a time and location for a meet."

<*Best to do that in person,*> Kodi advised, and Terrance heard a sound of protest coming from the Marine who stood beside him.

As he spun around to head for the lift at the end of the corridor outside the bridge, he wasn't surprised to find Khela on his heels.

"You don't need to shadow me. I'll behave," he promised her once the lift doors closed.

Dark eyes turned to scrutinize him as the conveyance began to move.

"It's not your behavior I'm worried about," she said, leaning into him and looking up into his eyes. Terrance wrapped one arm around her waist as she went up on tiptoe and kissed him. "It's you. If they could have captured Jason, they would have, you know that. I'd prefer it if my husband wasn't the next one they try to acquire."

She stepped back as the lift doors opened onto the *Vale*'s dock. "Understood?"

He smiled over at her. "Ma'am, yes ma'am."

She swatted his backside as he led the way out.

SETTING THE TRAP

STELLAR DATE: 03.09.3272 (Adjusted Gregorian)
LOCATION: Barat Citizen Guard HQ, Republican Compound
REGION: Phaethon Duty Station, Little River

Sergei stood at attention in the citizen lieutenant's office, located in the Republican Central Compound, housed deep inside Barat territory and more than a hundred kilometers away from the Godel marina.

He did his best to remain impassive, but knew he'd failed to keep the dumbfounded look off his face as he repeated the order.

"A lawyer, sir?" he parroted stupidly, and was rewarded with a flash of sharp annoyance crossing his superior's face.

"Our…guest…has requested legal representation," Maritz said. "We've been ordered to attempt a straightforward trade first, before we escalate any further. Therefore, we need to keep her unharmed and be willing to verify fair treatment until the *Avon Vale* delivers the stasis technology in exchange for her safe return."

Sergei nodded mutely, uncertain exactly why the citizen commander had singled him out from his guard unit to confer upon him this dubious honor.

He'd been surprised to see the woman escorted to the temporary lockup area at headquarters rather than to medical when they'd arrived. Truth be told, he'd rather assumed that the moment they returned to base, she'd be sent directly into one of their autodocs, in order to extract whatever tech they could mine from her. At the very least, to scan her more thoroughly than he'd been able to do on the maglev.

Belatedly, he realized he hadn't acknowledged his citizen lieutenant's order, and hastily added a "yes, sir" into the silence.

His superior stared at him with an expression that caused his balls to shrivel a bit before she continued with her instructions.

"Try to force her into requesting better representation than what you can provide. Get a holo of it that we can use if Enfield balks at handing over the stasis tech. We'll use it to claim that our hands are tied by the prisoner's own words when we ship her to Barat." The citizen lieutenant's chuckle was more of a sinister cackle as she added, "Our generosity in extending the same rights to an obvious criminal that we do to our own citizens will make a nice sound bite for the news nets."

He turned obediently at her dismissive wave with a brief salute, and then spun and headed down toward the cell block where their prisoner awaited his interrogation.

*****

Calista stood and once more began pacing the confines of her holding cell. She'd been doing so off and on ever since she'd been politely but firmly escorted there hours earlier. The drab four-by-four-meter plascrete room she'd been ushered into held all the charm of a military brig, down to the stained floor and the lumpy mattress on the single bunk.

She'd spotted an armed guard stationed in the hallway across from her cell the one time the door had slid open to admit her single visitor. That individual had conducted a second, more thorough scan. The soldier had refused to answer any of the questions Calista had rained down upon the woman; she'd merely grunted—once as the unit beeped when it located her Link, and then again when it had revealed the nano Jason had laced through her hair.

When ordered to strip for the scan, Calista had carelessly tossed her boots to one side but made a fuss over her jacket, reluctantly allowing it out of her possession. With any luck, Calista hoped the woman would assume it was something of value.

As she'd hoped, the jacket worked beautifully as a deflection, focusing the soldier away from the thing of real value. The boots—well-worn, scuffed, looking as if they'd seen better days at least a decade or so earlier—were returned to her after a cursory scan indicated they were comprised of nothing but inert materials.

Bless Jonesy for his brilliant engineering mind.

The soles of those shoes were comprised of a material patented by Enfield Holdings, and on the list of highly-marketable items the company intended to bring to market to the people of Little River: Elastene. Inside the shielded compartment was additional nano she could use to break out of her prison. Nano not likely to be detected and neutralized by her captors. She just needed to bide her time and wait for an opportunity to present itself.

She turned at the sound of the door sliding open. Standing in its entrance was the soldier who had taken her into custody in the bazaar earlier, and had then scanned her. She lifted a brow and waited imperiously for him to speak. Oddly enough, the man appeared uncomfortable. She filed that away, in case it might prove useful against him in the future.

After an awkwardly long pause, the man said in a heavily accented voice, "You asked for a lawyer; I am here to represent you."

A short, incredulous laugh escaped before she could stop it. "You're kidding, right? You? You're the one who planted those stolen goods on me in the first place." Calista lifted her arms in a wide gesture, then let them drop to her sides with a loud slap.

The man had the decency to look down as she glared accusingly at him, but then he straightened and stiffly informed her, "The Barat Procuratorate states that every individual has the right to plead their case with the citizen's court. That includes foreigners such as you."

"Procura—" Calista had never heard of such a word, but her embedded database supplied the term 'prosecutor general's office' at her subconscious query.

As she gawped at him, he gestured for her to take a seat on her bunk. He pulled over the one chair, crossed his leg, and unpocketed a hyfilm, which he then proceeded to scroll through as he cleared his throat.

"Now then. You claim you did not steal the very valuable and high-quality handwoven *tszatzkots* found in your possession—"

"I have no idea what the hell a *tszatzkots* is, for star's sake," she snarled at him as she stalked toward him and wrenched the hyfilm from his grasp and tossed it aside, "and I certainly didn't steal one of them."

"No, you stole *three* of them," the man said, and if she'd wondered if her cell was being monitored, the entrance of the guard, weapon pointed at her as she loomed over her seated 'lawyer' confirmed it.

She slowly settled onto the mattress as the man waved the guard back out and bent to retrieve the hyfilm.

Raising it again, he swiped until he found what he'd been looking for and nodded in satisfaction. Looking up once more, he made eye contact as he shook his head sadly.

"I must inform you that the evidence is not at all in your favor, and you will most likely be found guilty—that is, unless we can find a way to settle out of court…." The man lowered his hyfilm and studied her, brow raised in an unspoken question.

Ahhh, there it is.

"You're holding me hostage." Her voice was flat, accusing.

The man shrugged. "If you were to offer up something of value to the Republic—a novel new technology, for instance. Something that might benefit our way of life. Perhaps the Procuratorate could see fit to issue a pardon, as this is your first infraction."

"And if I refuse?"

He checked a date on the hyfilm. "Well then, let's see. Ah, yes. Your trial is scheduled to be held in a week's time. Until then—"

"Wait," Calista protested. "Is there no system of bail here on the station? Surely you don't plan to keep me locked up here for an entire week."

The man shrugged eloquently. "For robbery, Barat's justice system requires that the defendant be held without bail until such time as the case comes to trial."

"That's—! Surely there's some way I can appeal this. Let me talk to your superior."

The man's face shuttered, and he shrugged once more. "If you wish, you can appeal the decision and it will be remanded to a higher court. But you would have to officially request such a thing."

"Hell yes," she muttered, glaring at the man. "I don't want some soldier who was responsible for framing me in the first place representing me on a bunch of trumped-up charges."

The man leant forward, his gaze intent. "Is that an official request? Are you asking me to put you in contact with someone who has greater legal authority than I do? Someone, perhaps, better suited to represent your case?"

"Yes!"

Something about the man's demeanor warned Calista. She had the distinct impression she'd somehow been manipulated into saying exactly what he'd wanted her to say. Her gaze rested on the man's collar and she saw the telltale pip indicating a recording device embedded into it.

The man sat back with an air of satisfaction. "Done," the soldier said, one hand slapping the empty holster of his sidearm to emphasize the word, as if they'd sealed some sort of deal.

His eyes glinted in triumph as he nodded and rose to exit the room in which she was being held.

Calista groaned. *Dammit, I just played right into his hands!*

HOLDING ALL THE CARDS

STELLAR DATE: 03.09.3272 (Adjusted Gregorian)
LOCATION: ESS *Avon Vale*, Slip 512, Godel Trade Marina
REGION: Phaethon Duty Station, Little River

<*Hold up, there, lover.*>

Khela's words caused Terrance to slow his stride and glance down at her. She tucked her arm through his and melted into his side, looking up at him with a smile.

Her attitude and demeanor were nothing like they'd been yesterday when he'd set out to meet the trade commissioner. But then again, today's meet was covert; yesterday's hadn't been.

<*Tearing through a marina like a man on a mission is not the best way to approach a clandestine meeting,*> she pointed out, a teasing smile playing over her lips.

Kodi snickered as Terrance sent back a mental groan. Ignoring the AI, he sent a wave of apology to his wife.

<*Good call.*>

<*It's what you pay me for.*>

<*I pay you?*>

<*With interest.*> She winked at him suggestively, and he couldn't repress a grin as he followed her lead.

Damn, his wife in espionage mode was one sexy package. Almost as sexy as when she went full-on Marine, and that was saying something.

Glancing casually around the marina as if to get his bearings, he leant over and made a point to gesture toward the exit that led to the entertainment district as they reviewed the token Deb Weir had sent him.

<*Assume you're under surveillance at all times,*> the Godel trade commissioner had advised the day before, when they'd managed to track her down and set up today's rendezvous. <*Once you arrive*

at the location, tell your server that you've heard they have an excellent cherry stout you want to try. That'll get you escorted back to the secured room.>

Khela nodded in response to his gesture, and they began to stroll casually toward the district's large, reinforced archway, hand-in-hand. As they passed through, Terrance received notification that Phaethon had scanned them, acknowledging their presence in that sector.

Pulling up the token Weir had given him, he overlaid it on top of the station's map, then set out on a meandering path that would eventually lead them to their destination. Khela kept up a running commentary as they strolled the streets. She window shopped, pausing at a patisserie to exclaim over the pastries. She gestured at the ornamental trees in planters lining the walkway, wondering audibly about their varieties and if they were native to the system.

A few blocks up ahead, he could see a strand of local breweries. Most of them were named after various rivers back on Old Terra—Ganges, Danube, Yangtze. The one they were after was not.

It had a sign above its entrance that proclaimed it The Broken Hart, although he could see nothing broken about the holo of the stag's head that hovered above its name.

As they approached, he tilted his head toward its entrance.

"Thirsty, love?" Terrance knew his easy smile didn't quite reach his eyes, but he saw Khela nod as she leaned into him.

"Sounds good," she said aloud, tipping her head back to meet his gaze with a smile of her own.

<You're doing great, handsome,> her voice, warm and reassuring, filled his mind. She gave his forearm an encouraging squeeze, and he felt some of the tension leave him as they entered.

The interior was dimly lit, as opposed to the daylight that currently illuminated Phaethon. Terrance noted that it was just nearing seventeen-hundred station time, as he was greeted by a human waiter. They were a few minutes early, by design.

The man smiled amiably as Terrance used the code phrase.

"Our cherry stout is a favorite among locals. Follow me, and I'll get you set up." He turned and led Terrance and Khela along the outer wall of the establishment, skirting a crowd of milling people who'd gathered at the end of their workday to toss back a few brews.

Terrance noticed the lighting was dimmer in this corner, the entrance the man stopping at almost indistinguishable from the dark wall surrounding it. With a nod, he left them to retrace his steps as a door slid open in front of them.

Khela immediately ducked inside. After a moment's hesitation and a quick glance around, Terrance followed. The moment the doors slid shut behind him, a second set of doors on the opposing side slid open, and two individuals entered.

As the door slid shut behind them, the room shimmered faintly. The air quality shifted, and an anechoic silence filled the space, indicating jamming had been employed and security measures emplaced.

Terrance wasn't sure whether to be amused or offended when his wife silently interposed her petite form between him and the newcomers as a warning icon appeared inside his head, confirming they were cut off from the outside.

"I apologize for the cloak and dagger," Commissioner Weir began, "but this was the most expedient way I could think of to get you to a secured location where we could talk—and be certain we weren't overheard."

Her mouth twisted in chagrin. "As you probably suspect, the trade commission has a spy in its midst that we've been unable to identify as of yet."

Khela grunted once but Terrance knew her well; that single sound carried an abundance of opinion—none of it flattering. His lips twitched as he suppressed a smile, then he shifted her slightly to one side as he gestured from her to Deb.

"Commissioner, I'd like for you to meet Khela Sakai. She's—"

"—charged with ensuring Mister Enfield's safety while on

Phaethon Station," Khela interjected smoothly.

'Do not introduce me as your wife.' Message received loud and clear. Professional it is.

Deb nodded politely and then gestured to the individual accompanying her. "Mister Enfield, Kodi, and Miss Sakai," she said, smiling and glancing from Terrance to Khela and then back again, "I would like for you to meet Simone." She gestured to the AI standing quietly next to her, clad in a tunic and leggings of a chameleonlike material.

The AI bowed her head slightly in greeting, then motioned toward one of the three small tables scattered about the room before moving to take a seat.

"Shall we?" she said with a smile, pulling out a chair as the three humans joined her.

As she sank into her own chair, Khela leant forward, her gaze direct. "The security protocols in this room are more suited to an intelligence office than a trade commission." She didn't mince words.

Deb nodded. "You're right, of course." Gesturing toward Simone, she ceded the conversation to the AI, who promptly dropped a token to both him and Khela.

As Terrance reviewed it, Kodi made a sound like a low whistle.

<*If I were a betting creature,*> he guessed, <*I'd lay odds that your Directorate of Military Intelligence is an agency pretty high up inside Godel's government.*>

"You'd win that bet," Simone confirmed, crossing her forearms on the table and leaning toward them as she exchanged glances with Deb. "Commissioner Weir told me about your ship's captain," she continued, her expression pleasant but unreadable. "Unfortunately, this has happened with our own people on more than one occasion."

Terrance nodded but fell silent as a servitor trundled in, a pitcher of ale and four glasses brandished on the flat tray that was the top of its head.

They exchanged small talk until the unit disappeared and the room was once more sealed and warded against intrusive probes.

"You were saying that this has happened to your own people in the past," Terrance prompted, and Simone nodded.

"It has. In fact, they're currently holding a very important military advisor of ours that we'd like to have back," the AI said, reaching for a glass and filling it from the pitcher.

It registered in the back of Terrance's brain that Simone was pouring it properly, too—glass tilted so as to minimize the head of foam at the top.

Handing it to Terrance, she added, "We thought we might be able to pool our resources and, together, launch a rescue mission to retrieve both our people."

Khela's eyes narrowed as he reached to accept the glass. "What makes you think a civilian ship like ours would have the capacity—"

She stopped abruptly as Kodi yelled, *<Stop! Don't drink that!>*

Terrance froze as his wife flowed out of her chair, laser-dagger activated and inserted protectively between him and the Godel natives across from him.

Carefully, he set the glass down, but not before Kodi had wrapped a buffer around the nano Simone had dropped on the outside of the glass and screened it for harmful viruses.

Terrance waited for Kodi's analysis, his gaze shifting between Deb and her companion. Simone looked guarded but expectant. Deb looked hopeful.

<It's clean,> Kodi reported, and Terrance slid a glance up at Khela.

Her lips compressed, but she gave a reluctant nod.

With a mental tap, he accessed the nano. And then rocked back in his seat, utterly nonplussed.

<How the hell…?> Kodi's voice sounded shocked. It echoed the thrill that coursed through Terrance.

The token Simone had embedded in the nano on the glass

contained an official government seal. A familiar one. The seal of the office of the Prime Minister of El Dorado, back in Alpha Centauri.

Lysander's seal—the AI who had formed Phantom Blade.

"Might I suggest that we resume this conversation where you can more easily confirm our identities?" The AI smiled crookedly and with a little tilt to her head toward Khela, asked, "Do you think your guardian would mind too terribly if you invited us to tour your ship?"

BIG REVEAL

STELLAR DATE: 03.09.3272 (Adjusted Gregorian)
LOCATION: ESS *Avon Vale*, Slip 512, Godel Trade Marina
REGION: Phaethon Duty Station, Little River

After Terrance and Khela passed through the umbilical, through the *Avon Vale*'s airlock, and into the ship, Simone and Deb were cleared to follow, and entered the *Vale*'s airlock.

The Godel representatives had been told that the only way they'd be allowed aboard was if they agreed to undergo a thorough scan. All parties understood that this was happening in a place that could be easily secured should the scan reveal anything untoward.

When Logan was satisfied the two posed no existential threat to the ship, Terrance escorted their guests up to the command deck and into the ready room.

And then Simone and Deb dropped their bombshell onto the rest of Phantom Blade.

Terrance sat across from Jason and suppressed a flare of amusement as his executive officer stared, dumbfounded, at the seal of Lysander's office hovering before them on the ready room's holo.

"What the—? How—?" The Proxan native glanced from Simone to Deb and then over to Shannon.

The ship's AI shook her head, then glanced pointedly at the twins. Landon had nothing to offer, but Logan leant forward, looking intrigued.

Before he had a chance to speak, Jonesy did.

"What do you want to bet the prime minister sent data on our task force to allies in nearby star systems?" the engineer said slowly, his tone thoughtful.

Tobias nodded. "Aye, lad, I see where you're going with this, I think. To establish bona fides, in case Phantom Blade ever found itself in need of assistance." His tone lifted in the end, turning the statement into a question as he raised a brow at Simone.

The AI's nod gave the Weapon Born—and the rest of the team—the confirmation they sought.

"Huh." Jason sat back, eyes narrowed, then nodded once. "Sounds like something the Old Man would do."

" 'Old Man'?"

Terrance felt Khela's breath on the back of his neck as she leant forward to quietly murmur the question into his ear.

"Lysander was embedded with Jason's dad when he was a kid," Terrance explained in an equally low tone, leaning back into her shoulder. "Probably the only reason he's not feral, given Tobias's influence."

"Heard that," two voices spoke at once, one with an accent and one without.

"Ahh, that explains it," Khela replied, a thread of mirth in her tone as she sat back.

Terrance suppressed a brief grin, then straightened. "Okay, I'll buy that. It's exactly the kind of thing he'd do. I can assure you, though, that our mission parameters have been met." He gestured to Lysander's seal. "We entered this system just to set up trade with Epsilon Eridani—excuse me, Little River—nothing more. So, we're square on that count?"

The commissioner nodded firmly. "We believe you. But given what has transpired with your captain, and given our own missing person, we thought we might be able to help each other out."

Jason's expression darkened, and Simone hastened to put up a forestalling hand. "We'll do what we can to help you recover Captain Rhinehart, regardless. We won't place contingencies upon that; it's not our way."

Silence descended upon the ready room as those seated around the table processed what had just been said. Then Tobias stirred.

"What do you want from Phantom Blade, lass?"

"You're an outside agency. No chance that you've been compromised. It's obvious that Barat has managed to insinuate its people into our agencies, as yesterday's setup of your captain will attest."

Jason and Terrance exchanged glances.

"Lass, Phantom Blade isn't for hire," Tobias admonished, his tone mild.

"I don't believe the people in Tau Ceti would agree with you on that," Simone countered.

Terrance swept a glance around the table and over to where Shannon's avatar stood, her arms crossed and a doubtful look on her face. He caught her eye, and she nodded reluctantly.

Turning back to their guests, he sat back, elbows resting on the arms of his chair, hands folded across his abdomen. "We're listening."

Before they could begin, Hailey, who had the ship's conn, pinged them over the shipnet.

<Sirs? There's a communication coming through right now that I think you're going to want to take....>

*****

"It's in the queue," Hailey called tersely, her fingers flying once more across the board at her station on comm. "From the Barat Consulate on the station."

Jason drummed his fingers on the side of the captain's chair. Calista's chair. Technically, as executive officer and acting captain, the chair was his until such time as Calista returned.

He glanced sharply at Hailey. "Live, I assume?" As she sent her assent, he moved away from the chair and motioned Tobias over. "Might be better if I weren't the one to deal with them, given the circumstances." Glancing over at the people who had spilled out of the ready room, and then back at Hailey, he added, "Make sure the pickup on our end is narrow enough so that only Tobias is shown in the feed."

"Aye, sir. Woman says she's Citizen Consul Brentano."

As Tobias settled into the captain's seat, the AI nodded once to Hailey. "Let's see what they have to say, lass."

The image of a woman resolved on the bridge's forward holo, her face long, lean and spare, her expression severe.

"Counselor Brentano," Tobias greeted, and Jason saw the woman's face tighten in displeasure—although he couldn't yet tell what had spawned it. Maybe it was because Tobias had dropped the 'citizen' from his greeting. Hell, perhaps it was because Tobias was clearly an AI.

"*Avon Vale,* we regret to inform you that your captain has been caught stealing from one of our merchants and is being held for her crimes, pending her trial."

Woman doesn't mince words, Jason noted.

"Where we come from, lass, an individual is innocent until proven guilty," Tobias stated mildly, and Jason saw the woman's lips compress into a thin line.

Definitely not an AI lover.

"Calista Rhinehart was found in possession of stolen merchandise, and the merchants have identified her as the perpetrator." She spread her hands in a slight, disdainful shrug. "Really, it's only a formality at this point."

"And you're telling us this why, again?"

"Your people are new to Little River, and the Humans' Republic of Barat—" *Yes, there it is, a subtle emphasis on the word '**humans**',* Jason thought, "—can appreciate that your people might not be familiar with our ways."

The woman leant toward the holo pickups on her end. "It's possible we might be able to convince the court to be lenient with this first offense. But we would, of course, require some show of good faith in return."

Tobias placed an elbow on the arm of the captain's chair, resting his chin in his hand, and let the silence over the connection build. The woman stared back at him implacably.

When finally, he spoke, the Weapon Born's tone was mild, his enunciation precise and his brogue almost nonexistent.

"And what, might I ask, would the *Humans'* Republic consider a show of good faith?"

*Stars, Tobias is **pissed**.*

Surprisingly, that thought cleared the veil of red that had threatened to obscure Jason's own vision. His eyes narrowed as he studied the woman on the holo. Her expression had just subtly altered. He suspected the emotion behind it was one of satisfaction and knew it was because the people on the *Vale* were playing right to her script.

She gestured casually. "Oh, surely someone from a star system more than a dozen light years away has progressed with their skills, knowledge, and science in ways different from our own. Perhaps," she suggested in an offhanded manner, "we could arrange for a technology exchange. I hear your stasis tech is a bit different than ours?" She smiled, but it was a cold thing, not reaching her eyes. "Such a benefit to society could offset the dangerous influence a criminal might have on its citizens...."

Jason reached for Tobias over their private Link connection. *<Bull. Shit.>* His mental tone was incensed, and he felt a corresponding outrage from the Weapon Born.

The pretense was so threadbare that to call it a veiled threat was a real travesty. He could feel the AI seething, his ire barely contained.

But Tobias merely nodded, then paused as if to gather his thoughts. Jason figured it was more to rein in his temper before he spoke.

"You understand this is not within my authority to grant," Tobias began, and Jason saw the woman's lip curl ever so slightly. "I will need to run this past my employer, the owner of the company."

The woman's cold smile grew broader, her expression now one

of a predator locked onto its prey. "Please tell him it is best if he did not delay his decision. Your shipmate has petitioned her case be heard by a higher court than any we have here on the duty station." She sat back, eyes glinting in triumph. "We have no choice but to accommodate her wishes, you understand, as the citizens of the Republic pride ourselves on extending the courtesies of the State even to those incarcerated. We would hate for this to happen, of course, to someone less familiar with our laws. Especially if there are other…more amicable…ways we might resolve this."

Fuck. <They're forcing our hand, Tobe. If they ship her out before we have a chance to attempt a recovery op—>

<I see that, boyo.> The AI's thoughts were heavy in Jason's head. *<You can see it in her eyes, too. She believes she has us hemmed in.>* Tobias inclined his head toward the figure on the holo. "I'll pass that along, and we'll be in touch."

With a jerk of her head, the woman cut the connection.

BIG GAME

STELLAR DATE: 03.09.3272 (Adjusted Gregorian)
LOCATION: New Pejeta Game Preserve, equatorial region
REGION: Barat, Little River

Giovanni stood respectfully beside his premier as Rachelle Feretti leant against the railing of the hovercraft that was skimming slowly over the equatorial veldt. He could feel sweat beading on his brow and upper lip, but restrained himself from wiping at it.

Feretti, in contrast, was the only one on the skimmer who looked comfortable. Giovanni had suspected that Feretti had mods no one knew about; this confirmed it. No one, other than someone able to regulate their body's temperature, could manage to look so fresh in the wilting heat and high humidity of the New Pejeta Preserve.

They were observing a lioness as she crept up on a herd of unsuspecting gazelle. The predator would soon spring, bringing down the animal unlucky enough to be on the outside of the group, while those surrounding the inner core remained protected.

Reminds me of our political structure. Those inside the premier's political sphere, the ones who successfully curry her favor, are the ones that survive the longest, he thought as they watched the sleek, golden form of the big cat.

Moments later, powerful muscles bunched, then arced through the air. A massive paw slapped at the animal's rear, knocking it down. Adamantine jaws fastened onto the creature's neck, quickly draining it of life.

Feretti made a pleased sound as she observed the lioness's kill then turned and slanted a look toward Giovanni. Tilting her head to indicate the tableau, she murmured, "A successful kill requires forethought, cunning, and skill, does it not, Councilman?"

He nodded. "Indeed, Madam Premier." He paused, searching for the correct response. "Had she been stalking the doe upwind, the herd would have scented her and scattered. I rather suspect a predator learns such things early in life, or it will starve."

"Ah, but you're wrong." She turned to him, leaning against the railing, the slight breeze created by the movement of the craft stirring her cap of dark hair. "Lions don't take wind direction into account. Instead, they stay out of sight—and then they ambush. And when they do, the attack is swift, overwhelming, and decisive."

Her eyes narrowed. "I want there to be no misunderstanding between the two of us. It is good to stalk your prey, necessary even. But it would be most unfortunate should the prey scent the predator." She turned back to the lioness. The creature's head raised, one oversized paw on the haunch of the dead doe, muzzle red with her kill's blood. "Don't wait too long before committing to the Verdant acquisition, Giovanni. Councilmember Savin and General Jones have assured me that the Guard is ready to enact a swift and decisive takeover."

The threat could scarcely be considered veiled or implied—if Giovanni didn't act soon, *they* would.

The premier confirmed it with her last words on the subject.

"Let me be perfectly clear: that crystal *will* be ours."

"Yes, Madam Premier." Giovanni held himself stiffly, his tone stilted and constrained.

Feretti ignored it, turning back to the hunter and her prey.

"And what of this Enfield, from Alpha Centauri?" she murmured. "Your report this morning indicated his company has new tech to trade with Little River."

"They do. A new stasis tech," Giovanni confirmed, casting a glance across the vessel's deck to ensure there were no interested listeners nearby. "And possible military advances, too."

Feretti smiled in satisfaction, and Giovanni couldn't help but compare her to the leonine figure crouching in the tall savannah grasses.

"Excellent. And you have plans to acquire those as well?"

Her words hung between them, an expectation of compliance.

"Of course," he assured her, and his gaze slid from her penetrating gaze back to the carcass of the gazelle, where the lioness had buried her muzzle as she rent strips of flesh from its hide. "We have their captain in custody, on charges of theft. We will make an exchange."

Feretti nodded perfunctorily and motioned to the hovercraft's pilot. Immediately, the vessel picked up speed, its track curving back toward the Republic pinnace at the nearby spaceport, standing by to return them to the Presidium.

She turned her attention back to him, spearing him with an intense gaze. "How confident are you that Enfield will trade for his captain?" Her tone was sharp.

"Every bit of information we have on these people—although, granted, we don't have much—" Giovanni said carefully, his voice neutral, "leads us to believe that they are close-knit, and will do whatever is required to get her back."

Feretti's brows rose in frank disbelief. "Don't dissemble with me, Giovanni." Her reprimand stung, as she had intended it to. "If this doesn't work, then by what other means do you intend to acquire the tech?"

Giovanni hastened to reassure her. "They are a civilian ship, Madam Premier. They have no defenses against us and would be easily overtaken, should they, for some reason, decide to abandon their captain rather than trade for her."

She turned her face into the wind as the craft began its deceleration on approach to the pinnace. As it drew to a stop, she cut one final glance his way.

"Come to the mews tomorrow at seven. I wish to fly Tigan," she said, referring to the Harris's hawk that Giovanni had gifted her two years before when he had learned of her growing interest in the sport of falconry. "You can apprise me of the progress of our acquisitions—on both fronts—at that time."

He bowed his head slightly in acknowledgement of her order and then followed in her wake, surreptitiously wiping the sweat from both brow and lip as she disembarked and strode toward the craft waiting to return them to the governmental seat of the Humans' Republic.

PART THREE: INFILTRATION

THE ORIGIN OF SPECIES

STELLAR DATE: 03.10.3272 (Adjusted Gregorian), 0100 hours, local
LOCATION: ESS *Avon Vale*, Slip 512, Godel Trade Marina
REGION: Phaethon Duty Station, Epsilon Eridani

"Give me one good reason why we shouldn't trade the stasis tech for our captain."

Jason's words sounded sharply into the lull that had fallen after the Baratian woman cut the connection. They caused a ripple of reaction around the bridge.

Deb looked alarmed, and Simone looked—well, Logan still couldn't get a good read on the AI, which was a bit disconcerting, given that it was his job to profile others. But it also intrigued him.

Before things progressed, Terrance held up a hand. "Let's take this into the ready room, shall we?" He looked over at Landon in inquiry, and Logan's brother nodded then turned and headed for the captain's chair. Settling into it, he began to quietly issue orders to those that would remain behind.

The team and their guests drifted around the table as Terrance ordered coffee and tea from the room's servitor. Shannon placed her avatar into a chair near Jason, and Logan saw Tobi's sinewy length settle at the XO's feet.

Logan settled back, content to observe. The more data points he could gather, the more easily a situation resolved inside his own mind. Patterns exposed, motives revealed.

For a while, the servitor's quiet hum was the only sound that could be heard as it circled the table, delivering beverages.

After a moment, the Godel AI spoke.

"Your ship, Mister Enfield, and your crew, have just been drawn into a highly volatile situation. Barat intends to hold your captain hostage for whatever tech you came to Little River to sell. They will settle for nothing less." She glanced over at Deb. "Historically, though, we've had very little luck negotiating with them for the release of prisoners."

Deb nodded, one finger circling the rim of her coffee cup as she looked down into its depths. "Your chances of retrieving your captain are far better using the resources of Phantom Blade," she said, looking up at them intently, "than they are negotiating through Enfield Holdings."

Terrance sat back at that. "Why do you say that?" he asked, eyes tracking from one to the other.

Before either could respond, Shannon broke in, her avatar's silver eyes slitted in thought as her hair shifted restlessly behind her.

"I wonder," she mused. "Little River's an awfully young colony to be so polarized. Didn't the Generation Ship Service screen applicants for such things when they filled the colony ships' rosters, so this kind of situation wouldn't happen?"

Simone glanced over at Deb and then back at Shannon with a wry smile. "Under normal circumstances, you'd be right about that," the Godel AI admitted. "But this system was settled by two colony ships, backed by two different corporations, instead of just one."

<*Whoa. How'd that happen?*> Kodi asked, his tone curious.

Logan saw Jason shift impatiently, but Tobias held off the man's incipient protest with a gesture before the *Vale*'s acting captain could voice it.

"It wasn't originally supposed to be that way," Deb admitted. "Although it's rare, any government or corporation requesting an FGT terraforming project—one wealthy enough to afford more than one ship, that is—can petition the FGT for a second planet in its system."

"I take it that's what happened here, lass?" Tobias clarified, leaning forward, and Deb nodded.

The Weapon Born turned to the ready room's holowall and brought up the statistics of the two colony ships that had disgorged their passengers back in the late thirty-first and early thirty-second centuries.

The task force studied it a moment in silence, while their guests allowed them to assimilate the information on display.

By colonial standards, this system was a fledgling in comparison to the one from which Phantom Blade hailed, as Alpha Centauri was now in its sixth century of colonization.

It was also much younger than Tau Ceti, or even Sirius, as the other systems had been first stops for their respective FGT worldships. Epsilon Eridani was the second stop for the *Voyager* after it had completed its terraforming of Galene in Tau Ceti.

Interestingly enough, the *Avon Vale* had followed in the *Voyager*'s wake, making the same trip one hundred and forty years after the second planet had been handed over to its colonists.

Perspective. Logan wasn't sure how much Little River's comparative youth played in this situation, but information was the coin by which he plied his trade, and he stored it away as he worked to prise more intel out of their two guests.

"Obviously, neither colony ship had AIs aboard," he prompted, priming the pump.

<Kind of hard for them to, since they left in the twenty-sixth century, and we weren't common until the twenty-nine hundreds,> Kodi mused.

From her position next to Tobias, Shannon's avatar stirred, silver hair beginning to snap a bit in agitation. "From that last transmission on the bridge," she said, an edge in her voice, "I get the impression that the people of Barat don't like our kind very much."

"They don't," Simone confirmed.

"Why's that, lass?" Tobias's voice was mild, but Logan could tell by his expression that the way the Weapon Born had been treated by the Barat Guard rankled.

"Ah, well now, *that* is where we come to the purpose of this little history lesson," Deb said, swiveling her chair once more to the holodisplay at the end of the conference table.

The holo shifted, and two colony ships hovered in its depths. Icons appeared, identifying them by name, date, and planetary destination. Deb highlighted the first one.

"The *Manifest Destiny* was commissioned by a publicly-traded company in the mid-twenty-five hundreds, name of EpiGen."

<*Whoa,*> Kodi commented. <*That ship name just about says it all. They see AIs as an existential threat to human supremacy, I'll wager.*>

"You'd win that bet," Simone agreed. "Although, at the time the ship was commissioned, the AI singularity hadn't yet occurred. But it was projected to happen soon, and EpiGen was one of its main detractors. Their position on humanity is the source of much of the tension within the system, too. In fact, had they not leveraged their company so heavily back in Sol, we might be dealing with a completely different dynamic."

"How so?" Terrance asked.

"Because both planets would have been settled by EpiGen. Instead, by reinvesting all of its shareholders' profits into the building of two colony ships at once, as a proof of concept for its next generation of products," Simone leaned forward, gaze sweeping the room, "EpiGen overextended itself, and folded."

"It wouldn't have been a problem if the expedition had launched all at once," Deb explained, "but you see, they'd only just laid the keel for the second ship when they discovered the shipment of raw materials intended for its framework was inferior product."

She glanced over at Simone. "There was speculation at the time that the materials had been sabotaged by a competitor, but nothing came of the investigation."

The Godel AI shrugged, opening her hands, palms up, in a *"who knows?"* gesture. "Regardless, because of the trouble they ran into with the second ship, EpiGen decided to go ahead and send the settlers to the first planet and begin populating Barat."

"And then the company folded…?" Jason prompted, glancing from Simone to Deb to Terrance.

Terrance returned his gaze, his own speculative as he raised his coffee mug to his lips, then shifted to look over at Simone thoughtfully. "And there was a bidding war over the second ship," he guessed, then gestured with his mug before taking a sip. "Which meant that those slated to be colonists had to reapply all over again."

<*It was probably a mandatory requirement,*> Kodi mused. <*I'm sure the new company had its own mission statement, different from the original one that had won the bid.*>

Deb laughed. "Oh, you'd be right about that! And since the FGT had already begun terraforming two worlds in this system, the Generation Ship Service knew they had to fast-track their next round of colonists."

"But it wasn't like they were desperate for people to fill the contract, though, was it?" Khela interposed. "Colony ships have always had their pick of candidates to choose from."

There were murmurs of assent all around the table.

<*You laughed when I mentioned a different mission statement,*> Kodi asked. <*Why's that?*>

"Because," Simone's tone was wry, "you may have noticed that the EpiGen colonists evolved a much more rigid social structure than the one we practice on Godel."

Jason made a derisive noise no one would mistake for a laugh. "I kind of did, yes."

Deb took up the narrative. "Because of that, freedoms on Barat aren't as…easily obtained…as they are in the parts of Little River controlled by Godel."

She paused to take a sip of coffee, swallowed, then canted her head thoughtfully. "You know, even though Barat was colonized almost fifty years earlier than Godel, we've more than caught up to

Barat's technology; we've significantly surpassed it. Many believe their oppressive society is one of the reasons why."

At Jason's skeptical look, Deb smiled slightly.

"How familiar are you with the path of scientific advancement in such governments, as opposed to those that are more pluralistic?" she asked.

Logan saw Noa exchange a glance with his daughter. "Some of us," the quiet man offered in a soft voice, "are a bit more familiar with it than others might be. You refer to the concept of stagnant orthodoxy?"

Logan saw Deb nod in relief. "Yes, I do." She must have caught the perplexed look on the faces of some of her audience, for she added, "It's the concept that scientific advances become strangled when subjected to an arbitrary, authoritarian government. That those in power see the exploratory aspects of scientific advancement as frivolous waste, and contrary to the goals of the state."

"All governments have an impact upon science," Noa murmured. "In all of human history, they always have." Deb's nod conceded his point.

"So that happened here," Terrance speculated. "Godel supported research and innovation—including welcoming AIs with open arms—while Barat…?"

"Barat steals what it cannot create."

"How does this matter to us where Calista's concerned?" Shannon's words were direct. Based on the impatient jiggle Logan could see in Jason's leg, she'd barely beat him to the question.

"Yes," Khela agreed, her tone thoughtful, "why would this matter to us?" Her palms were carefully placed on either side of the mug in front of her and she was staring intently into its depths.

Her words could have been provocative, but they were delivered in a reflective, musing tone. It was clear she was working through the information they'd just shared.

Logan liked that about Terrance's wife.

He saw Deb and Simone exchange a glance.

"If you gave them your stasis tech," Simone cautioned, "it could alter the balance of power in this system and most likely start a war."

Jason had been sitting in a deceptive slouch, one leg crossed over the other, fingers tapping out a soundless beat on the leg of his shipsuit. At Simone's words, he sat up abruptly, all pretense erased.

The man who stared back at the Godel AI was laser-focused. All warrior.

"Explain that." The words were a command.

"Our intelligence suggests that Barat has been working on a plan to decimate Godel's economy for some time now. Your stasis tech could turn that plan into a reality."

"Getting Calista back is what matters here," Shannon's avatar straightened from where she'd projected it against the wall. She stepped forward, hands fisted at her sides. "I'm not concerned about your financial problems."

Jason held up a hand to stop the ship's AI, all without breaking eye contact with Simone.

"How?" A single, terse word shot like a bullet from the acting captain's lips.

Stars, and Landon thinks I'm stingy with what I say. Logan looked on admiringly as Shannon subsided and Jason's hand lowered. Not once had the XO looked over at Shannon as he continued to hold the other AI's gaze.

"Your tech," Simone confessed, "might just be the edge they need to come out ahead in any conflict that might erupt between the two planets."

Terrance held up both hands in protest. "Now, wait a minute. We didn't come here to get embroiled in a system-wide war. We just came to establish trade relations. Nothing more."

Simone nodded solemnly. "Understandable. But if you hand over that tech, that's exactly what will happen. Which is why our offer to help stands, even if you can't see your way to helping us free our analyst."

"Retrieving Calista's our top priority," Terrance began, pausing at Jason's muttered "damn straight".

"But if we can free your agent without compromising the operation," Terrance shot a glance around the table, and Logan saw nods of affirmation from the team, "then we'll get your agent back for you, too."

"Barat considers your captain a veritable gold mine," Simone warned, her expression grim. "They will have her under close guard. And—" Here, she paused, hesitating, her gaze shifting uncomfortably to Deb and then back. "If she has any modifications of any kind, they will seek to extract everything they can from them in an attempt to reverse-engineer your tech and appropriate it for their own use."

A stir went through the room. Logan exchanged looks with Terrance, who gave a slight nod. The profiler stood.

"Send us everything you have," he instructed the two from Godel as he moved toward the exit. "I'll be in the armory. We leave at oh-two-hundred tonight."

SHELL GAME

STELLAR DATE: 03.10.3272 (Adjusted Gregorian), 0200 hours, local
LOCATION: ESS *Avon Vale*, Slip 512, Godel Trade Marina
REGION: Phaethon Duty Station, Little River

The teams had been assigned. Terrance would accompany Deb back down to the station and begin a very loud and obvious series of protests with an entourage from the *Vale,* while Landon remained on the ship as acting captain.

Jason, Tobias, and Logan would board the *Vale*'s Icarus-class shuttle, the *Sable Wind.* A small cadre of Marines would accompany them, captained by Khela. Simone would go along in an advisory capacity. Charley would shadow the shuttle in the stealth fighter, *Mirage.*

Jason slid into the armory and headed for the cabinet where the ammunition was stored. His chameleon suit matched those Khela and her team wore, its hood dangling loosely from the back of his neck, awaiting activation.

He grabbed a holster and shrugged into it, the unit exchanging tokens with his suit as he did so. It faded into the background between one breath and the next as he tightened the holster's rig straps and slid a pulse pistol inside. Several EM grenades and a few small-yield shaped charges were next, tucked into the suit's bandolier.

A lightwand slid into each of the leg holsters he'd strapped into place when he'd hastily donned the suit in his quarters. He completed the ensemble by snapping on a pair of woven Elastene wrist cuffs, each filled with various types of breach and infiltration nano, protected behind the Faraday cage of the experimental new Enfield cloth.

"No light armor, boyo?"

Tobias's voice emanated from the armory's speakers as Charley worked to seat the Weapon Born's cylinder inside a stealth frame, while Landon did the same for his brother.

Jason shot the frame a grin. "I have you and our Marines to look out for me, Tobe. I'll just hide behind you if anyone starts shooting. Besides, you guys are going to be doing the advance work; I'm just along in case things go sideways and you need someone unaugmented to get the job done."

He caught Lena exchange a sardonic look with Ramon out of the corner of his eye as the Marines finished kitting up in light armor and their own artillery.

"Don't worry, squishie. We'll keep your tender hide from going splat," Lena assured him, slapping him on the back with one of her armored hands. Anticipating the move, Jason dipped just far enough into his enhanced abilities to deflect the blow and keep it from flattening him as the Marine had intended.

Lena's scowl telegraphed her disappointment as he grinned back at her. "Hey, I thought only armadillos and hardbody mod-jobs could call a guy a squishie," he complained, which caused Ramon to bark out a laugh.

"He's got you there, Lena," the Marine smirked at his comrade-in-arms. "Don't think our augmentations count for that. Especially if you're not fast enough to take him down."

Lena's eyes narrowed at her fellow Marine, and she shot a leg out to trip him as he passed, which he easily avoided. "Oh, he'd be down, all right—if I'd wanted him to be. Not like I was trying very hard."

"Not like I was evading very hard, either." Jason grinned back at her as she took a threatening step toward him.

The sound of a pulse rifle cycling drew their attention. "Bet even you couldn't outrun this…squishie," Khela's eyes twinkled as she joined in the conversation.

<*Seriously, though, Jason,*> she added privately. <*Terrance will kill me if I let anything happen to you. Won't you* **please** *consider wearing*

light armor?>

Jason knew the Marine captain wasn't fond of the idea of him going along, especially without the same protection her fireteams would have. He didn't particularly feel the need, but the concern in her eyes and the slight pleading look had him nodding his agreement.

She grinned impishly at him. *<See?>* she teased. *<That wasn't too hard, now was it…squishie?>*

He rolled his eyes as he reached for his armor and began donning it.

Landon slapped his brother on the back. "Good to go," he said.

The stealth frame powered up, and Logan tested its responsiveness. Nodding, he moved out of the armory, the Marines at his heels.

Jason stopped up next to the stealth frame that held the Weapon Born. "Ready, Tobe?" he asked, moving aside to give Charley room to kit up.

"Almost," Tobias said, twisting around to grab spare batts for his frame's twin E-SCARs—Electron-beam Special Combat Assault Rifles—before flipping each individual weapon up to check the current status of each charge. With a sound that approximated a satisfied grunt, the AI rose. "Let's go get your lass back, shall we, boyo?"

"You don't have to ask me twice," he agreed, then followed him down toward the hangar.

The ship's complement of smaller vessels were attached to rails, each one tied down to an auto-tow unit. Once the bay doors were opened, the rails would extend, and the auto-tows would tug their loads free of the ship, releasing them into the black.

Jason paused next to the first craft, a sleek, ultra-black fighter, while the rest continued on toward the Icarus-class shuttle, the *Sable Wind.* He could just make out the stasis field and shroud covering the second shuttle, the *Eidolon.*

Salvaged from the battlefield back in Tau Ceti as a jumbled

mess of parts and twisted electronics, he and Jonesy had set out to rebuild her on the long journey to Epsilon Eridani. Along the way, Shannon and Jonesy had taken the opportunity to tinker with her a bit. Jason was itching to test some of her new capabilities, but knew she wasn't quite ready yet.

Too bad, he mused. *She'd be a real asset on a mission like this.*

Turning back to the task at hand, he triggered the fighter's canopy, then turned to face the AI who would be flying the *Mirage.*

"Ready?" he asked Charley, and the AI sent his assent, then powered down his frame, releasing the panel where his cylinder was secured.

Jason leant down and detached the leads that connected Charley to his frame and pressed the release that would unseat the cylinder from its cushioned slot.

He then stepped into the lift that would take him level with the pilot's cradle and activated it, Charley in hand. When the lift came to rest, Jason leant into the cockpit and inserted the cylinder into the specially cushioned recess that had been created to allow an AI to embed inside the fighting machine.

He sent a handshake over the combat net to the *Mirage,* and the fighter powered up, accepting Charley's token.

"Ship's yours, Charley," Jason said.

<*I have the ship,*> the AI responded in the timeworn hand-off pilots used.

"Fair skies and tailwinds," Jason said, slapping the canopy closed and sending the lift back down to the hangar's deck.

<*Not really applicable to spacecraft, you know,*> Charley commented dryly, and Jason sent him a mental chuckle.

<*Tradition, Charl. We pilots love our traditions. Thought you knew that by now.*>

<*Oh, I do. Still doesn't make it applicable though.*>

<*Touché.*>

Jason spotted Simone at the hangar's entrance and waved her over as Charley remotely operated his frame, sending it into a protected area in the back of the bay.

"Everything set on Godel's side?" Jason queried as the two walked across the bay to join the team on the *Sable Wind.*

"It is. We have a nice shell game planned for any of our friends who might be monitoring your ship's activity." The AI glanced over at Jason as he led the way up the shuttle's ramp. "And I guarantee they're watching you right now."

"I don't doubt it," he replied, then switched over to the combat net.

<Charley's good to go,> he informed the team as he ducked through *Sable Wind*'s hatch, followed by Simone.

<Excellent,> he heard Terrance's voice from where he stood on the bridge of the *Vale. <Sure you don't need another hand?>*

<No!> came Khela's sharp response, and Jason saw Lena and Ramon turn away so that their captain didn't see their smirks.

<Very well, then. Shannon says you're clear to launch.>

"This is it, people. Stow your gear, take your seats. You launch in five," Landon announced as he strode down the ramp. Clapping Jason on the shoulder, he wished him luck and headed for the bridge.

Jason nodded at Simone and slipped past Tobias and the Marines to join Logan in the cockpit. As he did, he reached out to Comm on the bridge.

<All right, Hailey,> he sent. *<We're just about ready to get the heck outta Dodge down here.>*

<What, sir?> Hailey's voice came back to him, confused.

<Nevermind,> he responded, sending her avatar a smile. *<We're ready to launch. We'll stay close-in until our hitchhiker's secure, and then we'll bug out.>*

The hitchhiker Jason referred to was *Mirage.* As soon as both ships exited the bay, and while they were still within the *Avon Vale*'s radar signature, the two ships would perform their own docking maneuver. The fighter would attach itself to the belly of the shuttle and then turn off its universal ident, thus remaining undetectable by scans from Phaethon's STC.

<Ahh, got it, sir. I think,> Hailey responded. *<You're clear any time.>*

* * * * *

The Citizen controller monitoring Phaethon's Space Traffic Control sat up suddenly, the stack of plas films scattering on the console before her as she reached over to tap the icon that would send the feed to the main holo.

"Sir!" she called out, swiveling her chair around to face the commanding officer on duty. "The Centauri ship has launched a shuttle, and it's headed to our side of the station."

She nodded toward the holofeed that showed the icons representing the vessels in nearspace around the duty station.

Her fingers flew over the display in front of her as she highlighted the craft that had departed the *Avon Vale*. Captions scrolled beneath, recapping the interaction between the STC controller and the pilot of the vessel, the *Sable Wind.*

"What kind of a name is that for a proper spacecraft?" her superior scoffed as he glanced at the glowing ident the STC had tagged to the little ship.

In the next moment, she saw his eyes narrow as he read the text hovering beneath the radar map. Just then, they heard a comm sent from STC.

<Sable Wind, *this is Phaethon Control. Say destination.>*

<Just taking a tour of your fine station, Control,> came a lazy drawl in reply.

The unseen man sounded insolent and undisciplined to the Barat officer's ear, and she could tell her boss had taken an immediate dislike to it.

<Sable Wind, *you're nearing restricted space,>* STC warned, but the Centauri vessel seemed not to care that it was headed straight for the Barat side of the station's wheel.

The controller watching wondered briefly if it was a purposeful gambit. An attempt, perhaps, to try to obtain more information on the whereabouts of their ship's captain? She'd heard that the woman was currently in their custody, enjoying temporary accommodations inside the Republican Compound's lockup.

She saw her superior lean back in his seat as he watched the little craft approach, an expression of rapt attention on his face. Should it breach Barat sovereign territory, she rather suspected he'd enjoy the opportunity to have it shot out of the black.

In the next moment, however, she saw his expression morph into a scowl, as a Godel vessel more than twice the mass of the Centauri vessel veered from its flight path to intercept.

<Sable Wind,> the Godel ship called, *<Stand by to be escorted back to your ship.>*

<Thought this was open space.> The cocky male voice now held an edge of caution to it. *<We're good, Godel, no need for an escort.>*

<Well now, we wouldn't want you to stir up any incidents,> the Godel pilot responded with a drawl of her own. *<You don't know the rules in these parts, son.>*

As the Baratian controller watched, the icons identifying the two craft did a little wobble-and-dance, the Centauri ship attempting to evade, but the Godel craft snagging it and drawing it into its hold.

Her superior glowered at the screen as if highly offended that his entertainment had been snatched away from him. He waved the holo off, and with a glare at the controller monitoring the STC channels, ordered her not to bother him again with trivialities.

Abashed, the controller murmured her apologies to the citizen officer and went back to sorting the stack of films she'd been working on since beginning her shift late that afternoon.

*****

The tightbeam exchanged between the Godel transport and the

Sable Wind included the IFF ident of a few Godel pinnaces known to be in the area, should they need to use them during their operation.

With a final 'good luck!' the transport rolled to interpose itself between the Barat section of the station and the two *Avon Vale* spacecraft. At the same time, it slewed slightly to port, exposing just enough of its engine wash to spike the sensors Barat was using to monitor nearspace. The radiation from its engines would more than mask the two spacecrafts as they became stealthy, turning off all transponders and shutting off their own engines.

As the transport adjusted its heading for the Godel marina, two blacker-than-black shadows—lost to Barat's overwhelmed sensors—eased down toward the Barat side of the duty station.

*****

Just before the shuttle dropped below the horizon created by the wheel of the duty station, the fission-powered mini sun that controlled its circadian cycle from the center of the spoke-and-wheel assembly dimmed as the station went into official night.

From inside, the view through the thick plas dome revealed the spars that made up the station's spokes, the far view of the opposite side of the wheel, and the flickering lights of nearby space traffic.

The view from the shuttle's front holo, by contrast, swelled with the image of seamed metal shielding that comprised the station's underbelly as Jason piloted them ever closer to its surface.

He tapped the thrusters one last time, matching the *Sable Wind*'s angular velocity to that of the rotating surface of the duty station. Moments later, they hovered two meters above an out-of-service airlock, an entry point that had been sealed shut decades before, when Godel completed construction.

Simone assured them it would be the ideal entry point, and she'd brought the manufacturer's override codes to ensure their silent entrance.

<*Transferring control to you,*> Jason informed Charley, and the AI sent his acknowledgement as he took control of the *Sable Wind.*

Logan's stealth frame was hovering at the hatch, and Jason could sense a flurry of information pass between him and Charley on the periphery of his awareness as the two coordinated the seal of the shuttle's collar around the airlock's frame.

<*We have seal,*> Logan sent as he stepped back to give Simone access.

The Godel AI accessed the dormant panel and keyed in an override. <*You're good to go,*> she said over the net as the airlock doors slowly recessed back into the station's frame.

The shuttle sensors registered positive pressure, and Logan triggered the hatch.

The two teams filed off the shuttle and into the low-ceilinged, single-story underlayer that had been used as the foundation of the station.

<*Good hunting,*> Simone sent.

MOTOR POOL, SLUDGE POOL

STELLAR DATE: 03.10.3272 (Adjusted Gregorian) 0330 hours, local
LOCATION: Beneath Barat Sector
REGION: Phaethon Duty Station, Little River

The lowest deck below the inner 'surface' of Phaethon's ring was dimly lit and tall enough for the infiltrators to stand upright.

Well, most of us at least, Khela amended with a mental smile as she saw the two AIs adjust their frames to fit.

Intel had Calista housed in temporary lockup inside Republican HQ. Godel's agent was being held in the compound's long-term detention block. It was far enough from the main building that two fireteams were needed in order to extract them both.

Khela, Logan, and Ramon were Fireteam One. They were to go after the Godel agent, while Fireteam Two—Tobias, Jason, Lena and Tama—retrieved Calista. Calista was the primary target, so Khela's team would hold back, ready to provide assistance, until the captain was secured.

After a short trek, the two teams formed up one level below the station's main deck, around a pillar that housed the nearest node.

Lena slung her kit down by the pillar's base and began to pry off an access panel for Tama to make use of the software toolsets Godel had provided to breach Barat's network. Logan released reconnaissance drones down the length of the passage, while Khela pulled up the station map Simone had provided.

Tossing it onto the combat net, she highlighted the Republican Compound, then waited for the view to update based on the data Tama had just gleaned from behind Barat's firewalls.

<Looks like Godel's intel is solid,> she observed. *<Not much has changed. Is this where you'll breach?>* She dropped a pin on the far side of the compound and glanced up to catch Jason's nod.

<*Aye, lass,*> Tobias concurred. <*That's the service entrance we identified.*>

<*It's a bit of a haul,*> Khela noted. <*Once Lena's disabled Republican surveillance, head on out. We'll hold back until you have eyes on and have confirmed your location's secure. We breach on my mark.*>

She suppressed a smile at Lena's crisp, if distracted, <*Aye, cap'n*>, then let her gaze sweep the group until she received confirmation all around.

<*We're good,*> Lena announced as she straightened and shouldered her kit. <*Barat's eyes won't see us.*>

<*Electronic, no. Human, yes,*> Khela cautioned. <*Don't get careless just because we've hacked surveillance. There's always the chance Godel missed something. No one's sloppy and screwing up tonight, got it?*>

Tobias nodded, then pushed away from the wall. <*We'll be off, then.*>

Lena nodded to Khela and fell in behind Jason as the three disappeared down the corridor.

Khela consulted her overlay once more and tilted her head in the other direction. <*Okay, folks, it's our turn. Let's move out.*>

Ramon grinned at her as he followed Logan's frame into the dim recess. <*Ooo-rah, Cap'n!*>

* * * * *

Ten minutes later, and a kilometer further upspin, Jason raised himself up through an access hatch. It led to an area on the diagram graced with the uninspired label, 'Citizens Housing Section Twelve'.

Stars, did these people just completely run out of names?

He crouched next to Tobias, taking in their surroundings with a glance, even as his overlay began to populate with data, streaming in from the microdrones Lena had set aloft that Tama now controlled.

The drones carried an array of multi-spectrum cameras and

sensitive microphones. These would establish a surveillance perimeter that would warn of any humans approaching as the team infiltrated.

Each microdrone was hidden by its own cloud of colloid nanobots. These weren't capable of independent motion; they were much too small for that. The cloud, comprised of sound-dampening and light-scattering nano, was there to conceal the drones themselves from any passerby with augments that might catch such things.

The microdrone's thrusters handled the cloud's transport, pulling the colloids along in their wake turbulence as the drones slowly rose in accordance with their own mission objectives.

<*Stars, that's a lot of data to sift through,*> Jason murmured over the combat net as the sensor data began building a comprehensive picture of the ramshackle neighborhood.

<*Not any more than what you process every time you strap into the pilot's cradle, from what I hear,*> Tama countered as the three figures fanned out.

Tobias's frame cautiously crept toward the alleyway exit. Jason followed, lifting one shoulder in a half shrug.

<*I suppose you're right,*> he allowed. <*Guess it's all in the kind of information you're used to processing.*>

He looked back toward the recess of the darkened alleyway, then let his eyes sweep up and across the three-story apartment buildings they stood between. The structures were fashioned out of rough-poured, lightweight plascrete. In a time long past, their surfaces had been whitewashed, but the intervening years had not been kind, and the paint had begun to peel, irregular patches revealing the dingy grey of underlaying formation material.

Jason swiveled as a rustling noise behind them caught his attention, and his IR caught something small, a rodent probably, scurrying across from one pile of discarded debris to another. He could just make out a label on the crumpled side of plastic sheeting: 'beverage base powder—orange'. Its description reminded him more of institutional military rations than the type of refuse discarded by those living in a residential neighborhood.

<*Nice place they have here,*> he sent as Lena signaled it was safe to exit the alley.

<*Matches what Godel has told us of the Baratian lifestyle. Has the feel of a police state, doesn't it?*> Tobias's mental voice was grim.

They followed the drones to their objective, keeping to the shadows—a task surprisingly easy to do. As the service entrance came into focus, Jason's lips tightened in frustration.

<*Well, shit, guys. Even your maps suck.*>

The feed revealed what the purloined Republican diagram had failed to record: the service entrance had been sealed shut.

<*How much time would it take to unseal?*> Lena's mental tone was doubtful as they studied the situation from the shadows a block away.

<*More time than we would have without drawing attention,*> Jason responded, <*especially with that.*> He tagged the pool of light spilling out from a coffee shop across the street.

That, too, hadn't been listed on the map. The light was bright enough to illuminate the recessed entrance clearly—as well as several passersby—which meant there was no way their tampering would go unnoticed.

<*Okay, so what are our options?*> Jason asked as he eyed the compound's wall. <*What about another service entrance?*>

<*Too far. But there's an exhaust grill up at the top of that plant just past our entrance that should work,*> Tobias countered. <*We can enter through there.*>

<*Wait,*> Lena said, her mental tone doubtful, <*isn't that the waste reclamation plant?*>

Jason shot her an amused look. <*Doesn't mean we'll be slogging our way through shit. Maybe we could crawl through a ventilation shaft.*>

She shot him a dark look. <*That only happens in holo vids, sir. Not real life.*>

Jason shrugged and followed Tobias around the back of the coffee shop until they were once more in the shadows and could cross over safely.

<Dude's a Weapon Born; I'll trust him to figure it out.>

* * * * *

As soon as the other team disappeared, Khela motioned for Logan and Ramon to take point. Both had their E-SCAR rifles at the ready, barrels describing slow arcs before them, clearing sweeps as they went.

As they traversed the shorter distance to their destination, Logan reached down periodically to adhere packets to the seam where the bulkhead met the station's deck. These would serve as countermeasures to deter pursuers, should they find themselves under attack during their planned exfiltration.

They reached the access panel that would bring them up through the deck above and into the Baratian garrison's garage. At a nod from Khela, Logan released a nanofilament to check the panel for any sensors, and when none were found, he and Ramon began to work the panel free.

It came loose with a soft scraping sound, and the pair carefully rotated the rectangular slab and pulled it down. Above, a troop transport that looked like it had seen better days concealed the greater part of the cavernous garage.

One by one, the three members of the fireteam carefully pulled themselves through the hole, laying prone beneath the transport. Khela updated Simone and Charley, while Logan released a set of surveillance drones and colloids identical to those Lena controlled.

The motor pool appeared to suffer the same fate as most did across the known star systems. It was dark and damp, smelled of ozone and maintenance grease, and was infrequently occupied. It made a perfect infiltration point.

Khela rather suspected the transport had been left to rust, good only to scavenge parts for the occasional repair of other transports. She'd be surprised if it would even start, given its outward appearance.

That was fine by her; something that was in disrepair or obviously not in use was less likely to be monitored; certainly, the area around it would see less traffic than other areas within the garage.

<We have a patrol headed our way,> Charley warned. *<Unless they change their route, they'll pass close enough to detect an anomaly on the station's hull an hour from now.>*

Khela pursed her lips in thought, running the numbers in her head. *<Understood. We have a hard out in thirty minutes, mark. I'll let Fireteam Two know.>*

A single click was Charley's response.

As she updated Tobias on their accelerated timetable, Logan cleared the garage of sensors, and Ramon advanced to the outer doors, where he threaded nano to peer out onto the compound's common grounds.

<I have eyes on,> Ramon announced. *<We're clear.>*

Khela nodded and he slid the door open. Logan directed the drone cloud out into the compound proper; there, they would provide an eye in the sky overwatch.

This would also provide a real-world test of Enfield stealth capabilities against Barat's security measures.

Nothing of any great security was ever exposed to the dome, Simone had told them. Neither Godel nor Barat dared risk sensitive material being captured by surveillance cameras or sensors peering down through the clear dome from above.

Both Barat and Godel employed regular security sweeps, using sniffer bots to locate and destroy any spy-drones around their most secured areas. The two also politely refrained from commenting on the number of surveillance devices neutralized on a weekly basis, although both clearly deployed them. It was likely that private concerns and corporations did so as well.

<*Still amazes me how desperately people feel they need to know what the other side is doing,*> Ramon commented, his mental tone flavored with a wry humor. <*Friend or foe.*>

<*Can't argue that one. Curiosity's a trait both our species share in equal measure,*> Simone chimed in from where she monitored both teams on the shuttle.

They settled in at the motor pool to wait for Fireteam Two to be in position.

* * * * *

Fireteam Two stood at the base of the waste reclamation plant, looking up at the release valve Tobias had identified as their best entry point. Jason reviewed the diagram one last time, but the result was the same: there was no other path from where they stood into the compound except through the belly of the beast.

The 'beast' was a microbial biomass filled with anaerobic bacteria busily working to convert organic waste matter into an activated sludge.

The 'belly' was the secondary treatment tank, where methane could be extracted for fuel and solid products could be stabilized and used in hydroponics for fertilizer.

<*Okay,*> he sighed. <*Let's just get this over with.*>

Tobias turned and began to scale the metal rungs that led up to the release valve. He reached for the grille and pulled. With a low screech, the covering gave way, providing access to the wonderland of goo that was their ticket inside the compound.

<*Don't forget, methane's not a particularly stable gas when mixed with air,*> Tobias reminded them, <*so don't scrape anything that might set off a spark. And be sure to have your chameleon suit filter out the smell.*>

Jason snorted a laugh. <*Thanks, Tobe. Not the kind of thing we're about to forget, trust me.*>

Tobias just grunted before sliding his frame through the

opening. After a moment, the Weapon Born waved him in.

<Step inside, but be sure to hug the outer rim,> he cautioned.

Jason ducked his head inside and peered around, as Tobias reached a narrow, twenty-centimeter shelf—something a charitable person might call a catwalk—that ringed the tank. It had no railing, so a single misstep would send a person plummeting into the slowly churning slurry of materials with dubious origin. Two meters below the ledge, a series of four rakes stirred the sludge in a steady counter-rotational motion.

<Holy shit, Tobe!>

<Quite literally, boyo,> Tobias agreed with a chuckle.

Jason didn't bother to respond. After a pause to study the situation, he added, *<It's going to be tricky, but it's doable.>*

<Agreed,> Tobias concurred.

Jason stepped inside, shifting to the other side of the valve to make room for Lena and Tama.

Lena joined them, then shifted to close the grille behind her. She caught herself before she lost her balance.

<Careful, Lena,> Tama cautioned. *<I don't want my eulogy to read 'lost inside a pile of shit'.>*

Jason stifled a snicker, then realized he hadn't been too successful when he caught Lena's glower. Turning back to examine the tank's interior, he willed himself to ignore the steady sweep of the rakes that churned the tank's contents beneath them.

<Intake pipe on the other side,> he pointed out. *<Looks like it'll accommodate your frame.>*

<It'll do, boyo,> Tobias agreed. *<But we'll need to maneuver halfway around this ledge to get to it. Ready?>*

<Stars, yes,> Lena said. *<Get me out of here.>*

*****

<Fireteam Two in place,> Tobias told Khela as her feed updated.

It now showed their three-person team twenty meters across

the open compound from her, in position and ready to breach the main building. Her own team's objective was the third floor of the building next to the motor pool.

<Lena, how are we for untraceable encryption back to the shuttle?> Khela asked.

<Got a web of relays set up that'll give 'em one big headache if they try to follow. Any source from within the compound's going to lead them to someone's grammy's pot pie recipe.>

<Good. Route me a hot comm line, then, will you? I want to confirm there's no new intel on where the prisoners are being held before we move out.>

A few seconds later, Khela heard Simone's voice.

<Location confirmed. Extraction is a go.>

Khela sent her acknowledgement as she motioned her team forward. *<Okay, people,>* she addressed both fireteams over the combat net. *<We have fifteen minutes to exfil. Make them count.>* She pushed a countdown clock to their HUDs and activated it.

Logan triggered the breaching nano and was through the door of the long-term detention block with Ramon on his heels. Khela followed behind, sparing a last glance at the silent exterior before sliding the door shut behind her.

The building had NSAI-monitored surveillance inside, but Logan released a cloud of jamming colloids to spoof them. He then slapped a packet of nano onto a stairwell, paused for it to bypass the sensor that would report the door had been opened, then slipped through.

<Clear,> he reported, and Ramon and Khela joined him.

<Ramon,> Khela pointed to the door, and the Marine nodded, adopting a watchful stance as Logan passed him the tokens to control the nano he'd emplaced on the door's exterior.

Her overlay updated as Simone fed it more data, the AI's voice whispering in her head.

<There are twenty holding cells to a block, and three different blocks branching away from the lift exit. As of shift change, our analyst was

listed as being held here.> She dropped a pin on the leftmost corridor, fourth cell. <*We've been told she's been worked over and may need medical care before transport.*>

Khela waved Logan forward, their advance coordinated so that one covered the other as they moved deeper into the cell block. As they approached the fourth cell, she hoped to stars the woman was stable enough to move; they were running out of time.

* * * * *

Jason followed Tobias into the headquarters building, Lena bringing up the rear. The three leapfrogged across through to the back of the building where a pin hovered over a cell in the small temporary lockup area.

As they approached a security checkpoint, Simone's voice came to them from the shuttle.

<*Fireteam Two, your captain, at last report, was here.*>

Something about Simone's tone snagged Jason's attention.

<*Last report?*> His words were sharp, he knew, with an edge to them he couldn't help.

He tensed at the regret in Simone's voice as she replied.

<*The information on her location was not updated along with the other prisoner's. It is her last known location.*>

Jason lurched for the entrance, but Tobias reached a gauntleted hand out and pulled him back.

<*Patience, boyo,*> he cautioned. <*We'll nae have come this far, and through so much shit, to make a misstep now.*>

Jason sucked in a lungful of air then nodded silently back at his friend.

<*I'm sending colloids out now,*> Lena informed them. <*And…we're clear.*>

The door slid open soundlessly, and they slipped through, swiftly but methodically searching each cell.

* * * * *

Khela paused behind Logan's frame until he pivoted, his E-SCAR sweeping the room before coming to rest on what looked like a pile of cloth in one corner of the room.

Closer examination revealed a severely-beaten human huddled beneath.

Khela slapped her suit's medkit open as Logan bent to examine her. The data he sent from his scan indicated that the woman's mednano had been all but obliterated. Several broken ribs, an arm fractured in three places, and a concussion. The myelin sheath surrounding the axons in her brain registered as loose and decompacted from the head trauma.

<*Unconscious,*> came Logan's terse appraisal, as Khela studied the medical readout.

<*It's no wonder,*> she remarked. <*She's in bad shape, but no spinal insult, so she's okay to move. She'll need to be carried out,*> she added unnecessarily, as Logan had already gathered her in his arms and rose.

Khela paused at the entrance to the cell, knowing that the interrupted feed would not go unnoticed for much longer, and once they departed, the NSAI would report the empty cell to those in charge.

<*Seven minutes! We're on a clock, people. Jason?*>

There was no answer.

IF IT WEREN'T FOR BAD LUCK

STELLAR DATE: 03.09.3272 (Adjusted Gregorian) 2030 hours, local
LOCATION: Unknown
REGION: Unknown

Calista's restless pacing kept a steady measure of her cell's dimensions: three meters wide, seven down, then three to the other side. Seven more brought her back to the door. The faint glow of the ES shield reinforcing its seal was discouragement enough to keep her from attempting to breach it.

As her captors knew it would be.

It also conveniently sealed her inside a room in which an EMP could be unleashed against her—and which regularly was—preventing her mednano from replicating itself in large enough numbers to neutralize the neuroparalytic they had employed more than once.

The soft slippers she now wore allowed the cold surface beneath her feet to seep into her soles, and the shapeless coveralls were thin enough to make her wish for a blanket to wrap herself in so that she could ward off the chill.

She'd almost made it.

She'd have to tell Jonesy how well his new nano had worked. He'd taken the nanotech that had run rampant in Tau Ceti, the stuff that nearly brought the planet Galene to its knees, and adapted it. What was once a nanophage was now a sweet little deployable weapons package.

Terrance had blanched when the engineer had first mentioned his latest project, but Jonesy had just grinned and said something about 'eating the fish and spitting out the bones'.

She'd nearly laughed at the look on Enfield's face—a weird mixture of horrified and confused—until Shannon had backed up Jonesy's claim with a more coherent explanation, and his expression had cleared.

The end result had been a tidy little package of Elastene-clad colloidenes, a special breed of lighter-than-air colloids that employed some of the click-assembly tricks used in chemistry. Pre-loaded common codes, or 'bricks', that gave nano creation a jump-start.

The result was a nanobot programmed to rapidly alter existing nano to whatever the person controlling it needed it to be. Considering how ubiquitous nano was—the stuff was practically everywhere, you could hardly inhale without breathing some in wherever you went—it was like having your own personal unlimited supply of whatever you wanted, whenever and wherever you were.

Calista didn't pretend to understand nanotransfection. The whole concept was a little bit like waving a magic wand, as far as she was concerned. But she'd become a believer just five short hours ago.

She'd waited until after dinner had been served and the hallway outside her cell had quieted before accessing the stockpile inside the compartment Jonesy had fashioned inside their combat boots.

This little trick had elicited a laugh from Jason, who had accused Jonesy of 'playing at being Q again' when he'd revealed the design to them. The engineer had responded by reminding him that martinis were to be served shaken, not stirred, which made no sense to her whatsoever.

But the real marvel hadn't been the hidden Faraday cage that prevented scans from finding the cache of nano.... It had been the nanotransfection colloidene bots themselves.

She'd been stunned at how rapidly the microscopic machines had subverted the nano in her immediate surroundings to her control. Calista felt like she had a full arsenal at her disposal as the bots disabled the sensors monitoring her cell, released its door, and blanketed her progression with a satisfying array of suppression that covered the full spectrum of EM emissions.

She'd sent a passel of nano into a nearby node, the nanotransfection bots hybridizing Barat's own systems until the heavily censored public net run by the Humans' Republic lay open before her. From there, she'd begun to lay a web of relays that snaked their way outward toward Godel and freedom.

A part of her mind was occupied with a search for a relay that would give her access to the marina and the ships moored there. She'd anchored the relay with her own ident, and encrypted a brief missive updating the team on what had transpired, then had instructed the little buggers to notify her when they'd connected to the *Avon Vale*.

All this had been done while she slipped from shadow to shadow down the long hallway where she'd been held. The lifts were no good; she daren't risk such an obvious exit point. The electronic monitoring, she could spoof; humans, on the other hand.... Those, she was trying to avoid. The stairwell next to the lifts would do just fine.

Her divided attention may have been to blame for her inability to drop both soldiers that entered the stairwell's third floor landing just after she'd rounded the corner and had begun her descent. But then again, it could have been sheer, dumb luck—the bad kind.

That they were hoping to steal a few moments away from their posts for a bit of fun was evident in their whispered words, which came to an abrupt stop as she whirled to face them.

Had they been in a public place, Calista might have bluffed her way down the steps, hoping her garb and the back of her head were nondescript enough to hide her identity. Here, though, where every citizen soldier wore the same uniform, there was no chance of that happening. She'd had no option but to rush them.

Both paused as their minds reconciled what they had expected to find with what they'd actually found. This allowed Calista the time to launch herself from her position on the third step, jabbing a straight-knuckled chisel fist strike to the first soldier's throat.

The man stumbled back into his companion, his hands reflexively going to his neck as he knocked the second man back out into the hallway. Before Calista could reach past the first man, the second one had pivoted and bolted, sounding the alarm.

The soldier she'd felled had a crushed windpipe. He might survive—if he had mednano, and if it was any good. Calista frisked him, relieving him of a short blade and one biolocked pulse pistol.

With one hand, she loosed a passel of nano colloidenes onto the weapon's biolock, as she leapt over the railing, bracing herself with her other hand, and plunged two stories down to the bottom level.

She hit the deck running, flash-sighting the now-unlocked pulse pistol at two soldiers racing to meet her head-on. They dropped, and she hurdled their bodies as the sound of pounding feet informed her that the alarm had been sounded on her escape.

Five minutes later, she plowed face-first onto a dirt quad ringed by half a dozen drab plascrete buildings, her body twitching and numb from the riot control pulse cannon that had felled her from the guard's tower twenty meters away.

Moments later, a pair of grey uniform slacks, black piping running the length of their sides, swam into her vision, above a pair of tidy, yet utilitarian, black boots.

Their owner spoke; it was a voice she recognized.

"You're turning out to be more trouble than you're worth, thief. Looks like we'll need to move you somewhere a bit more secure."

She was lifted roughly as two soldiers hooked a hand underneath her armpits and dragged her off toward an awaiting transport.

INTELLIGENCE SNAFU

STELLAR DATE: 03.10.3272 (Adjusted Gregorian) 0400 hours, local
LOCATION: Beneath Barat Sector
REGION: Phaethon Duty Station, Little River

<*She's not here. Dammit, she's not **here**.*> Jason's movements took on a fevered urgency as he raced from cell to cell, confirming that the few occupants in this block weren't the woman he sought.

<*Time's up. Move out.*> Khela's mental voice came to them from the *Sable Wind*, her tone unyielding.

Jason began to protest even as Tobias tugged on his arm and they began to jog toward the stairwell. <*We have to keep searching. Once the element of surprise is gone, they'll triple the guard around her, and we'll never—*>

<*Think, Jason.*> Khela talked over him, cutting him off. <*If we can get out undetected, they'll assume this was purely a Godel op. We won't have tipped our hand.*> She paused, then added, <*To them, we're still just a civilian ship, shaking the trees with loud protests in the only way we know to get her back.*>

<*It's true, boyo,*> Tobias sent privately, and Jason hated that he was right. <*Best to make a clean exit now and leave our options open for a later recovery.*>

They met up with the rest as they crouched, waiting in the shadows of the motor pool's exterior.

<*Logan's loosing a few microdrones to seed a bit of misdirection that will lead them away from our exit point,*> Khela informed them, nodding in the general direction of the compound's nearest ten-meter-high wall.

<*Ramon's inside, setting up a seam-repair program for the access panel, for after we slip back into the underlayer.*> She turned back to the unconscious form she was kneeling beside.

<*Need some help with her, lass?*>

Not waiting for an answer, the Weapon Born bent and gently lifted the woman into his arms. Khela thanked him with a nod, then rose.

<Let's go.>

Silently, she slipped through the side door into the cavernous garage where the Humans' Republic kept its vehicles.

*****

While the infiltration team crept back along the passageway to the shuttle awaiting them, Terrance and Kodi were engaged in a campaign of distraction.

Earlier, Deb Weir had helpfully supplied them with a list of the various types of legal motions they could file against Barat. Shortly thereafter, Terrance had appeared at the entrance to Barat's customs offices, holojournalists in tow.

He'd vociferously demanded the return of his ship's captain, while Kodi flooded the system with every legal filing against Barat that he could contrive. Affidavit of complaints, interrogatories, discoveries, motions to examine judgments and the like were heaped upon the hapless citizen soldier on duty. The AI had even sent messages across the interstellar relays that would—in decades hence—file suits against the nation of Barat on behalf of the Enfield Corporation in three different star systems. One after another, they rapidly stacked up, while, across the street in Godel territory, picketers began chanting slogans and hoisting signs.

Terrance was all too aware that the cameras hovering behind the crowd were likely the only things that prevented the soldiers from employing aggressive crowd control. That, plus the platoon of Godel peacekeepers who stood, weapons in hand, guarding their backs.

He also was aware that the Enfield name made him an attractive target. He didn't doubt Barat would love to take him prisoner, too—held hostage for his own damn IP. Although, at this point, they might just do it to shut him up.

Terrance stepped back as Hailey—posing as a news reporter for the Tau Ceti Sentinel, a fictitious news net—finished the wrap-up for her latest color commentary.

<*She's doing a stand-up job at this,*> he commented as she ad-libbed her way through her latest fake news report. <*Hailey's an accomplished actress.*>

<*We'll have to keep that in mind,*> Kodi agreed. <*Who knows when we might need that skill set again.*>

Terrance snorted mentally. <*Given our track record, that just might be soon.*>

He prepared to launch into another round of protests, but pulled up short as Jonesy's voice came across the ship's net.

<*Package not retrieved,*> he informed them. <*Ships are en route back, ETA thirty mikes.*>

His gaze swept their group, gathering them with a look, and received slight nods in response. Hailey's eyelids flickered, but she gave no other indication she'd heard, as she smoothly drew her broadcast to a close.

"I think we're done here, people," Terrance said, shooting the Barat patrol a look of anger and frustration that, for the first time since they had arrived, wasn't feigned. <*Dammit. I was so sure we'd be able to retrieve her.*>

<*I've been chatting with Landon. From what he's told me, it wasn't a problem on our end. She simply wasn't there to retrieve.*>

* * * * *

<*I think I've found something,*> Tama announced as the two fireteams approached the station airlock where the *Sable Wind* had docked. <*I went back and accessed the historical data feeds in the Baratian compound since Calista's arrest. This happened earlier today.*>

A recording popped up on Jason's HUD, a view of the ground floor lifts in the building where they'd found the Godel analyst.

The corridor just off the entrance was empty—until two soldiers walked into view. They glanced around and then slipped inside the stairwell, the one behind already reaching his arm around the other's waist for a few stolen moments together.

Before the door could close behind them, the rearmost soldier stumbled back, an alarmed look on his face as he turned to call out. Moments later, Calista burst through the door, pulse pistol in hand. She raised it toward a small group of soldiers rushing toward her. Firing off a series of shots, she leapt over them, and then raced out of the camera's frame, several soldiers in hot pursuit.

<Hold on, switching feeds.>

The image flickered, stabilized. Now the view was of the grounds outside, and Jason could see from the angle that the camera was either mounted on the waste reclamation building or the guard tower just south of it.

Calista sped toward the main exit, her path zig-zagging to evade fire coming at her from behind. He sucked in a breath as he saw the IR signature of a ranging beam emitted from the tower across the grounds.

In the next moment, Calista's body jerked twice, then she face-planted into the ground as a pulse cannon hit her. An officer he recognized, the leader of the three who had stopped them in the bazaar, approached and motioned her soldiers toward Calista.

They lifted the insensate woman high enough for the officer to bend down and whisper something into Calista's ear. The woman then straightened and motioned her soldiers to load their barely conscious prisoner onto a transport.

His mouth tightened in dismay as the transport exited through the compound's main gates.

<Any way to track it?>

<Working on tapping into the eyes that Barat has scattered throughout their sector,> Tama said, referencing the sensor drones that canvassed Barat's environs. There was a pause, and then she

added quietly, <*That transport…it drove right into the cargo bay of a ship docked at the Barat marina.*>

<*Slip number?*> Simone broke into the conversation. Moments after Tama passed the information to her, the Godel AI responded with a sound suspiciously like a sigh. <*I'm truly sorry. That ship left for Barat five hours ago.*>

The team cycled through the airlock and loaded into the shuttle in silence, Simone helping Ramon stabilize the rescued Godel analyst with the shuttle's triage kit.

The ultra-black shape disengaged from the surface of the duty station, joined by its sleek shadow. Half an hour later and more than a hundred kilometers away, both began their descent into an open hangar bay on the other side of the rotating wheel. The two ships settled onto their rails, and the bay doors began to close just as the fusion-powered mini sun began to blaze, heralding the start of another day.

PART FOUR: THE PLOT

INTERIM PLAN

STELLAR DATE: 03.10.3272 (Adjusted Gregorian) 0600 hours, local
LOCATION: ESS *Avon Vale*, en route to Godel
REGION: Inner System, Little River

Sable Wind was on final approach, the amidships bay doors open and waiting for them. Jason spied Terrance and Jonesy standing behind the secondary ES shield as Logan and Charley piloted the two ships into their cradles. As soon as atmosphere was restored to the ship's bay, both men strode forward.

Jason exchanged silent nods with Jonesy as Landon released the shuttle's hatch and extended its ramp. Too wired to stand still, he leapt to the shuttle bay's deck and began a walkaround, visually inspecting the *Sable Wind* while the rest of the team unloaded.

He saw Jonesy maneuver Charley's frame next to the *Mirage* and ride the lift to the fighter's cockpit to extract the AI. Turning back, he caught Terrance's eye as the man stood, feet braced at an almost parade rest while waiting for the crew to clean up the shuttle and disembark.

Shannon's holopresence appeared on the deck between the two ships, and her words distracted them both, cutting into the weary silence that had befallen the team on their way back. "If we leave now, we can intercept them," she said as her avatar appeared next to Terrance.

Her thoughts echoed Jason's own desperate need to take action, but he had enough presence of mind to realize that reckless haste was ill-advised.

Besides, no one in Little River knew the *Avon Vale*'s true capabilities. Her antimatter-pion drive had been disguised, as had her not-insignificant weapons array. Eight massive, twenty-five-centimeter lasers were paired, four at the bow and four aft, and she had a dozen ten-centimeter rails emplaced along her three-kilometer length. Missile tubes had been incorporated into the fore and aft decks, with a rate of fire at four per second. All of these armaments had been hidden behind plates of Elastene cladding; the hull plating could be slid aside in seconds to free the ports for use.

And that didn't take into account the number of tactical nuclear warheads Landon had insisted on outfitting the ship with prior to its departure from Tau Ceti.

In other words, the ESS *Avon Vale* was one big, three-kilometer-long Q-ship.

Jason shot Shannon a warning look, but before he could say anything, Jonesy did.

The engineer straightened, Charlie's cylinder in hand, and shot the ship's AI a repressive scowl. "Shannon, we're a civilian ship." His tone was one of warning, as his gaze flicked pointedly to Simone and then back.

Jason could tell Simone was studiously ignoring the exchange. Her attention appeared to be focused entirely on helping Marta secure the rescued Godel agent onto a gurney for her transfer to a Phaethon medical team that was standing by at the marina. Simone was doing a good imitation of someone completely absorbed in her task, but he knew she was well aware of the conversations around her.

"We can catch those bastards," Shannon insisted, "and we can board their ship and take Calista."

At that, Simone reluctantly stirred. "I…don't think that's your best use of resources," she began, but Shannon stopped her with a thunderous expression.

"You have no idea what we're capable of," she flung at Simone and then turned pleading eyes to Terrance. "We've got to at least *try....*"

Terrance looked from the ship's AI to Simone and then back again. "What do you suggest, then?" he asked, his tone neutral.

"There are a few places where you might intercept their ship before it reaches Barat," Simone admitted, "but honestly, your best chance is after they reach the planet."

Jason crossed his arms and leant back against the *Sable Wind*'s cowling as he did a bit of spatial math. He didn't like the result.

"Doing that means we leave Calista to Barat's mercy for another three days," he scowled, advancing slowly upon Simone. "Explain to me why that's a good idea."

"Because you still hold all the cards. They won't want to hurt her," the AI explained, "and risk not making the tech exchange."

Jason glanced at Tobias, who had descended the ramp and now stood, shoulder to shoulder alongside him. The Weapon Born's emotions were closed to Jason, his expression unreadable.

No help from that quadrant.

"There's another thing to consider," Simone added. "If you wait until they arrive on Barat, we'll have the resources of an entire underground network on that planet ready to assist you."

The AI's expression was earnest as she attempted to convince them to follow her advice.

"Barat is a rigidly structured society; because of that, there are things in place that we can exploit. Their penal colonies, while heavily guarded, are also run on a software that uses a long-forgotten codebase, stolen from Godel decades ago. We can get you in and then out again, with no one the wiser."

Terrance nodded slowly, his gaze sweeping the team, and Jason knew the man saw the fatigue that plagued them all. Unconsciously, he straightened into a stance of readiness, his look daring Terrance to say otherwise.

The executive sighed.

"The good news is that any in-system departure from Phaethon right now is going to be along the same path, given the station's current position. So we're headed in the same direction, regardless. Hailey's already asked for an expedited departure, so we'll be on our way very soon."

*****

Two hours later, Jason found himself scowling at his hazy reflection in the brushed-metal surface of the lift doors as he stood waiting for one to take him from the cargo area down to the engineering deck, where the armory was located.

They'd received clearance from the STC for departure and filed a flight path for Godel. As acting captain, Jason had shepherded the *Avon Vale* out of nearspace and onto their current heading and then handed the bridge over to Landon.

The humans who had participated in the infiltration operation had been awake more than twenty-seven hours. He'd taken himself off-shift for the next ten.

Though he knew sack time was a must, Jason was too tightly strung for sleep. He knew that if he didn't work off some of the energy coiled within him, sleep would evade him altogether.

There's always the firing range…or I could jam some iron in the weight room.

If all else failed, he could turn on the holo and beat the hell out of the sim with a few Kai-Eskrima moves.

What he *wasn't* going to do was stand around waiting all day for the stars-be-damned lift. He turned on his heel, heading for the access shaft and the ladder that would take him there, albeit not as quickly.

"In a hurry?"

The voice at his shoulder came without warning, and served as a catalyst for his L2 reflexes. He had Lena shoved up against the bulkhead, his arm across her throat and his fist pulled back, ready to pound, before she had time to take a breath.

"Sorry," he muttered, releasing her and stalking toward the stairs.

The lift chimed and he pivoted, reversing his direction before the Marine had time to blink.

Before the doors slid shut, she raced forward and joined him, one hand massaging her throat.

<Guess that answers my other question,> Tama said into the silence that fell between the two humans as the lift resumed its course.

Opting to use the Link, most likely to give her ravaged throat a chance to recover, Jason heard Lena sigh before responding to the AI paired with her. *<Okay, I'll bite. What other question?>*

<The one about whether or not the rumors about L2 human reflexes is true. Guess it is.>

Jason only grunted at Tama's comment as he slid Lena a sidelong look. He considered apologizing again, but he just couldn't work up the energy.

He heard her swallow. The sound was overly loud, and he knew from past experience that a throat block like the one he'd just given her would make swallowing a painful experience for another hour or so.

<Don't shoot the messenger, Andrews,> Lena's voice was tart, but not overly so, and Jason figured that meant the apology had been accepted.

Movement at her waist caught his attention, and he saw her slide the carbon-fiber blade that all Marines carried back into its sheath. She caught his gaze and gave him a wink.

<You're lucky I like you, sir. Anyone else would have been scooping up their intestines.>

Looks like I'm not the only one with fast reflexes. He gave her a respectful nod. "I'm impressed."

<Training kicks in, you know how it is.>

The lift stopped at the deck that held the common area, and he gestured for the Marine to exit first, then strode toward the nearest galley. Stopping in front of a chiller, he grabbed a bottle of water and held it out to her.

"Sorry," he said again and winced mentally at the surly tone he heard in his own voice. "Rough day."

The Marine nodded her thanks as she uncapped the bottle and took a long pull from it.

"Killer reflexes," she finally said, her voice raspy. "And I do mean that literally."

She gestured over to a table, brows raised in a questioning look. Jason hesitated, then nodded and followed her over, slumping into a chair. Lena set the bottle of water down and sat across from him.

"Where were you headed just now?" she asked.

Jason shrugged. "It's a three-day trip to Godel from Phaethon. Thought I'd use the time to do some range work in the armory."

<*Thought so,*> Tama sounded smug, as if she'd just won a bet with the Marine over his destination.

What he didn't mention—what was on everyone's mind—was that it would only take seven hours more to travel to Barat, given the current orbital locations of the planets relative to Phaethon.

"You're pissed that we're not headed directly there," Lena guessed.

Although it sounded more like a statement, he nodded anyway, fingers sliding back and forth across the edge of the table, his hands restless with pent-up rage.

"What's there to say? Simone talked Terrance into letting her come along with us," he slammed his palms flat on the table's surface as he growled, "and then she did her damnedest to convince everyone that the best way to get Calista back was to go to Godel first."

Lena raised an eyebrow skeptically as Tama observed, *<I believe Mister Enfield said something about going off half-cocked and without all the intel being a stupid-ass plan.>*

"Actually, lass," a voice came from behind Jason, and he turned to see Tobias approaching. "What he said was that hope was not a plan, and charging out with little more than that as your strategy was a piss-poor way to get her back."

Jason glared at his friend. "Don't recall asking your opinion on the matter."

"Don't recall you doing much opinion-asking at any stage of your life, boyo."

The Weapon Born's tone was mild. He crossed behind Jason, settling a hand on his shoulder briefly as he folded his frame into a chair.

"The thing is," he continued, "you and I both know that the best possible plan is the one that has the backing and support of Godel's intelligence community behind it."

"Fine."

Lena caught Tobias's eye. "Is he always this stubborn and surly?"

Tobias made a sound that was a cross between a snort and a laugh. "Only when we don't let him charge off into the black on his own."

"Well, gee, Tobe," Jason let his voice sink into heavy sarcasm. "If I'd known this was shit-on-Jason hour, I woulda looked you up sooner."

The AI fell still and stared pointedly at him.

Jason slouched back in his chair, dragging his hands through the snarls of his short-cropped, dirty blonde hair. His scalp felt gritty, and his hands came back feeling greasy.

"Huh, speaking of shit," he responded absently, rubbing his fingers together. He'd almost forgotten their trek through the tank of sludge six hours earlier.

His comment had Lena reaching up to her own hair. She made a face, then pushed back from the table.

"That's it. I'm hitting the shower and then getting some rack time." Lena paused as she stood, pinning Jason with a look. But before she could say anything, Tama beat her to it.

<Stars, sir. For all our sakes, please do the same.>

"What? I just got here, and now everyone's leaving?" Tobias asked.

"Must be your winning charm," Jason said as he rose. "Once I'm rested, let's hit the sims for some friendly competition."

"Sure thing, boyo. You go rest that fragile, organic body. You're going to need it if you think you can beat me."

A SPORT AS OLD AS GILGAMESH

STELLAR DATE: 03.10.3272 (Adjusted Gregorian)
LOCATION: Premier's Estate, Hauptstadt
REGION: Barat, Little River

Giovanni looked to the sky, noting that Epsilon was riding low in the west, its ruddy glow lengthening the shadows of the guards around Rachelle Feretti. The premier stood facing a stand of trees on the other side of the field, her arm raised and gloved hand fisted.

Sitting in a bough high in one of those trees was a Harris's hawk, a band of white gracing the tips of its tailfeathers. The hawk, named Tigan, had a mild temperament that was best-suited for novice falconers.

Of all the birds housed in the mews on the premier's estate, Tigan was the only one that the master falconer trusted Feretti to handle. Even then, the falconer ensured that someone more experienced was always present when Feretti chose, like today, to go hunting.

This afternoon, it was Giovanni's turn. He, too, wore a glove, and on it perched a second chestnut-shouldered Harris's hawk. This one's gaze was fixed upon the distant tree where its companion sat.

"Tigan!" the premier commanded to the Harris's hawk across the field. Extending her arm, she pivoted her shoulder toward the tree, her voice imperious and carrying. "To me!"

Giovanni knew better than to allow any hint of censure or amusement to color his expression. He merely stepped closer to Feretti and rose his hand behind her so that she could not see the visual cue he sent to Tigan.

Tigan was imprinted to the master falconer; the bird wouldn't come to any other voice. Thankfully, the premier rarely went hunting like this, and all raptors kept within the mews had been trained to respond to visual commands as well.

It appeared Feretti had forgotten this.

Giovanni signaled once more to the bird perched in the trees. Tigan launched into the air, sweeping across the meadow with powerful strokes of its meter-wide wingspan.

Giovanni began an internal mantra, mentally urging Feretti to not flinch or duck as the Harris's hawk swooped toward them at an incredible speed. He cupped his hand just behind the woman's elbow, ready to steady her should she make the mistake of moving out of the bird's path.

Raptors such as Tigan devoted up to eighty-five percent of their brain power to their vision, and he knew the hawk had his flight path dialed in with precision. At his rate of speed, deviation could mean injury to both bird and human.

Giovanni suspected that allowing Feretti to be injured might not help his chances at career advancement.

He released a silent breath as the raptor alighted onto her fisted hand, scraping his reward off the base of Premier Feretti's glove with his beak. Faust, the hawk on Giovanni's own fist, shifted slightly at Tigan's approach, turning a bright and inquisitive eye toward her fellow raptor.

"There," Ferreti said, her eyes glinting in satisfaction as she glanced over at him, one brow arched. "*That* is how you call a falcon to you, Giovanni."

He bowed his head respectfully. "Impressive, ma'am. Tigan is a fine specimen." *Stars, she can't even tell a hawk from a falcon!* Giovanni looked down at the chestnut-colored hawk on his wrist and sighed mentally. *It's a good thing they* ***aren't*** *falcons; those are solitary hunters and don't exactly play well with others, even of their own species. Not like our two Harris's hawks here.*

The pair of humans turned and began trudging along the brush that edged the tree line, Feretti's security detail fanning out behind them.

Giovanni murmured to Faust, then launched her into the air. The raptor alighted on a tree a few meters ahead of them, her gaze intent upon the ground, prepared for the moment her human rousted a small animal from the brush.

It was a routine the two performed regularly. His job was to startle the small animals from their hiding spots; hers was to kill.

He dutifully plied his walking stick, sweeping it into the bushes, rustling the foliage as they walked. Feretti *tsk*ed, glancing pointedly down at the hand that was beating the bushes.

"It's no wonder your bird took off, with all the racket you're making." She turned to address the hawk on her fist, cooing at it. "Such a good bird, Tigan. So well-trained, unlike your sister up there."

Giovanni arranged his face into an expression more appropriately respectful than his thoughts allowed.

"He knows power when he sees it," he murmured in response and, with a mental apology to Faust, limited his rustling to the occasional light whack against the foliage as they passed.

"Speaking of power," she began, and Giovanni arrested his motion, his attention now fully on his premier. "I understand our prisoner on Phaethon almost managed to escape yesterday afternoon." She glanced his way, her expression appraising.

"She did," he admitted. "But she has been secured, and the offer to exchange her for Enfield's stasis tech has been tendered."

Feretti pursed her lips, flashing him an astute, measuring look through narrowed eyes. He reminded himself that this woman was not all affectation. Despite her pretentions, Feretti was a shrewd politician.

"I hear that an exchange may no longer be possible," the premier said, tossing Tigan carelessly into the air and turning to face him.

Giovanni tensed at the action, then relaxed as the hawk joined Faust on a nearby branch. Quickly, he sent the master falconer instructions to come retrieve the hawks. He hoped they were still there when the woman arrived.

Though Feretti had yet to internalize the concept, hawks weren't truly ever trained; each time a hawk was released, one risked them returning to the wild, never to be seen again.

Abruptly, he realized what the premier had just said.

Mentally berating himself for allowing the Harris's hawk to distract him, he asked cautiously, "Not possible?"

Feretti took her time unfastening the glove and handing it to one of her attendants. "No, Giovanni, it would seem not."

Her voice held disapproval, and he tensed once more, this time for entirely different reasons.

"Apparently," she said coldly, "your man on Phaethon had not made the situation clear to the citizen commander at our duty station's compound. She deemed the prisoner too much of a flight risk and shipped her here."

"Madam Premier, Enfield need not know this," he assured her. "We can still use her as a bargaining chip for the stasis—" His words stumbled to a halt as she began to shake her head.

"No, Citizen Perelman, we cannot."

Giovanni looked at her blankly, not understanding what the woman's location had to do with her value in trade.

"Giovanni, Giovanni," the premier chided, shaking her head. "Any possible chance we might have had to treat this as a simple exchange went out the airlock when your people initiated standard interrogation procedures on her."

Shock reverberated through him at the news. Those had *not* been his standing orders.

Feretti pointed an accusing finger at his chest, and he wondered if a pistol shot from one of her detail would follow in its wake. "How do we return such damaged goods and expect any reciprocity?" she demanded.

She turned suddenly and began walking back toward the estate. When he made to follow, she halted him with her hand.

"I'm sure you are much too busy cleaning up the mess your

people have made to join us at tonight's dinner, Citizen Perlman. Citizen soldier Marsden will see you to your transport."

Giovanni swallowed hard at the rebuff, as he realized his dinner invitation had been revoked. The premier's retinue closed around her retreating form as she returned to the mansion, save for the single soldier—the one of lowest rank—who stood, waiting to escort him off the estate.

He nodded stiffly to Marsden and then trudged behind her as she turned sharply on her heel, marching toward the estate's general parking area.

As they walked, his mind raced.

How did this go off the rails so quickly, when mere hours ago, everything was proceeding so smoothly?

More importantly, who on my staff has been feeding the premier information from my own offices before it gets to me?

DEAD SHORT

STELLAR DATE: Unknown
LOCATION: Unknown
REGION: Unknown, Little River

Calista knew she was in trouble.

She had no idea how long she'd been out, nor where the ship was taking her. She could feel the subtle vibration through the soles of her feet as she paced in her cell, and knew they were underway.

She recalled, as through a fog, her attempted escape back on the duty station. The memory of a pair of crisp grey pants swam into view in her mind's eye, of being hauled up to face their owner—Citizen Lieutenant Maritz, the one from the bazaar.

Another face had registered, that of the soldier who had posed as her lawyer—Sergei, his name was. He'd been one of the ones who had hauled her aboard this ship. She'd been barely conscious at the time.

There had been some sort of medical or research area. She'd been stripped, injected with a paralytic. Then agony, as every muscle in her body seized when they subjected her to a strong electrical current, strong enough to fry her mednano. It was a crude but effective way to remove any chance she had of neutralizing the pharmaceutical cocktail the autodoc sent coursing through her veins, far more effective than the EMPs they'd hit her with back in her cell.

Through a drug-induced haze, she heard voices discussing the autodoc's scan, as the unit pinpointed every modification the El Dorado Space Force had given her, and the ones Task Force Phantom Blade had upgraded.

And then the extractions had begun.

First, they went after the superconducting batteries embedded within her body. These ran the length of both femur and tibia, of humerus and ulna. They were excised for study and comparison to existing tech.

The sample of retractable CNT lattice that protected her organs—a mod she'd received when she became a fighter pilot with El Dorado's Space Force—had been acquired by the simple expediency of removing one of her kidneys.

Her optical implant went next.

"Just one, though," she heard a voice instruct the medic who was programming the autodoc. "It's too much of an inconvenience to have a blind prisoner."

Stars forbid I inconvenience you, she thought sardonically, although she couldn't make her mouth form the words.

Then they moved on to her musculoskeletal frame. A plug of bone containing carbon nanothreads had been removed from her femur—that had been fun. She heard one of the medics note that it was to compare Barat's CNT with the ones Alpha Centauri used. Why, she had no idea; the tech was hundreds of years old.

Tissue from artificial sinews was next, harvested from enhanced ligaments and tendons. And then the Baratians harvested the specialized nano laced throughout her brain.

It was designer nano, custom-tailored to the unique folds of her brain's peaks and valleys, predetermined by her parents before she'd been born, and she had no idea how it could possibly be of use to them. She'd overheard enough to know they intended to try their hand at reverse-engineering the tech.

Stars, haven't they heard of patented anti-tampering code? she thought foggily, but then she heard one of the chop-shop crew bragging about the Godel scientist whose studies on retroviruses looked promising as a tool to neutralize security programs.

Had she the energy to cringe, she would have, for Calista couldn't fathom equipping these monsters with advantages of any kind.

When they'd extracted what they could from her, a dead short had been deliberately induced in the remaining SC batts. Sabotaged, they were turned into slag so she couldn't use them to power the active modifications laced throughout her body.

The resulting surge across each low-resistance connection released a tremendous amount of energy. Those handling the procedure hadn't cared about her comfort. After the first searing discharge, she'd slipped into blessed unconsciousness.

They must have been instructed not to allow her mind to be damaged, though, for they had discharged the batts near her brain stem much more carefully.

Or so she thought.

It was a bit difficult to tell, given that some of her modifications were ones that augmented the speed at which her mind processed information. Without them, she felt as sluggish as if she were treading through a morass.

It had been decades since she'd last had only her own natural-born neurons to call upon; it was frightening how handicapped she felt.

Her hand shook as she ran it through her short tresses, wincing as her fingers touched the tender spot where they had invaded her head.

"Stars, that hurts," she said aloud, but the words sounded more like "shtharths tha hurth." She felt an edge of hysteria build within her as she heard the garbled words. *What if I'm damaged beyond repair, and this is permanent?*

Calista shuffled away from the entrance of her cell and slid down the wall, resting her wrists on top of her knees, her hands dangling uselessly. Her one good eye closed, she gently banged her head back up against the wall, a physical mimicry of what she was attempting to do mentally: knock the wool from around her thoughts.

She recalled as through a fever dream the interrogation that had followed the medical exam. Relentless questions hammering at her over and over again, all the while, her body strapped into the autodoc as drugs poured through her system. Her ESF mods, standard for every soldier, included anti interrogation filters; she was certain those in charge had attempted to bypass them.

If she recalled accurately from within the dream, they'd even attempted to hack her Link—a fact that boggled her befogged mind, as it was common knowledge that such a thing was impossible to do.

What kind of crazy, messed-up society has taken me captive?

With effort, she stood and gave herself a shake, much like her Space Force roommate's dog did when wet. Despite her aching body, she paced and tried to ignore the fact that one leg dragged slightly and her speech was slurred.

She suspected that the ruthless manner in which they'd defanged her may have triggered a mild stroke or transient ischemic attack, damaging a brain now bereft of the resources it required to repair itself.

Resolutely, she worked her body as best she could, cycling through sets of calisthenics while doing much the same inside her mind.

It is the duty of every soldier to resist to the utmost of their ability. To remain in the best possible shape in order to take advantage of every opportunity.

As Calista paced, she recited the words inside her head as a mantra.

* * * * *

Jason was still in a foul mood and he knew it.

The team had spent the second full day on their journey to Godel being briefed by Simone. The analyst possessed a thorough knowledge of Barat—an invaluable tool as they planned how best to conduct Calista's rescue.

"A smaller team, assisted by some of our local assets, will have a much better chance of infiltrating Gehenna," Simone informed them, mentioning the name of the prison Barat used to house spies and outworlders. "Our people know how to get you in without detection. They can provide passage into the area, a few local guides, and a safe house."

Terrance nodded. "Sounds solid. How many is it safe to send in, then? Three? Four?"

Simone paused, her gaze traveling from Terrance over to the Marines in the room. Jason waited impatiently as her gaze shifted to him and then Tobias.

"One," she said abruptly.

"*One?*" Jason erupted. "That's—"

"One human, one AI," she interrupted, then paused and glanced down at where Tobi sat next to him. "And one cat."

"Why the cat?" Noa was the first to recover. The physicist voiced the question that Jason was sure had sprung to many of their minds.

<Yes, why me? Not that I mind,> Tobi's mental voice descended into a growl. *<I'm happy to shed Barat blood for Calista.>*

Jason heard the sound of nails puncture the carpeting that lined the ship's deck, and saw Terrance wince at the sound.

By way of reply, Simone turned to the holo and brought up a visual of the animal life around Gehenna.

"Take a look. You're a bit smaller than some of the local predators that live on the veldt, but no one from Barat has ever heard of an uplifted animal, so you'd be far better equipped to blend into the surroundings than a human," she explained. "Because of that, you should be able to get much closer to the prison camp than a human could."

<I can do it. I might be smaller, but I'm smarter. Faster.> The big cat's mental tone was smug.

Jason exchanged a glance with Tobias. "I don't know," he began. "It makes more sense to me to have more people along—"

<Hold on, there, boyo,> the AI interrupted, his tone musing. *<I think Simone may be onto something. It's true some of them outweigh her*

three-to-one, but Tobi's faster, more agile, and smarter than the larger predators are. They also tend to be a bit lazy. It could be worth the risk.>

Jason narrowed his eyes at the Weapon Born, then shifted abruptly back to Simone.

"How fast can we get there?"

Simone smiled wryly. "Speed's not going to be the issue, as much as a human's—or cat's—tolerance of it will be," she said, indicating Tobi. "I can get you passage on any number of container ships that travel between Godel and Barat daily, but a lot of them are drone ships that use the fast lanes to transit between our two worlds."

"And…." Jason pressed.

"And a lot of them are transiting at twenty, up to thirty *g*s or more."

"Not a problem," he said instantly. "I have pilot's mods, I can take it."

"And Tobi, boyo?" Tobias asked gently.

Jason thought a moment, shooting Terrance a glance. "A stasis pod," he said abruptly. "That should take care of our problem, shouldn't it?"

Noa leant forward, a concerned look on his face. "Do we want to risk having the very tech they want there for them to take, if you're discovered?"

Jason felt irritation at the physicist for throwing a wrench into the plan, but before he could voice it, Jonesy interrupted.

"Actually…." Jonesy drew the word out, his tone thoughtful. "We can insert a command code, one that can trigger a self-destruct, if you find you need to scuttle it."

"Bonus points if it can be used as a tac-nuke." Jason's tone was dry.

Jonesy shook his head with a grin. "Sorry, sir, it'll be a standard detonation," he said. "But I'll be sure to make it a nice, earth-shattering kaboom."

The session went on for another two hours, Jason pressing

Simone to go back over minor details, until finally Terrance stopped him.

"Enough," the exec said wearily. "We're rehashing old information. We need a break. Food. Rest. We'll reconvene tomorrow before we arrive."

"I'm fine," Jason said shortly. "I want to go over the New Pejeta terrain one more—"

"Jason." Terrance's voice, sharp and hard, cut him off. "Stand down. That's an order."

Jason's head snapped back, his eyes hot with anger. "Not a normal human, dude. And I'm not about to waste precious time feeding my goddamn face," his voice rose, "or sleeping with my goddamn wife, when I could—"

Terrance's fist shot out as Jason sprang away from the table. Tobias leapt up at the same time Khela, Landon and Logan did. Jonesy just sat there, mouth hanging open, while Logan held Khela back, Landon went for Terrance, and Tobias wrapped an arm around Jason's cocked fist.

"Haud yer wheesht!" the Weapon Born bellowed.

Silence descended upon the ready room.

Shannon's avatar appeared. Her arms were crossed, her silver eyes solemn.

"First," the ship's AI said quietly to the room as her eyes swept the tableau before her, "no one wants Calista back more than I do."

She looked squarely at Jason as she approached him, silvery hair drifting softly around her, her eyes holding a sympathy rarely seen in the spirited, sharp-tongued AI.

"I've known her longer than you have, Jason. A lot longer. She's like a sister to me."

Jason took a breath and then nodded at Shannon. He released his clenched fist, and Tobias relaxed his hold.

"Second...." She turned to Tobias, one eyebrow cocked, as she planted her hands on her waist, all attitude once again. "Seriously? 'Haud yer wheesht'? That is *so* not Irish."

The comment had its desired effect. A ripple ran through the humans—a nervous cough from Jonesy, a short bark of a laugh out of Terrance, even a snort from Jason.

The Weapon Born managed to look embarrassed. "I, ah…it's a long story, lass…."

"Well," Khela shot one final glare Jason's way, and he raised a shoulder in a half-shrug of apology that she chose to ignore. "If everyone is ready to act their age now, I'm going to grab something to eat and get some sleep."

"Good idea, love. I'll join you…." Terrance began, but Khela threw him a dark look, and Jason smirked as Terrance's voice trailed off. "What? He started it!"

"And that's our cue to leave, boyo," the Weapon Born said. He hooked an arm around Jason's neck, steering him out of the room.

Tobias forced him to eat, get some sleep, and then refused to allow him back on the bridge. Instead, he dragged Jason down to the bay to help certify that the newly-rebuilt shuttle, *Eidolon,* was ready for flight. It had most likely kept Terrance from throwing another punch at him—and Khela from poisoning him.

THIMBLERIGGING

STELLAR DATE: 03.12.3272 (Adjusted Gregorian)
LOCATION: Presidium Offices, Humans' Republic
REGION: Barat, Little River

As Giovanni entered the premier's oak-paneled conference room in the Presidium, his attention was arrested by the sight of a woman sitting in the chair he usually occupied. He looked around, realizing the only open seats were against the wall among a sea of aides.

On the outside, looking in.

He seethed silently at one more indication that he had been replaced—as if the fact that he had not been informed about this meeting wasn't indication enough.

Back ramrod straight and pride stung, Giovanni made his way stiffly to the single remaining chair as the premier's inner circle of advisors began recapping for the group at large the strategies being enacted.

He glared at the profile of Citizen General Jones, the soldier who sat in the chair he'd occupied just yesterday, her expression one of veiled triumph.

Giovanni had figured out what had transpired the night before. In retrospect, it had clearly been a setup. It was the only possible conclusion he could come to—once he'd found the missives that had been sent out in his name. All official correspondence, from the offices of Public Safety and Information.

His organization. Compromised.

He'd discovered the agent Jones had subverted and had neutralized her—permanently. He'd backtraced a forgery of his own auth token, convincingly done. The instructions sent to Phaethon's outpost ordered his agent to ship the *Avon Vale* captain to Gehenna. En route, they were to interrogate the subject, and harvest all available tech. He raged inside, knowing that last had been what had sealed his removal from the premier's ranks.

Jones knew it, too. She'd passed him a single, shrewd look as he entered the chambers just now, and then a visual dismissal, as if his influence on Barat was a chapter that had ended.

"And where do we stand on our acquisition of the stasis tech?" he heard the premier ask, her gaze settling squarely on Jones and ignoring him completely.

The snub did not go unremarked. Giovanni caught side glances from both Willa Savin and Natasha Coletti as Jones began her report.

"We are doing what we can to salvage the situation by harvesting as much tech from the subject as possible, given the unfortunate mishandling of the prisoner," Jones replied. Her voice rang with confidence as she added, "Our doctors tell us they've harvested a few promising bits already, including a superconducting battery more efficient than our own."

"*Very* good, General," the premier practically purred. "It is gratifying to hear you've achieved so much in such a short time."

Her words soured Giovanni's stomach, more so because it had been *Jones* who had mishandled the *Avon Vale*'s captain—not him. He'd advocated that they leave the prisoner unharmed. Her cadre of generals had been the ones to botch the situation.

"As for the stasis tech itself," Jones continued, "our agents inside State House tell us the Centauri ship should reach Godel late tomorrow. Once the tech has been traded to Godel, it should be an easy matter to relieve our neighbors of it."

"Speaking of relieving our neighbors of something they hold and we need, where are we on obtaining that vein of high purity silica?" Natasha Coletti leant forward, eager to hear news of the Verdant mining operation.

Giovanni noted with some satisfaction that the question caused Jones to deflate a bit. "Our friends on Godel suspect our hand in the uprisings there. They've sent notice that they will defend the asteroid, if we approach," the general admitted. "But I've devised a solution that will effectively divert them."

"Oh?" The premier cocked her head. "And what would that be?"

Jones's confidence rallied, and she sat taller, leaning forward to deliver the news. "We've instructed patrols along the shipping lanes to renew their harassment of Godel container vessels, and have sent orders for our ships to execute close passes on three other mining concerns."

The premier crossed her arms, blood-red nails tapping a finely-tailored sleeve in irritation. "This has been done before, General," she reminded the woman.

"It has," Jones agreed. "And they may even recognize the ploy for the tactic it is. But they cannot let the aggression go unanswered, which means their forces will have to be spread across greater distances. In the meantime…."

She drew her lips back, baring her teeth in a feral grin. "We go forward with our plan to destroy their planetary storehouses. That distraction—combined with the thinning of their forces—will leave Verdant poorly defended." Jones sat back, raising a hand in dismissal. "A simple conquest."

Giovanni caught the look of avarice shining in Natasha Coletti's eyes and knew the general had made a convert by doing nothing more than co-opting his own plan and adding a bit more firepower—something she had conveniently refused to give to *him* a week earlier, claiming she had no vessels available for the task. Now he knew why.

Well, shit.

A glance around the table showed the general had managed to gain the approval of everyone else, as well.

But Jones wasn't done.

"Of course, it would be a shame," she added with a studied nonchalance, "to have Godel in such a uniquely vulnerable position and not take full advantage of it…."

Her voice trailed off, and she looked over at Feretti, her expression calculating.

The premier returned the gaze, her own eyes narrowing. "Go on," she said, after a moment.

"It would be interesting, would it not, to have Godel dependent on *us* for a critical resource for a change, and not the other way around?"

Jones now had the complete attention of everyone in the room, including Giovanni. She nodded, as if she'd received unanimous agreement to her statement.

Their attention surely implies tacit agreement, at the least, was Giovanni's passing thought.

"We've expanded our planetary operation to include their top farming operations, in addition to the planetary storehouses. Additional Digital-to-Biological units, DBCs, are en route now and will soon be emplaced. With a single encrypted signal sent, we will be able to decimate Godel's food supply."

It took a moment for the implications of her statement to sink in. Once it did, Giovanni felt gut-punched at the general's words. This wasn't warfare; it wasn't even terrorism. The scale to which Jones had escalated the situation threatened to wipe out a large portion of Godel's population.

Have we no decency? Or, at the very least, a sense of self-preservation?

There was a reason the ancient saying 'don't poke the bear' existed. A world facing an existential threat could feel they had nothing to lose….

And then Jones upped the ante.

"Consider this." The general's face was intense as she leant toward those seated at the table. "Once we acquire Enfield's stasis tech, we will have the ability to preserve fresh produce in a way cryogenics has never allowed. No cellular damage of delicate fruits and vegetables. For the first time, we will truly be able to store up reserves in case of famine."

She paused for effect. "Or for famine on another world. Which would place us in a position to render assistance to a neighboring planet that finds itself faced with a food shortage. For a price, of course."

Stars, the woman is a greedy, ambitious bitch, Giovanni *thought. High risk does yield high reward, but what she has orchestrated could also galvanize Godel against us and plunge us into war.*

He sat up suddenly as realization hit him.

She knows this. She's been lobbying for a stronger military presence against Godel for years. She wants this.

The nods of the people around the table gave him chills. Jones's madness was a contagion that was spreading, he could see it happening before his very eyes.

He knew then what he had to do.

To save his people, he would first need to betray them.

* * * * *

That evening, junior analyst Molly Chaudry checked her internal chrono one last time before boarding the elevator that would take her to the New Kells Spaceport. She cursed the last-minute string of reports that had showed up unexpectedly, demanding her attention.

Charlotte, the AI aboard the courier ship *Charade,* had assured Molly that her brother's two girls could wait in the diplomatic lounge just off the main concourse if their timing didn't quite match up, but she hated the thought of leaving them alone any longer than necessary.

It had been kind of Simone to take an interest in Molly's nieces and check on them on her way to Phaethon. Molly had very nearly cried when Simone had sent her a message saying the girls would arrive on Godel in three days' time. She owed her.

Molly exited the elevator and pinged the spaceport's NSAI for directions to the diplomatic lounge. A map appeared on her overlay, and she reversed her course, turning down a side corridor and taking a lift up two levels.

Her steps quickened as she approached the lounge, a smile playing over her face. Twenty meters from the lounge, she received a priority ping. Automatically, she accepted the token, realizing just as she did so that the sender's tag had been truncated.

<*Your brother's children are in our care,*> the voice began, and Molly stumbled to a halt. <*They will remain unharmed so long as you do as we say. Do you understand?*>

Her eyes widened and her heart began pounding. She looked around wildly, then bolted for the lounge at a dead run.

<*You will stop, **now**, if you wish to see them alive.*>

She ground to a halt, hands fisted at her sides, her breaths coming quick and shallow.

<*Very good,*> the voice said approvingly. <*Now, here is what you are going to do. I have a message for your director of intelligence. You will find a way to get it to her without anyone being the wiser, or these charming little girls will never see their father again. Am I understood?*>

* * * * *

"Citizen General!"

Jones looked up irritably as one of Giovanni's Citizen intelligence officers came barreling into her Combat Ready Room.

Jones jerked her head at the Citizen major standing guard by the door, and the woman moved to cut off the interloper.

"But, sir," the young man protested as the major crowded him and began pushing him bodily back through the entrance, "it's about the DBCs!"

Jones had returned her attention to the Godel map she'd been studying, but at the man's words, she blanked the holo and swiveled to meet his gaze.

<*Stop. Let him speak,*> Jones instructed the major, who immediately snapped to attention, inclined her head, and resumed

her watchful position at the door.

The young man took a nervous breath, his eyes darting about the room as he straightened his uniform. Licking his lips, he turned back to lock eyes with Jones, the adam's apple just above his uniform's neckline bobbing as he swallowed.

"I'm listening," the general prodded, and her tone held a clear "this better be good" warning. She crossed her arms and raised one brow, waiting impatiently for the man to speak.

"I…we just intercepted a transmission to Godel, Citizen General," he began. "It relayed the locations of each of the Digital-to-Biological Converter units that our agents have planted in Godel's food supply chain."

"What?" Jones's two-star demanded from where he stood next to her.

Fury engulfed Jones at the news of this betrayal. She had not worked on this plan so hard and for so long to see it destroyed from within by some spineless traitor.

She swiveled, pinning the Citizen major-general beside her with a look. "Go with him," she instructed, tilting her head to indicate the twitchy intelligence officer. "Track the traitor down. I want that leak plugged!"

The major-general drew himself up with a crisp salute before double-timing it toward the door and waving the young man back through it with an impatient gesture.

Jones pivoted, allowing a glare to sweep the occupants of the room. "If Godel is aware of the DBCs, then find me another solution, and find it now." Her words were harsh and staccato, striking with the force of a projectile, and several in the room flinched as if struck. "One way or another, their food supply *will* be taken out. Am I understood?"

Heads nodded vigorously as suggestions began to fly around the room. Jones braced her hands on the War Room's holotable as she silently observed the interchange.

"Nanophage?" one suggested, and another dismissed it with a

wave of her hand.

"Too slow," she countered. "What about a fast-acting poison?"

"The DBCs could have printed that," another pointed out. "And besides, if we introduced a toxin, they could quickly engineer a cognate antitoxin to neutralize."

"True, what about—"

"Enough!" Jones interrupted the debate, clenching her teeth in annoyance. "We have neither the time nor the margin for error to rely upon clever solutions. I want a decisive victory, Citizens."

Her fierce gaze swept the room and, when she was certain she had captured their undivided attention, she spoke once more.

"This time, we use a blunt instrument. Have our agents plant explosives *everywhere.* No food storage facility, no processing plant, no stars-be-damned farmer's market is to be left out, am I understood? I want their food supply taken *down,* Citizens. And if that means we take a tac-nuke to a knife fight—then so be it."

FOOD FOR THOUGHT

STELLAR DATE: 03.13.3272 (Adjusted Gregorian)
LOCATION: State House, New Kells
REGION: Godel, Little River

<*Director Mastai is here to see you, sir,*> Elie, Edouard Zola's chief assistant, informed the president.

Zola sent her a swift thank you and then consulted the calendar on his HUD. It was as he'd thought; there was no meeting scheduled with Celia today.

He knew the woman wouldn't interrupt him except for something important, so he excused himself from the conference holo he'd been attending with his staff and pushed away from his desk.

His office door slid open, admitting the tall, slender form of the intelligence director as he stood to welcome her.

"Mister President," Celia greeted as she strode toward him, the sleek folds of her tailored, sage-green dress alternately hiding and revealing the well-toned legs of the athletic, auburn-haired woman as she approached.

Her hand dipped inside her jacket pocket, and then she reached out as if to shake his hand. He caught a flash of white and then felt the crisp lines of the sheet of rapid-degrade-plas she'd passed to him.

Zola palmed it, glancing down briefly. He could just make out a thin line of neat handwriting in the inside of the fold.

"I do believe spring has finally left us for summertime," she murmured, and he looked up in time to see her glance out the window then return her gaze to him, tipping her head meaningfully toward the paper he held.

"Seems so," he agreed absently, his thumb flipping the creased page open so that he could read what she'd written.

Find a reason to be in the Situation Room in half an hour. Alone.

He refolded it, tucking it into a trouser pocket as he eyed her quizzically.

"I was on my way over to deliver a few case files to your protection detail," she said, "and thought I'd stop in to see if there was anything I could do to help prepare for our guests' arrival this afternoon."

Her gaze was guileless. Why she felt the need for such secrecy, within State House of all places, was beyond him. But Edouard Zola had learned long ago the value of his intelligence director's instincts, so he merely nodded while wracking his brain for something banal to say in response.

"I fear they won't be up to much pomp or circumstance, given their concern over the arrest of their ship's captain," he said, settling for the obvious. "I asked Elie if she would have the presidential steward arrange for a quiet meal here in one of the smaller dining rooms."

Celia nodded in satisfaction. "Ah, well, it sounds like you have things well in hand over here, as usual. I'll just be on my way, then."

With a raised brow, Zola nodded and escorted her to the door.

Now, what is this all about, I wonder? he mused.

Half an hour later, excuse invented, Edouard's detail palmed open the door to the Situation Room, glanced inside, nodded once to its lone inhabitant, and then stepped aside to allow Edouard to enter.

"Sir! I'm sorry, I didn't realize you had planned to use the Sit Room today." Celia's voice carried into the hall, its tone one of carefully crafted surprise. "I'll just see myself ou—"

Playing along, he raised a restraining hand. "No, no, please. This was just a whim on my part. Purely spontaneous. I had a moment, and thought of something I might have left in here. Please, finish what you were doing. I'll wait."

"Well, if you're sure." Her tone was pitched perfectly,

delivering a flawless mix of hesitance and doubt. "I'll only be a moment."

Zola smiled and waved for her to continue, nodded amiably at his detail, then indicated they seal the doors as he strolled over and took a seat.

Well, at least ***her*** *acting was superb. Not sure I convinced my detail that this was a chance meeting….*

As the Situation Room sealed them in, Celia triggered its security protocols. Her casual pretense fell from her like a cloak, and she turned a bleak look his way.

"What's with the skulking, Celie?" he said, invoking a nickname he rarely used. He slipped his hand inside his pocket and pulled out the thin sheet of plas, waggling it at her. "Going old-school on me, now?"

Celia's mouth twisted in a wry smile that did not meet her eyes. "Sometimes, if you want to ensure something absolutely cannot be hacked, the best way for it to remain secure is the most antiquated of them all."

A shaft of alarm shot through him as he considered the implications of what she'd just said. He looked down at the note he held in his hands, folding it carefully. He slid the crease through thumb and forefinger as he turned her words over in his head.

Shooting her a glance from lowered brows, he said quietly, "That's quite something, considering where we are standing right now. You suspect we've been compromised?"

Celia began to pace. It wasn't a nervous kind of thing, more the type of measured step that came as one pondered a weighty matter.

"One of our most trusted assets on Barat appears to have sent us an encrypted TS/SCI message," she stated.

His head snapped up at her use of the acronym. Celia had just referenced the most elite security classification Godel had: Top-Secret, Sensitive Compartmentalized Intelligence.

Well, that's one way to get my attention….

His gaze locked with hers. "You said *appears to have*."

"It was from Giovanni Perelman."

Her words had him inhaling sharply. "Your counterpart on Barat," he said in a flat tone.

"If the message he sent is to be believed, our agent was compromised six months ago." She crossed her arms and shot him a sardonic look. "As a 'show of good faith'," her fingers air-quoted the words, "and to prove his sincerity, he has provided us with the tokens of three assets here in State House who have been compromised—one of whom was actively turned by their agents here on Godel."

The plas fluttered to the ground as Edouard gaped at her. She bent and scooped it up, pocketing it in a fluid motion.

"Stars, why?"

Celia crossed her arms, running her hands up and down them as if she were suddenly cold. Then, as if realizing her movements were revealing too much of her state of mind, she straightened, dropping her hands to her sides.

"Edouard, he claims Barat has infiltrated our planetary storehouses with a biological weapon capable of destroying half of Godel's food supplies within a matter of hours. Worse, they've upped the ante, and are prepared to decimate the crops of our largest and most productive farming operations."

A silence fell between them as what she'd said sank in.

"Celia…this…it's verified?" Zola struggled to verbalize the question, the shock he felt at the news causing his normally facile tongue to stumble over the words.

The director nodded once, her gaze somber. "It came directly to me through one of our compromised assets using a one-time cypher. I backtraced it and cross-checked the signal myself."

Zola stepped back, bumping into the table set into the center of the room. Blindly, he fumbled for a chair and collapsed into it, his mind racing.

"Okay. Okay," he muttered, eyes flickering back and forth as he mentally catalogued the information and its impact on the planet. He shot a glance up at the woman who stood, waiting silently for his response. "You were right to take precautions. If it were to get back to Barat that somehow we'd learned of this before they executed their plan…."

Celia nodded. "They'd go ahead and pull the trigger on those devices before we had a chance in hell of finding them—much less stopping them."

Zola drummed his fingers lightly against the table, leaning back in his seat in thought. "This needs to be handled, quickly and very quietly."

"And by a small, elite task force, yes," Celia concurred. Then she smiled crookedly, tilting her head to one side. "I hear there's a new arrival that just might fit that description."

Zola shifted his eyes from her jacket pocket, the one that held the plas, to her face. A speculative light gleamed in his eyes.

"You think the team from Alpha Centauri is our best option?"

She nodded. "I do. I've forwarded Simone's report on their operation to recover our agent and their captain. According to her," she added lightly, "Phantom Blade has some mad covert skills. Between you and me, I think she might be coming down with a mild case of hero worship for at least two of their AI members. Weapon Born of some sort or other, she said."

Zola studied his thumb as he ran it along the table's edge, contemplating what she'd just told him. Looking back up at her, he frowned. "They're coming here to ask for our help to recover their captain," he warned.

She shrugged elegantly. "Quid pro quo."

Stepping up to the table, she perched on its edge, folded her arms in her lap, and sent him a level look.

"Simone says they're decent people. Given the circumstances, I can't really see them turning us down, can you? Hell, Edouard," she said, lifting a hand in a sweeping gesture, "you'd have to be some sort of stars-be-damned *monster* to be willing to consign millions to death by starvation."

His steady glance and slow nod conceded her point. "Very well, then," he sighed. "Will you coordinate with the State House steward on a revised guest list for this afternoon's welcome?"

She murmured her assent as he stood, straightened his suit, and glanced at his internal chrono before sending her a grimace.

"I have to get back before I'm missed," he told her.

She nodded, but then held up a hand. "We're going to have to handle this carefully, Edouard. We can't let on, even to your security detail—possibly even *especially* to them—that this afternoon is anything more than a state visit."

He frowned, shoving his hands in his pockets. "That could be challenging."

She smiled. "Yes, but I have an idea…."

PART FIVE: ARRIVAL

WET CAT, ANGRY MARINE

STELLAR DATE: 03.13.3272 (Adjusted Gregorian)
LOCATION: ESS *Avon Vale*, Main Spaceport
REGION: Godel, Little River

The insistent chime came across Terrance's Link, the sound slowly growing from a gentle reminder to an annoying buzzsaw-like noise that not even he could sleep through.

Sending the mental command for it to shut off, his half-awake brain toyed with the idea of rolling over and burying his face into the silky black strands of hair that teased his neck, while catching another hour of sleep.

And then he remembered. Today was the day the *Vale* was scheduled to arrive at Godel. He couldn't afford to sleep in, but he could spare a few extra stolen moments with his wife.

His hands skimmed feather-light over Khela's body, tracing from her neck, down across the strong muscled shoulders of a Marine. Across the gentle curves of her breasts, down the tapering length of a trim yet well-muscled torso, her skin impossibly smooth against the coarser texture of his hands.

She turned into him, running her hands up his bare chest. Strong hands that knew a hundred different ways to kill locked around the back of his neck, pulling his face down to meet hers as she pressed herself up against him in a quick embrace—and then she was gone, flowing out of their bed like water, her naked form stealing the breath from his body and making other parts stand up and salute.

Khela glanced back at him, her eyes dark and inviting.

"Planning to sleep in, lover, or can I talk you into joining me in the san?" Her tone was serene, even as she shot him a suggestive look.

Their san had been modified during their journey to include a real-water shower that they could use during the times when their cabin experienced at least a half-*g*, as it did when the ship's habitat spun during cruise, or while they were docked at a station like Phaethon.

Khela had modeled it after a spa back in Tau Ceti, and Terrance had to admit it was pretty amazing. It was an indulgence, but she had assured him she'd make it worth his while—and she had.

He smiled in anticipation as she stretched languidly, her body all supple motion and tranquil harmony. It belied the backlash she'd endured the night before, the shuddering episodes wracking her petite frame. His smile faded as he recalled them.

A parting gift, those attacks were, a vestigal curse from the nanophage. Memory fragments, incompletely removed, left over from the AI who had perished while embedded inside Khela's brain.

Marta, the ship's medical officer, had assured him they weren't harmful, although the doctor hadn't been able to fully excise Hana's lattice from around Khela's brain stem, nor from the neural pathways they had wrapped themselves around. So far, the seizures—for lack of a better term—seemed only to occur after Khela had completed a mission.

Marta conjectured they were activated by some sort of neural dysphagia, a deeply integrated trigger rooted in the training she and Hana had received together in Marine country back on Galene.

As Khela slipped into the san, Terrance breathed a prayer of thanks that the remnant had yet to claim her while she was deployed on a mission. He still held out hope that one day Marta could find a way to fully neutralize the remnants that had been left inside his wife when the nanophage infected the joined pair.

Only then, he knew, would Khela truly be free, when the

portions of Hana that remained could be put to rest for good.

Terrance snapped out of his reverie when he heard a yelp, followed by his wife's muffled shriek from inside the san.

"Khela!"

He threw the covers back and was halfway to his destination when the san door slid open and forty kilos of wet Proxima cat came hurtling through.

Spying Terrance, Beck altered his trajectory and slid to a stop behind his legs.

"What the—"

"There's a *dead rat* in our shower!"

Terrance tried and failed to hide a smirk. "Aren't Marines supposed to be too tough to be afraid of a little—"

Abruptly, Khela appeared at the san entrance, one hundred and seventy centimeters of avenging fury, dripping wet and brandishing a bloody body part, entrails hanging loosely from one end.

"Finish that sentence," she bit off as she advanced, pointing the carcass at his bare chest, "and you won't be getting any." Terrance's eyes were glued in fascination to the thing she held in her hand. "Ever—" the carcass hit his bare chest with a wet *splat,* "again."

Reflexively, his hand reached up to grab the squishy mess, smirk gone as he shook his head. "Getting any?"

Her gaze flicked meaningfully to their bed and then back.

He swallowed. "Wouldn't think of it, love."

Black eyes glittered as they held his in a fulminating glare. Into the silence, one paw crept around from behind him, angled toward the dead animal cradled against his chest. With his other hand, he eased it away.

He saw Khela's lips twitch at the sight, but she fought valiantly to hold onto her righteous anger.

"Your cat—" Her voice quivered slightly with laughter before she cleared her throat and glared down at Beck, flinging wet hair out of her eyes, "was having breakfast all over the shower floor."

<*Wasn't in the closet this time,*> Beck argued. <*In the shower, all the blood washes off, easy.*>

"He's got a point there," Terrance volunteered. "At least now, he's not ruining our clothes...." His voice trailed off the moment she turned her glare back on him.

<*Would now be a good time to intervene?*>

"Not now, Kodi."

<*Because you're about to have a visitor pop in, and two wet, naked humans holding the intestines of a rat between them looks like some sort of—*>

"KODI!"

Khela's shout had a snap to it that only a Marine could dish out.

<*I'm gone. Was never here. Didn't see a thing.*>

<*Kodi,*> Terrance said privately, and the AI sent him a smirk.

<*Don't say I didn't warn you. Shannon'll be showing up in three...two...*> He heard the AI's laughter echo in his head as he withdrew.

In the next instant, a chime sounded, followed by Shannon's voice.

<*Good morning! I—Whoa. I've heard of humans using whipped cream, or chocolate sauce. But dead rodent carcasses...? Wow, Terrance. Kinky!*>

Terrance closed his eyes and tilted his head back as Shannon's holo faded away. Khela let out an exasperated sigh and disappeared back into the san.

<*Does that mean no shower time, hon?*>

<*Want to come help me clean this mess up first?*>

<*Uhmmm, is that a trick question?*>

Khela sent him a mental snort as he felt a wet nose nudging at his hand.

He looked down to see Beck tilt his head and delicately extract the chunk of flesh from Terrance's hands. He trotted to the door of their quarters, bloody carcass dangling between sharp incisors.

Nosing the door controls, he slipped through as it slid open, just as one of the crew walked past. The woman glanced down at Beck then up at the naked man standing in the middle of the room. Terrance could just make out her grin as she backtracked, craning her neck for a better look before the door slid closed behind the cat.

With a sigh, he glanced at the message flashing on his HUD—the one Shannon had come to deliver personally—and realized he was about to be late for a meeting.

* * * * *

Knowing they'd be docked at the New Kells Spaceport by noon made a huge difference in Jason's outlook. He'd agreed to go along for a brief visit planetside to press the flesh with Godel's president, but only after being assured they would be on their way to Barat shortly thereafter.

Finally.

He'd tried to get out of the presidential luncheon, but Tobias had reminded him that they needed Godel's help to get Calista back.

The AI had also had a few choice things to say about Jason's almost-fight with Terrance the day before. A flare of guilt arose at that, which he firmly squelched.

Not like I actually punched him…. Jason grinned at that thought.

He realized that he felt good for the first time since he'd left the bazaar. He consciously avoided labeling the incident at the bazaar as 'abandoning Calista', even though his gut kept insisting on calling it that.

<Thanks again, by the way, for keeping me from turning into a complete ass over the last few days.> He sent the thought, accompanied by a warm dose of appreciation, down the private pathway he shared with Tobias. The Weapon Born returned the

emotion, the same way they'd done throughout the countless years they'd been friends.

<Oh, you were still an ass, boyo. Just not a complete one. Be there in a trice.>

Jason sent an acknowledgement, whistling a soundless tune as he strode into the dining hall and giving an amiable wave to crew personnel just exiting. A glance around the room showed their guest seated alone at a table with Jonesy. He steered toward them, greeting them as he approached.

"Mister Andrews," Simone greeted, her voice cautious but welcoming.

Jason squelched a brief flare of remorse for his behavior over the past few days; he knew he'd come across as curt, bordering on hostile.

Now's as good a time as any to mend those bridges.

"May I join you?" he asked with an easy smile and saw Simone's expression relax.

She nodded and returned his smile with one of her own.

"I'd like that," the AI invited, gesturing to a chair.

Jason pointed toward the buffet set up at the back of the dining hall. "Let me just grab something and I'll be right with you."

He grinned at Tobias as the Weapon Born stepped into the room, inclined his head toward the table where he intended to sit, and sent the AI a sloppy salute.

As he turned toward the enticing smells wafting from the warming platters lined up along the half wall that separated the kitchen from the dining area, he received a ping from Terrance.

<Shannon says Simone wants to brief us on our meeting with President Zola, but I'm running a bit late.> The man's voice sounded harried.

Jason hid a grin at the stressed tone in Terrance's mental voice and wondered briefly what had caused it. He snagged a plate and began to fill it from the variety of breakfast foods, both savory and sweet, before him. Sliding his gaze back across to their visitor seated at the table, he offered, <*I'm just grabbing some breakfast in the main dining hall. Simone's here with Jonesy. Why don't we just meet here, instead?*>

He could sense Terrance's relief. <*Great idea. I haven't had time to grab anything yet, myself, so that'd be perfect.*> There was a pause, followed by, <*Any way you could ask whoever's on duty in the kitchen to scare up a pot of hot cocoa for Khela, too?*>

Jason's brow rose, and his grin settled into a smirk as he slid a couple of fried eggs on top of his gravy-laden biscuits. <*In trouble, are we? Don't you usually tease her about that stuff? Something about 'real Marines drink coffee'? Maybe I should order you a side of flowers to go along with it. Or maybe a Hallmark card?*>

<*A what card?*> Terrance replied. <*Nevermind, and yes, I'm trying to make nice. But it wasn't anything I did this time. It's all Beck's fault.*>

<*Uh-huh,*> Jason drawled. <*Sure. Blame the cat. Care to share what really happened?*>

<*Not in this lifetime, buddy.*> Terrance's voice was vehement. <*And I'll deny any rumors you hear circulating about it, too. Hey, is Vi still managing the kitchen this week?*> he asked, steering the subject away from the doghouse he seemed to be in at the moment.

Originally from Tau Ceti's third planet, Eione, Vi had bartered part of her ticket to Epsilon Eridani for her services as a chef. None of the humans aboard the *Vale* had minded in the least; what the woman could do with fresh ingredients was a gastronomic delight.

Jason sent Terrance a shot of the spread before him and heard him groan a <*Thank the stars!*> before hurriedly cutting the connection.

Plate balanced precariously on top of his steaming mug of coffee, Jason snagged one of the thermal carafes of coffee for refills later on. He then charted a course through the sea of tables between the buffet and where their guest sat. After settling his plate, he gestured to Jonesy's cup with the carafe.

"Can I top you off?" he asked, and the engineer smiled and proffered his mug.

Setting the carafe down, Jason ambled back over to the station where one of Vi's AI sous-chefs was prepping some vegetables for a lunch dish.

"Hey, Nick, Terrance asked if there was any way he could get a to-go order for hot cocoa."

Nick looked up, knife poised as he cocked his head. "In trouble with Khela, is he?"

Jason chuckled. "Actually, I hear it's Beck's fault. If you get the story out of that cat, let me know. I'm sure it's a good one."

Nick shook his head. "Tell Terrance I'll have a servitor send a fresh pot right up."

Jason sent the AI a sloppy two-fingered salute, then snagged a few more strips of bacon off the platter sitting under a warmer before returning to the table.

<Cocoa's on its way.>

"Thanks," Terrance called out as he entered the dining hall. He nodded hello to a few Enfield employees at a table across the room, straightening the cuff of one sleeve as he approached.

"Morning, Jonesy. Simone," Terrance greeted, nodding to them both. "I apologize for running late. Mind if I grab a bite? I'll be right with you."

"Not at all." With a wave of her hand, Simone gestured to Jonesy's charcuterie plate. "I understand this isn't considered breakfast food in Alpha Centauri, but Jonesy asked about Godel customs, so Nick fixed him a carpaccio platter. I highly recommend it. Jonesy tells me it's delicious."

Jason saw the expression on Terrance's face as he glanced down at the remains of the chopped, raw meat on the engineer's plate, and he suddenly had an idea what Beck might have done.

Coughing to hide a laugh, he supplied, "Yes, well, Terrance is more of a bacon-and-eggs kind of guy. What you recommended for Jonesy is what they call Mediterranean-style, isn't it?"

Terrance didn't wait to hear Simone's response; he beat a hasty retreat to the buffet line. Jason used Terrance's escape as an opportunity to dig into his own plate.

"He seems a bit frazzled," Simone observed, as Jason lifted his fork and cut through the rich, runny yolk of fried egg. "Is everything all right?"

Jason left Tobias to field that question as he dug into his meal. A twist of his utensil had a bite-sized piece of egg loaded onto the fork, which was then dipped into the gravy until suitably coated. Popping the load into his mouth, he paused to savor the morsel before chasing it with a swig of coffee and a bite of bacon.

"Just a wee bit of mischief from one of our uplifted crew members," Tobias offered, and Tobi stirred from where she lay under his feet.

<It was The Brat, wasn't it? I ***knew*** *it.>* The cat's voice was dripping with disgust.

Simone looked bemused while Jonesy paused, a forkful of carpaccio halfway to his mouth. "Uplifted animals," he mused, his tone thoughtful. "You never told us why you don't have them here in this system."

Simone shook her head. "I think it's simply because no one ever considered it. Why, I couldn't tell you. If I recall my pre-Sentience War history correctly, weren't some companies experimenting with this back in Sol, around the time the first SAIs were created?" She shot Tobias a questioning glance.

The AI nodded. "Heartbridge, Psion, a few others." He shot a glance over toward where Terrance was filling his plate with a pile of fluffy, golden, scrambled eggs and a generous side of bacon. "Including Enfield Scientific."

Jason winced. "Yeah, that was Terrance's great-great-someone, wasn't it, Tobe?"

"Aye, it was at that." The Weapon Born turned back to the AI from Godel. "The owners were left out of some critical decisions by management, I'm afraid. As a result, the family bought out the shareholders and took the company private. It's also when they pulled up roots and moved to Alpha Centauri."

Simone spared a sympathetic glance toward the approaching Enfield. "So I recall from my history lessons. But ever since, the company has had an upstanding reputation." She smiled as Terrance rejoined them.

"But back to uplifted animals," she continued. "All of the initial experimentation happened centuries after our colony ships left for Little River. But the ones back in Sol, weren't they an avian species? Parrots, if I recall."

Tobias laughed, the sound a rueful one. "Ah, yes," the AI recalled. "One of the very few pleasant memories I have of my time there. There was one bird in particular, Crash, his name was. Had quite a thing for numbers, he did."

An unreadable look crossed his face, and then he stirred, glanced at Jason, and redirected the topic.

"As far as uplifted felines go, Tobi here is one of the first. Jason's mum back in Proxima did the work. You may have heard of her," he turned to Simone. "Cara Sykes's daughter, Jane. A neuroscientist, quite skilled."

Simone's expression lightened, and she favored Jason with an approving look. "I must admit, I've only met Tobi and Beck so far since I've been aboard. How many are on the *Avon Vale*?"

<*One more than we need,*> Tobi growled from under the table, and Jason saw Jonesy's mouth twitch as he hid a grin, while Terrance coughed after swallowing a mouthful of coffee.

"Ahhh. I take it there's no love lost between you two, Tobi?" Simone directed to the cat, twisting her head to peer under the table.

<*You could say that, yes.*>

Jason smirked at Kodi's dry riposte as the AI joined their conversation.

"As riveting as it is to discuss uplifted cats," Jason tilted his head to peer down at Tobi with a wink, "I'd rather talk about the plan once we arrive."

Kodi chuckled. <*I think my meat-suit here would agree with you,*

Jason.>

Terrance merely rolled his eyes, stabbing a forkful of egg and chasing it around the plate to sop up some of the bacon grease as Simone nodded her understanding.

<*Landon informed us earlier this morning that Godel STC has given the* Vale *an approach window,*> Kodi informed them. <*We should be docked at your spaceport spindle in another three hours.*>

"Good," Jason said, eyes narrowing in thought. "How soon before the container ship's ready to transfer us over?"

"We'll have a tug waiting to push a container up to your starboard bay as soon as you're docked," Simone assured them. "We can transfer you over immediately after our meeting on Godel."

"Excellent," he smiled, tipping his mug back to down the last of his coffee. "We'll be ready."

<*Yes. We will.*> Tobi punctuated her comment with a snap of her teeth, and Jason slid Tobias a grin.

"Don't get cocky, Tobi, understand?" Terrance set his fork down and craned his neck to peer under the table at the big cat. "You come back to us in one piece, you hear me?" he added as he slipped Tobi a piece of sausage.

<*I will, don't worr—oooh, sausage, YUM. Got any bacon left?*>

She took the offered piece from him and swallowed it with a gulp, then licked his hand in thanks. Terrance grimaced and wiped his hand before pushing his plate aside.

Jason smirked, then grabbed a half-eaten slice of bacon off his plate and handed it to her.

He shot Simone a look. "In the meantime, if you have any specs for the container ship, that'd be helpful." His gaze grew concerned. "The lunch isn't going to be one of those several-hours-long state dinners, is it?"

A brief smile lit the AI's face. "I promise it won't. Although, it wasn't easy to arrange. We don't have much opportunity to entertain foreign nations outside Barat on our little planet, so representatives from Alpha Centauri—"

"And Tau Ceti," Khela interjected with a smile as she approached.

"And Tau Ceti," Simone agreed, nodding, "are a real treat for us."

Jason grabbed his empty plate and rose, offering the chair to the Marine. She nodded her thanks as she sat.

"Sorry to eat and run, folks," he said, as Tobias and Tobi rose to follow him. "But we have a mission to prep. You know, for when we're in the wilds of New Pejeta, sweating our asses off."

<*Speak for yourself,*> Tobi said. <*Cats don't sweat.*>

"You do through your paws," Jason countered.

<*Details.*>

"Good hunting," Simone said to Tobi, her tone solemn, then turned to Jason and Tobias. "I promise you, we'll keep the rest of your crew very busy while you're away."

Something about the way she said it had Jason peering at her sharply and wondering just exactly what the AI meant by that.

A SOLEMN CHARGE

STELLAR DATE: 03.13.3272 (Adjusted Gregorian)
LOCATION: *ESS Avon Vale*
REGION: Godel nearspace, Little River

"Welcome to Godel," Simone said quietly from where she stood on the bridge of the *Avon Vale*. The main holoscreen revealed the frenetic chaos of Godel's main spaceport as they came in on final approach.

Landon shot a quick glance over at the AI as she dropped a file to him on the ship's net.

"Thought your team might like a quick refresher before we land," she explained with a smile.

At Jason's nod, Landon tossed it up onto the bridge's main holo.

The image shifted from the bustling activity of nearspace to a more sedate view of the planet, slowly turning against the black backdrop of space. Dressed in cool blues and whites, with a belt of lush green spanning its equator, Godel looked like an oasis.

"The FGT had to wrap it in stasis, you know," Simone confided conversationally to the bridge crew. "That's how they kept it from being pulled apart as they wrestled it into place."

From his position at scan, Landon saw Hailey's head turn and shoot Simone a curious look.

"Oh, not Enfield-grade stasis, mind you," the AI's eyes crinkled in a smile as she returned the comm officer's look, eliciting a few chuckles from the rest on the bridge. "But they had to do something to protect it as they nudged it into the habitable zone from its original orbit farther out."

As the image zoomed into the planetary terrain, it morphed into majestic, snow-covered peaks that thrust their jagged way into the air, far above the tree line. The mountain range was met on both sides by tundra that seemed to go on forever.

The image shifted and the frozen climes slowly gave way to green, moss-covered fells that rimmed chilled, glassy seas. Rivers traced their way through the terrain, drifts of fog hanging low and heavy in their folds.

"Eire," Tobias uttered in a quiet voice from where he stood next to the captain's chair, and Landon saw Jason shoot the Weapon Born a sharp look.

"Very similar, yes," Simone agreed.

Curious, Landon ran a query and discovered a reference to lands back on High Terra, a region where those of Irish descent had settled. His gaze rested thoughtfully on Tobias, the Weapon Born with the Irish accent, but the AI offered up nothing more.

On the holo, the verdant land mass gave way to chains of islands, a delicate archipelago of brilliant greens. Oceans clung to their shores, plunging steeply into the deepest marine blue as the holo shifted closer to the slight bulge at Godel's equator. Here the blueness of the water turned a deep green as it ran ashore against the lavish greenery of an equatorial landmass.

"If you'd like to compare Godel with Barat," Simone added to Landon quietly, "there's a file that does that, too."

Landon backed out of the first file and accessed the second. An image coalesced of the star's inner system, showing two planets in the habitable zone. Barat was barely over an AU from the star, whereas Godel, the larger of the two, was located a little under two AUs away.

Data floating under the image indicated Godel had a mass that gave the planet a gravity of 1.2 *g*s, while Barat's was the standard 1 *g*. Godel had a moon, Escher, and orbiting Escher was a single moon-moon, Bach. Landon found it curious that the moniker moon-moon—something that dated back to Earth's twentieth century, if he recalled correctly—was still in use.

"Barat is closest to our star," Simone explained, "and it's slightly warmer. It was the first to be terraformed by the FGT.

They completed it fifty years before Godel was ready for habitation."

The system map dissolved, replaced by satellite imagery showing a planet painted in browns and golds. Splashes of blue indicated oceans and, at its poles, the orb was accented by areas of green with just the barest hint of white.

The holoimages progressed, and Landon felt as though he were aloft, skimming past the tops of trees. Trees gave way to the rolling hills of the planet's northlands, covered in a riot of gloriously colored vegetation. These in turn morphed into vast swaths of savannah. Its equatorial region consisted of a single, planet encircling veldt, the open, grassy range broken by occasional clumps of trees and low scrub.

Simone continued the narrative as fresh images resolved on the bridge holo.

"For the most part, the population prefers the more moderate climates found nearer the poles, although the Humans' Republic has a few urban areas that have been built up around the two elevators, placed at equidistance at the equator."

The file ended, and Landon returned the view to the image of the planet they were approaching.

"Godel, as you can see," Simone added quietly, "is a bit cooler in its climate, with its most populated areas encircling its equatorial region. Of the two, Godel should actually be marginally less agriculturally productive, but historically, the opposite has proven to be true."

Interesting comparisons. How much of Godel's success, he wondered, *has to do with its mindset, as opposed to its circumstances?*

Just then, Hailey straightened, flipping her long braid over her shoulder. "We're being hailed by the New Kells Spaceport, sir," she informed Jason with a glance back at the captain's chair. "They have our transponder ident and are sending us routing instructions."

The XO straightened, nodding to the comm officer. "Thanks,

Hailey." He then nodded to the AI running the nav boards. "Handshake with them, will you, Flo, and set up our approach. Give me an ETA when you have it."

* * * * *

Simone was as good as her word. The moment the *Avon Vale*'s amidships port dock connected with its umbilical at Godel's New Kells Spaceport, the AI forwarded the token of a tug operator to Hailey. A container was scheduled for delivery to the *Vale*'s starboard dock in two hours. At that point, they'd load the *Eidolon* into the container, with Jason and Tobias onboard, Tobi tucked securely into the stasis pod.

From where he sat in the captain's seat, Jason released a breath he hadn't realized he'd held as Hailey updated him on the container's ETA. He smiled and nodded his thanks to Simone once again, then looked up as the doors to the bridge slid open and Terrance entered. Khela was by his side, Beck trailing behind.

The executive looked ready for a state dinner, as did Khela, her raven hair swept into a loose bun. Elegant hairsticks he'd bet a week's cred chit were really a pair of stilettos in disguise pinned her sleek locks in place, and she wore a turquoise sheath, slit to allow convenient movement should she need it.

She stood just inside the doors, her dark eyes following Terrance's progress as the man gathered the team with a glance and a slight jerk of his head. Jason nodded and stood. He, Tobias, and Logan would be the only three to accompany the couple down to State House.

"Conn's yours, Landon," he said, handing over the captain's seat before nodding to Noa, and following them out.

<*We'll bring back food,*> Beck announced, just to pique Tobi.

Jason chuckled as he heard the big cat's answering growl from where she lay on the deck next to Hailey's console.

<*It was his turn,*> he reminded Tobi. <*Besides, it's a consolation*

prize. You're the one going along to Barat, not him.>

Tobi chuffed and subsided. A soft, surly voice reached them over the ship's net just as the lift doors slid shut.

<*In case anyone wonders, I prefer fish, not chicken.*>

*****

<*Your guests have arrived and are in the presidential drawing room,*> Elie announced, and not for the first time did Edouard wonder what drawing had to do with a formal room set aside for the reception of visitors of state.

<*Thank you, Elie,*> he responded and, with a thought, closed the file updating him on the latest developments at Gehenna that Celia had brought when she'd arrived for this evening's dinner. The data vanished from within his mind, the icon sliding into a secured file he tagged for later review.

Celia was waiting for him out in the hall, standing alongside his detail. She nodded to him and, without a word, fell into step as he strode toward the drawing room to meet the recent arrivals.

His first impression as he entered was of a petite woman with blue-black hair and exotically uptilted eyes, flanked by two men—one whose bearing held a distinguished air, the other with a smooth, almost predatory grace. Both carried themselves as if they'd seen combat before, and both had short, blondish hair. But there, the similarities ended.

The first man had straightened as Edouard entered, his arm reaching behind the woman to lay his hand at the small of her back, as if he was preparing to introduce her. A side glance from darkly-lashed eyes arrested his movement, and Edouard saw him glance down at her, blue eyes flashing with humor. He saw her lift one shoulder in a slight shrug and quirk a resigned smile up at him before linking her arm in his.

The other man, standing a bit farther away from the woman, caught the interplay and lifted his hand to hide a smirk. As he shifted, he revealed the humanoid frame of a red-headed male with the greenest eyes Edouard had ever seen, accompanied by a cat whose chest easily came to the male's knees. On the cat's other side stood a second AI, dark countenance unreadable, one hand resting lightly atop the cat's head.

The animal stared back at Edouard with keenly intelligent aqua eyes framed in fur of the palest cream. The cat took a step forward and then settled on its haunches, fur rippling with a platinum-like sheen.

This must be the uplifted Proxima cat from Simone's report, he mused, fascinated by the thought.

His eyes returned to meet those of the first man as Celia began the introductions.

"President Zola," Celia said formally, stepping forward and raising a hand to indicate the first man. "Terrance Enfield, from Alpha Centauri, and Lieutenant Kodi, the AI with whom he is paired."

Terrance nodded with a smile as Kodi spoke over State House's Guest Net.

<Greetings, sir. It's a pleasure to make your acquaintance.>

<Hello, Lieutenant,> Edouard sent as he stepped forward to clasp Terrance's outstretched hand.

"I agree with Kodi. It's a pleasure, sir," Terrance said. He turned to the woman. "I'd like for you to meet—"

The woman stepped forward, interrupting him in a crisp, almost military tone as she thrust her hand forward for him to shake. "Khela Sakai, sir, in charge of Mister Enfield's personal security," she said and the second man coughed, the sound suspiciously like a strangled laugh.

"—*and* my wife," Terrance continued, as he placed his arm around her and drew her to his side. "Although she insists on hiding that fact until we get to know people a bit better."

"Something to do with ensuring your ass is better protected," came the casual, amused comment from the other man.

Edouard saw Terrance suppress a smile at the sardonic remark. "And this," the executive nodded toward the other man, "is our acting captain, Jason Andrews."

Edouard nodded and extended his hand to the man, surprised at the measured strength behind Andrews' grip—almost as if he were controlling it to prevent harm.

"It is entirely my pleasure, I assure you," he said to the three as Jason stepped aside to make room for the AIs and their feline companion.

"Tobias," the redhead said with a genial nod, and Edouard's eyebrows rose.

"Simone's told us a bit about you and your history, Tobias," he said, striding forward and proffering a hand to the AI. "The legends of the Weapon Born have made it all the way to Godel," he said, eyeing his intelligence director. "Haven't they, Celia?"

The woman smiled at Tobias. "Indeed they have, sir. I think you'll find a very warm reception here, especially among our own military, who've had cause to study some of your people's strategies."

The lead agent for Edouard's detail, Hanson, stirred. "Required reading at the Citadel, sir," the agent said with a respectful nod and smile before returning to her ever-watchful stance.

Edouard hid a flash of amusement at the Weapon Born's apparent discomfiture, as Tobias turned to the AI next to him to introduce the final member of their party.

"This is Commander Logan." The dark-skinned one nodded as Tobias reached down to tweak the ear of the cat seated between the two. "And this young rascal is Beck."

<*Hullo,*> the cat said, rising to his feet and ignoring the moves Edouard's detail made for their pulse weapons, as they recognized the deadly power inherent in the predator approaching the person they were sworn to protect. <*Jason said there'd be food after everyone shakes paws. So when do we get to eat?*>

PRESIDENTIAL EXPANSE

STELLAR DATE: 03.13.3272 (Adjusted Gregorian)
LOCATION: State House, New Kells
REGION: Godel, Little River

The remains of native dishes, exquisitely prepared, sat on china bearing the presidential seal of Godel. That same president sat across from Jason, face etched with concern as he listened to his intelligence director's report.

"One of our agents is on the ship bound for Barat and has confirmed that your captain is onboard. They've made a positive ID."

The words, uttered by Godel's Director of Intelligence, sat for a beat in the silence of the private dining hall where they'd been escorted an hour earlier.

"Positive. That's an oddly inappropriate word," Jason heard Terrance mutter as he saw the man lift the black linen napkin he'd plucked from his lap and set it alongside his plate.

"I wish we had better news," Zola murmured, and the food in Jason's stomach suddenly soured as he considered the prison camp where Calista was headed. He pushed his plate away and sat back in his chair.

<Hold up, boyo,> Tobias cautioned. *<We don't know that Barat has lifted a finger against her yet. Don't jump to conclusions. >*

<We should be boosting for Barat right now,> he raged, *<not eating fancy pastries and chatting over coffee.>*

<And we will,> Terrance assured him. *<You're scheduled to arrive slightly ahead of them, so this delay does no harm, and you know it.>*

Celia placed her own napkin next to her plate as she sent a token to the three. "Everything we have on Gehenna," she informed them, then added privately, *<plus a proposition.>*

Jason's brows rose and he traded glances with Terrance before thanking Celia and accessing the file.

It was surprisingly thorough, with everything from blackout corridors they could use to enter Barat's ionosphere once the container ship disgorged its passenger, to the number of soldiers stationed at the outpost, and weaponry loads.

<*You sent that last privately, lass,*> Tobias sent, shifting his eyes from the security detail back to Mastai, regarding her through thoughtful eyes. <Why is that?>

Jason had followed the direction of Tobias's glance. As he saw Celia return the AI's look with a probing one of her own, he knew a distraction was in order.

As he began a light conversation with the president about the origins of various foods they'd eaten, he listened in on the exchange between the intelligence director and the Weapon Born.

<*Is it true,*> Celia asked, <*that Weapon Born can create expanses that include humans? And that they're unbreachable?*>

Jason's eyes flicked up to Hanson, and the agent tensed slightly under his regard. He sent the agent an easy smile as he responded to Zola's comment about a particularly obscure dish, while a separate part of his mind mulled over the curious exclusion of the president's watchdogs.

Fortunately, he was one of the few unmodified humans who could multitask, thanks to a disproportionately high number of nodes interspersed throughout the axons of his brain. What passed for multitasking in L0 humans was, in reality, more like serial unitasking. Not so in him.

As he monitored the heightened awareness of the presidential detail, he worked to abate their suspicion and draw it away from the tension radiating from Celia Mastai. Zola must have sensed it, too, for the president willingly engaged in a spirited debate with Jason over the refinement of the Godel palette over Proxan ones.

Tobias joined in, making a jocular reference to Jason's obsession with chicken fingers when he'd been a teen, causing him to scowl in mock dismay at the Weapon Born just before the AI asked Celia,

<Why do you feel the need for such secrecy, from your own trusted guards?>

Celia's forehead creased in a worried frown. *<We recently learned we've been compromised,>* she admitted, her glance shifting briefly to the guard, Hanson, and then back. *<And the situation is too critical to risk discovery.>*

<Understood,> the Weapon Born sent with a mental nod.

In the next moment, Jason saw the president start as his detail vanished and his surroundings abruptly changed.

* * * * *

The expanse was an experience utterly unique to Edouard. He found himself standing next to Celia outside the very dining hall he knew himself to be seated in. He wasn't really surprised to see that Simone had joined them. She nodded respectfully as he acknowledged her presence.

With a raised brow, he gestured to the door. "After you," he invited, and she smiled and walked through.

Inside sat the delegation from the *Avon Vale*, just as they'd been moments before, only without the remains of the excellent meal strewn about. And without the presence of his security detail.

The Weapon Born looked different here, as did the one called Logan. And a stranger was present, someone who hadn't been there before—a young man with military bearing, golden eyes, and close-cropped brown hair. He wore a uniform unfamiliar to Edouard. Abruptly, he realized this must be Kodi.

Tobias stood, gesturing to the table. "Mister president, madam. Please join us." His voice held a power behind it that rolled throughout the room, echoing slightly.

Terrance leant forward as they took their seats. "Since we're on the clock, here, let's dispense with formalities. What kind of a proposition are you referring to, exactly?"

Simone gestured, and a single sheet of hyfilm appeared before each of the *Vale*'s complement. Edouard waited as they skimmed the information on the DBCs and their targets, surprised that Jason appeared to assimilate it almost as quickly as the AIs did. The acting captain's head snapped up sharply in alarm and suddenly, Edouard found four pairs of eyes—one human, the rest AI—regarding him intently.

Another few minutes passed, and he felt Terrance and Khela do the same. He nodded slowly in response to the expressions on their faces.

"Their plan, it would seem, is twofold," he noted. "They want what a Godel corporation has found out in the inner belt—"

"High purity quartz silica," interposed Celia, who then motioned for him to continue.

"—and they will stop at nothing to get it," he finished grimly. "Including destroying our entire food supply."

"This..." Kodi's voice sounded shocked. "It's tantamount to genocide!"

Celia smiled grimly. "Well, we do have some stores. And I suppose Barat would be willing to sell us rations, for a price. But at least now you see why we need the help of Phantom Blade."

"Because any attempt by your own agencies would be leaked back to Barat, and the devices would be triggered before you could reach them to disarm." Logan's voice held certainty, and Celia nodded.

"We've already promised our assets' assistance in recovering your captain. It is our hope that, while your small tactical team heads to Barat to fulfill that mission, we can convince the rest of Phantom Blade to help us neutralize our threat here on Godel."

Tobias stirred, eyes resting thoughtfully on Logan for a moment before returning to Celia. "Your suggestion of an expanse was a good one, lass. Tell you what; give us an hour to review this, and we'll invite you to another one, up on the *Vale*."

Edouard saw the Weapon Born cock his head and affix him with a gaze, eyes twinkling in sudden humor.

"Not, I think, with you, though, Mister President." His voice took on a droll tone and tapped the side of his head. "It would be difficult to separate you from your watchdogs, and though we could pull you in from wherever you are in State House, I would assume your brain waves are somehow being monitored?"

Edouard grimaced at the reminder of one of the more intimate forms of protective monitoring required of his office.

"They are," he confirmed.

"Then even if you were to decide to, say, get away for an unscheduled nap," the AI's eyes laughed at the unlikelihood of that, "they would know something was up. And, begging your pardon, sir, but I don't think anyone on the *Avon Vale* would enjoy being shot at, should your detail suspect something amiss."

Simone looked impressed. "You could pull him in from down here, even while in orbit?" she inquired, and Tobias nodded.

"Aye, lass, I can. Or, rather, those of us on the *Vale* can. I'll be on my way by then, so it'll be Charley who will generate it."

Simone subsided with a secret smile that had Edouard wondering.

"Another Weapon Born?" he asked, curiosity piqued.

Tobias smiled. "The child of one. A powerful ally, our Charley."

"I can imagine," Celia murmured with a quick glance at Simone, whose smile broadened as she nodded.

Terrance turned to Edouard with an expectant look on his face. "What do you say, sir?"

He felt Celia's eyes on him and turned to see her nod her head at him in quick affirmation.

Turning back to Enfield and the rest, he smiled. "I say let's do it."

He felt a pang of disappointment that he would miss out on another such experience, but knew the issue was in capable hands.

*****

Celia waited until she was inside her own secured residence before sending Simone an encrypted missive that it was safe to begin. Simone sent the location up to the Centauri ship, where an expanse replicating the ship's ready room awaited them; moments later, she received an invitation to join.

And then she was there, standing next to Simone, shaking her head in amazement at the detail of the ship surrounding her. Simone introduced her to Charley, the powerful scion of a Weapon Born and a multinodal AI.

Charley had given her a small, courtly bow, his humanoid frame that of a simple, young man. When she complimented him on the incredible realism of the construct, he dissembled, claiming it was due in large part to a foundation laid by Proxima Centauri's AI Council more than a hundred years earlier.

"Welcome, Madam Director, to the *Avon Vale*," he said with a smile as he gestured her toward the entrance that slid open as they approached.

As Celia joined the rest at the table, she noticed that the AI standing at its head looked uncannily like the taciturn AI who had joined them at lunch. He introduced himself as Landon.

<Logan's identical twin,> Simone sent, and Celia shot her a confused look. *AIs don't have twins…do they?*

She was pulled away from that train of thought by Landon, as he sent a file to the ready room's holo wall and an image appeared. It was one that Celia's counterpart on Barat had sent, of a design schematic for the Digital-to-Biological Converters.

"This," Landon informed the team, gesturing toward the holo, "is a DBC. The weapon we need to locate and disable." He glanced around the room at those assembled. "We'll send you out singly, each one of you to your own location. Logan and I," he indicated the taciturn AI whom Celia had met, "will take the ones planted at the storehouses in the most heavily-populated areas here and here."

Icons flashed over the storehouse closest to State House, in the heart of New Kells, and at the one nearest Godel's main elevator.

"Khela and her Marines," he nodded to the four humans lined up and kitted out in the same military garb, "Ramon, Lena and Tama, will take the three farms."

Those icons flashed, updating the locations with individual names assigned to each.

"Jonesy, you, Charley, Terrance and—" he glanced over as an avatar flickered into existence, "Shannon will take the remaining four warehouses."

There was a stir at that last announcement that Celia didn't understand, but she noticed several individuals glance over at the newcomer with speculative eyes.

"Godel's infrastructure is as agrarian as it is industrial," Landon informed them. "Much of their economy is driven by the export of their harvests." He glanced over at Celia for confirmation.

She nodded. "Although Barat grows much of its own food as well," she explained, "the rest of the system relies upon Godel for its supplies."

She took a deep breath, expelled it in one short explosive burst.

"As do our inhabitants. We have a population of almost five billion mouths to feed, as well as ranchers with livestock." She smiled sadly. "The animals need to eat, too, you know."

Celia saw glances being exchanged as what she said sank in. Landon acknowledged her words with a slow nod.

"I suppose I don't need to tell you how important this operation is, nor how critical it is that we get it right." His eyes swept the room. "Failure is not an option."

Celia breathed a mental sigh of relief when she saw the resolve reflected in the eyes of the people sitting at the table. She returned her attention to Landon as the AI continued.

"Candidly, this whole situation sucks. I hate the idea of sending you out alone, without any form of backup. And I sure as hell hate that I'm sending some of you out on an op you've never run before."

She sat up in alarm when she heard that, but Logan, seated next to her, placed a restraining hand on her arm.

"But to be frank, we have no choice. If these aren't destroyed within seconds of each other, their destruction could trigger a warning back to Barat agents here on Godel. If that occurs, and they're able to send an execute command out to the remainder of the DBCs before we can locate them and shut them down…."

He didn't need to spell it out to them; they knew the ramifications. Celia could see it on their faces.

A man who looked strikingly like Terrance's wife stirred, and the woman next to him, clad in what appeared to be a lab coat, cleared her throat. "Noa and I," she said, indicating the man next to her, "are working on synthesizing a counteragent for the most likely vectors Barat will have the DBCs generate."

<Marta, our ship's doctor,> Logan informed her privately from where he sat beside her. *<Noa is Khela's father and a formidable scientist.>*

Celia sent her thanks as Marta continued.

"This process is a bit like throwing a dart blindfolded," the doctor cautioned. "The only way to *guarantee* that these things are stopped is to destroy them before they have a chance to release a biological agent."

Silence filled the air as those in the room digested what had just been said. Then Landon spoke once more, his tone final.

"Simone has files for each of you on your targets. Study them. Solidify your plan. No points for style on this," Landon warned. "Get in, neutralize, get out. Understood?"

All of them—human and AI alike—nodded.

"Good. Be ready with any questions an hour from now. One other thing," he added, his gaze spearing each individual. "This isn't a black op. It's black-on-black. No one outside the people right here, right now in this expanse, is to ever know a thing about this operation, understood?"

GEHENNA

STELLAR DATE: 03.13.3272 (Adjusted Gregorian)
LOCATION: approaching Barat Main Spaceport
REGION: Barat, Little River

Calista gripped the side of her bunk with her one good hand as the warning chimes sounded, indicating the imminent loss of gravity as deceleration was cut.

At least I now know what those tones signify, she thought as she recalled the first time they had sounded at turnover, and she'd been caught unprepared.

Granted, her mind had still been fogged, and her body sluggish and aching from its abuse at the hands of her captors. She'd been woefully ill-equipped to deal with the sudden loss of apparent gravity…and its equally sudden return.

She'd suffered a fractured arm as a result—something her mednano would have repaired with ease, if she'd had any. Instead, her arm had hung useless at her side, and at an awkward angle, until they'd gathered her for another round of interrogation inside the autodoc.

The orderly had been annoyed at her involuntary cry when he'd attempted to immobilize her for the next round of examinations, and had tossed a temporary cast at her, ordering her to put it on. She'd been forced to wrestle it into place one-handed, and had very nearly passed out when the cast had inflated.

Then the next round of invasive exploration had begun.

That had been yesterday. By her reckoning, she'd been aboard this ship for three days now, the exact amount of time it would take to transit from the duty station to Barat.

She had no doubt this was her destination, and as her hand kept her now-floating body relatively stationary, she felt the minute adjustments only a pilot would notice, sure indication of a docking procedure underway.

As the ship settled into its mooring and came under the influence of a low-grav station, she released her hold and shuffled toward the plas window of her cell to stare through it with her one remaining eye. Her right hand clenched, while the fingers of her left hand, now immobilized by a rigid nano cast programmed to deteriorate within six weeks' time, bent and flexed.

She tensed as, moments later, she felt the reverberation of footsteps through the sole of the deck as they approached her cell.

Showtime.

* * * * *

Hundreds of kilometers below, in the capital city of Hauptstadt, a chauffeured aircar pulled away from the exclusive penthouse that was Giovanni's home. It was bound for the block of offices reserved for the executive committee, behind the walls of the Presidium.

Wiping the humid air from his brow, Giovanni settled back into the plush faux leather cushion of the rear compartment, breathing in the blessedly cool and dehumidified air. He clutched his brief in his lap, eyes staring out the tinted and CNT-reinforced windows. But his mind wasn't on the view as the car descended to street level and merged efficiently with the city's traffic.

I never wanted this. I didn't ask to be born into this station. Stars! he thought morosely, *I'm not even certain I buy the party line that 'AIs threaten human supremacy' in the galaxy.*

Giovanni had been just a child when the first colony ship bound for Epsilon Eridani was commissioned. The chief information officer for EpiGen had been instrumental in the colony's transition from corporate organization to Barat's governmental structure. The woman had successfully parlayed her role as CIO into that of the Office of Safety and Information, and had appointed herself as the first Council member to hold the position.

What remained unspoken as Giovanni had grown was the fact that his mother, Julia Perelman, fully intended to be the first of many Perelmans to hold that position after she retired, thus guaranteeing the furtherance of her own lineage, her own ambitions.

Julia—indeed, all of the senior executives of EpiGen—believed that the scientists back in Sol would soon reach an AI singularity, and it was just a matter of time before artificial intelligence became reality. EpiGen's mission statement was the advancement of *human*kind, and they perceived AIs as a threat to the dominance of humans as a species.

The colony was meant to ensure humanity's preeminence in the galaxy. It had been a major blow to the endeavor when the company overextended itself and lost its bid for the second planet.

But AIs have been around for hundreds of years now, he mused, *and, except for the Solar Wars—where many AIs fought in defense of humans—they've been no threat to us.*

In fact, if information from neighboring systems was to be believed, AIs not only lived in peaceful coexistence with humans, but their partnerships had been beneficial, and both sides had thrived.

Even on Godel, his agents' reports indicated much the same—if one read between the lines. He very carefully refrained from mentioning these observations whenever he had occasion to visit his mother, or any of her cronies....

Giovanni's thoughts returned to the treason he'd committed mere hours ago.

No one suspects. Just behave normally, he reminded himself sternly, resisting the urge to check once more that his security taps had not been traced. *Besides, what has been done cannot be undone.*

Through the front windscreen, Giovanni could see the Presidium growing larger as the car approached. The gleaming, rounded edifice stood in stark relief, framed by regimented rows of buildings along their avenue of approach.

To each side of him stood crisp, sharp-edged structures, tinted in what had once been EpiGen's brand colors but were now referred to as the premier's colors. Each edifice had before it a prescribed amount of landscaping. The greenspace exactly gave back to its surroundings the amount offset by the building itself, so that the structure remained environmentally neutral.

In theory, it made sense. In practice, it held an unimaginative rigidity that seemed to suck both life and creativity from the soul.

The Presidium was the single exception to that. There were no sharp angles here, none at all. From above, its curved façade appeared as the pupil of a giant, unblinking, all-seeing eye. The mental comparison sent an uncomfortable ripple through Giovanni, just as the car descended into its subterranean depths. Here, the first of many security tokens would be exchanged before he would be permitted entrance to his own offices.

Just as the car's interior passed from daylight into night, a flashing icon appeared on his HUD, an updated timetable for the ship's arrival from Phaethon. With it came an information update that the prisoner would be transferred directly to Gehenna.

He grimaced mentally at the unnecessary waste. Had Jones not interfered, he was certain his people could have managed an equitable trade of the Centauri captain for their stasis tech.

It did not occur to him to regret the unnecessary harm brought to a fellow being. He was, after all, from Barat.

* * * * *

Hundreds of kilometers away near the equator, a Barat shuttle fought its way through severe turbulence and near-zero visibility to land at Gehenna. Gusts buffeted the craft, and a microburst of wind shear momentarily overpowered the craft, bringing it down with a hard *thump*. The craft's maneuvering thrusters kicked up clouds of dust that rose, billowing, on either side of the vessel, but the contribution was barely noticed for the dust storm raging outside.

The hatch opened and Calista was prodded forward into a maelstrom. Fine particles of dust and sand beat at her exposed face and neck with a million tiny stings. The biofilters in her lungs no longer functioned, so she used the front of her prison coveralls to cover her mouth and nose. Behind her, the shuttle's thrusters roared, and the craft took off moments after disgorging its single passenger.

Dirt and sand were everywhere. She could feel it coating her eyelashes when she squinted against the diffuse glare of sun that broke through the tempest now and again. She could taste grit between her teeth as she clenched them in her determination to remain upright, despite the wind that battered at her mercilessly.

An arm appeared from out of the dust, waving her forward. Then, impatience winning, its owner grabbed her roughly by the arm and herded her toward the nearest building.

"Stupid noob," the voice grunted as they entered, "outside's no place to be when a dust storm's starting."

The person disappeared, leaving her standing inside the prefab structure, blinking the grit from her eyes as her single working one registered the presence of others in the room.

Interesting form of due process they have here, she mused with a bitter edge, as she took in the roomful of men and women garbed in the same prison coveralls she wore. *Welcome to Barat, enjoy your stay in hell.*

"Better get used to the weather on Gehenna if you expect to survive the dry season," a gruff voice sounded on her blind side, and she turned toward it.

A crusty woman with weathered skin and sun-bleached, shorn hair approached. She circled Calista once, eyes sharp and assessing, then came to a stop in front of her.

"You're not Baratian, then," the woman mused, and Calista wondered what about her appearance had given her away. The woman motioned to her dead eye. "You have—*had*—mods," she explained, then gestured around her at the others.

Calista followed the movement, studying the room before returning her attention to the woman before her, one brow raised in question.

"No one on Barat gets mods unless they're former Citizen Guard," the woman explained. "And, although we do get the occasional political prisoner, they'd just as soon shoot a soldier."

Calista nodded, returning her gaze to those inhabiting the dusty space. "All human?"

The woman barked a short laugh and then spit to one side. "Any AI foolish enough to be caught on Barat gets terminated. If they made it here," she added, a malicious gleam in her eye, "we'd do the same." She laughed once more at the shocked expression on Calista's face. "Just because I'm a prisoner doesn't mean I'm stupid," she said, derision in her tone. "Everyone knows those machines will end up destroying us if we don't destroy them first."

Calista merely nodded, keeping her thoughts to herself until she had a better feel for the place.

"You a spy, or military?" Another voice asked, this one from a gaunt, unshaven man, his coveralls hacked off at the knees in deference to the stifling heat.

"Military's my guess," another hazarded. "Lookit the way she's standing, even all beat-up like that."

The man coughed, then spat. His eyes narrowed as he assessed her. "Huh. You think the Citizen Guard finally grew a pair and went after that second planet of ours? The one we ordered terraformed and the AI-loving bastards stole out from under us?"

History of Barat in one easy lesson, Calista thought sardonically, keeping her mouth shut and watching the interplay.

She shifted slightly, standing hipshot to take the stress off her weaker leg as she unconsciously cradled her broken arm.

Wonder what else I can learn if I just keep my mouth shut.

She grimaced as she tasted the fine grains of sand that had worked their way between her teeth, and glanced around for a source of water.

No need to brush my teeth while I'm here; I can just have them sandblasted clean.

The blonde woman must have noticed. She pulled out a battered canteen, removed its lid and proffered it. "Take a swig, swish, and spit," she instructed, pointing to the floor. "Not as we'd notice much anyways. It's not like you're going to track any more dirt in here than the diablo blows in."

Calista took it and did as instructed, then handed the canteen back. The woman nodded to the kit Calista had slung over her shoulder, a pack the prison guard had thrust at her as she exited, but that she had forgotten about in the interval following her arrival.

"You have one of your own in there, along with a few other survival necessities." The woman lifted the lid she held in her hand, waggling it at Calista to get her attention. "Top's a water extraction and purification cone, so be careful not to damage it. Not a lot of water around here otherwise."

Doesn't look like there's much of anything around here, Calista thought privately, *except for heat, humidity, and dust.*

* * * * *

Giovanni sat before his secured office holoscreen and regarded the icon hovering on his HUD as if it were a viper, coiled to strike. Its color pulsed a red-gold warning at him, indicating it had been tampered with.

He didn't need to open the data packet to know what it contained; the ident associated with it was enough to tell him that he'd been compromised. Someone else knew he'd leaked Barat's planned attack on the farms and food storehouses to Godel.

A noise alerted him to the presence of others, individuals

who'd managed to bypass his office's security. As he turned to the entrance, the Republican guard who usually stood sentry outside his office approached, his hand on his weapon.

"You are wanted outside, citizen," the young man informed him, face expressionless.

No cordial deference to his title, as the soldier had always given. Not even a drawn weapon, as if the concept of Giovanni being a threat was ludicrous.

Giovanni stood, bile rising in his throat, and mechanically reached for his uniform jacket. As he did so, he saw the soldier tense; he raised his hands to show he was weaponless.

Then an individual who had been standing in the shadows behind the soldier stepped forward.

The premier's citizen general.

"I wouldn't bother with that, if I were you," Jones advised with a humorless smile. "You won't need that where you're going." The look she gave him spoke volumes.

Oh yes, Citizen General Jones knew what he'd done; not only had she toppled him from his aerie, now she'd caught him leaking information.

He could see it in her eyes. There would be no mercy from that front.

* * * * *

Three hours later, Giovanni stumbled out of the prison shuttle, his hand shading his eyes from the relentless sun that beat down upon the Gehenna equatorial region. The small kit slung over his shoulder contained the bare minimum he would need to survive, but at least the prison coveralls he wore were made of wear-resistant, moisture-wicking nanomaterial.

Thank the stars for small favors, he thought humorlessly as he wiped the beads of sweat already forming on his forehead and upper lip. He rather suspected the prison garb had more to do with convenience than the prisoners' comfort. It would be an annoyance—and an unnecessary expense—to have to supply changes of clothing for people who the Republic considered expendable.

His arrival had been delayed due to a diablo, a dust storm that plagued the region during its dry season. But the winds had died down now, and in the waning sunlight—*still far too damned hot, even at this time of day*—he could just make out the prisoners milling about, curious eyes alighting on the newest arrival.

Wonder if anyone will recognize me, he thought with a fleeting gallows humor, fingering the slight alterations that had been done to change his appearance.

His mother's influence, no doubt. He'd expected a firing squad, not a quick trip to an autodoc, followed by a one-way shuttle to Gehenna.

Bet dear old mom managed to convince them I might be of use to them someday. He shook his head. *Wonder how long I'd last if this disguise fails to conceal my true identity?*

He harbored no illusions on that count; Safety and Information had consigned hundreds to the camps for their breach of Barat's Social Laws. People deemed 'Untrustworthies' based on their aggression, irresponsible behavior, or association with others who exhibited such traits.

Minutes, he decided. *My life would be counted in minutes once they knew who I really was.*

Movement caught his eye, a lithe figure slipping from the nearest hut, graceful movement marred by a slightly irregular gait. He cocked his head, interest piqued.

She was dark-haired, with the build of a warrior. If he ignored the limp, something about her movements reminded him vaguely of every Republican aviator who'd ever piloted a vessel he'd been on.

The Centauri captain, he guessed, and altered the direction of his steps so that they would meet up with hers.

RECONNAISSANCE

STELLAR DATE: 03.13.3272 (Adjusted Gregorian)
LOCATION: Commercial lanes between Barat and Godel
REGION: Little River Inner System

Jason hadn't been lying when he told Simone that he could handle the accel of the container ship. But he never said he enjoyed it. If he could, he'd be gritting his teeth against the immense pressure 50gs afforded. As it was, he could barely hold onto consciousness.

His body slewed in the pilot's cradle as the ship abruptly changed course and speed.

<Tobe…?>

<Tapping into their feeds now.> After a pause, Tobias's voice returned, this time with a grim edge. *<Looks like we have company.>*

<By your tone, I'm guessing it's not the friendly kind?>

Instead of responding, the Weapon Born sent him a stream from the container's external sensors. Two Republican ships were approaching, encroaching upon the lanes and forcing the merchant ships to change vector.

<Stars, we can't afford a detour! We'll just beat the ship from Phaethon to Barat as it is,> Jason fumed, glaring at the oncoming vessels.

<What we can't afford is for them to find us, boyo,> Tobias countered.

<That too. Not like we have any say in the matter, though. We're trapped in here like sardines in a tin.>

<Always wondered what that would look like.> Tobias's comment was an absent afterthought that Jason ignored as another ship caught his attention.

<Is that…?> He zoomed in, and would have breathed a sigh of relief if he could. Scan had picked up a pair of Godel warships,

and the container ship had once more resumed its course and acceleration.

<*That was too close for comfort.*>

<*Agreed, boyo. Agreed.*>

* * * * *

Their exit from the container ship occurred without incident, the blackout windows included in the intel packet providing Jason with an unchallenged atmospheric entry. Jason and Tobias set the shuttle down on the backside of an old maglev sorting yard, between a row of beat-up cars and a large repair warehouse. There, they met with one of Godel's agents, whose eyes widened in surprise when he caught sight of the spare battleframe Tobias had stored in the back of the shuttle.

He waited for the hatch to close behind him before he shook his head at them. "That's some real shit, man. Dumb as fuck, too. I assume that battleframe means one of you is an AI? Anyone tell you? There are no AIs on Barat—period."

Jason just stood, arms folded, glaring at the man, who shook his head and then shrugged. "Your loss. Should have sent all humans, though. You've just cut your team's effectiveness in half if they find out."

The agent propped his shoulder against the frame of the shuttle's hatch and eyed them warily. "We're short of manpower, too. Got no one to spare to assist you."

Tobias stirred, causing the man to jump. The Weapon Born wore an organic frame Jonesy had assured them would pass as human under standard scrutiny.

"No worries, lad." Tobias's brogue was virtually nonexistent; a sure indication that the man's attitude had irritated the AI as well. "We can handle it."

"As long as you have the intel we were promised," Jason qualified, his words sharper than he'd intended.

The agent's gaze swung back to him. An eyebrow rose in insolent query, but the man remained silent otherwise.

"Our contact on Godel told us you've had eyes on Gehenna for the past four days," Jason prodded. "Correct?"

After a beat, the man nodded, then flipped a silver disc toward him with a fast wrist snap. Jason's hand blurred as he caught it, and he noted the slight dilation in the man's eyes—the only outward indication of his surprise.

"Modded," he muttered with a shake of his head. "They scan for that here, too, you know."

Jason smirked. "Not going to be a problem, dude."

He dropped nano on the token, and the cypher Simone had provided unlocked it. With a thought, he shifted it to a small holo installed above the weapons locker of the newly reconstructed *Eidolon*.

An image resolved of a prison camp, matching the aerial view they'd been shown by Celia Mastai back on Godel. From there, the image morphed into a series of closeups from within the camp.

Jason shot him an assessing look. "You have a man on the inside?"

It was the man's turn to smirk. "A woman, yes."

"A Barat national? She can be trusted?" Tobias said sharply, and the man frowned at the criticism in his tone.

"She was arrested when the Guard busted her smuggling ring wide open," he informed them. "We'd heard in advance it was going to happen. Republican Guard went in, pulsers blazing, and shot her lover."

At Jason's skeptical expression, he shrugged and continued.

"Smuggler thought the citizen soldiers had killed her," he explained, "and they would have if we hadn't intervened right quick."

He nodded as an image of a woman—tough, blonde, and with weathered features—appeared on the holo.

"Our smuggler already had plenty of reason to despise Barat's finest. But when she heard her lover was alive, and that we'd patched her up, she was more than happy to turn on the assholes who'd shot her."

"Pretty altruistic for a smuggler," Jason muttered, eyeing the woman's visage skeptically.

The man sent him an amused look. "Smuggler's in for ten years. She does her time, she gets out. Then she can join her girlfriend, if she's still interested. We snuck her off Barat and set her up at a fabrication plant on Bach," he added, mentioning the moon-moon that orbited Escher, Godel's single satellite.

Then his eyes narrowed. "But the only thing you should care about is the fact that she," he pointed to the holo, "is in Gehenna. She's already made contact with your woman. Now, do you want our help or not?"

Tobias raised a calming hand. "Easy, friend. We're just a bit cautious is all. We appreciate any help you can give us." The AI nodded toward the holo. "Walk us through what you know of the camp, if you would please."

Half an hour later, they had the location of a small clearing twenty kilometers from the camp where they could leave the shuttle. The agent also promised to insert a small, stealthed airframe half a klick inside the rainforest that bordered the veldt surrounding Gehenna.

Now all they needed to do was figure out how to traverse the two-kilometer swath of open grassland ringing the prison without the guards stationed at Gehenna's bunker spotting them.

"If this shuttle is all the shit my superior says it is," the agent paused as he prepared to leave, "then why not just fly up, blast your way in, and get her out that way?"

"Because, lad," Tobias's voice held a note of weary annoyance, "she's as big as a bus, and even though they wouldn't be able to see her, or register her on sensors, they sure as hell would see the displacement of the grasses once we bring her down."

"And," Jason added, "the goal is to get our captain out alive.

They'd know instantly who we were there to retrieve. Not going to chance them killing her before we can intervene."

The man's eyes narrowed in thought, and then he nodded. "Suit yourself," he said as the hatch began to open. "We'll have your stuff in place before sunset."

<*I should have taken a bite out of him,*> came an angry voice from the cockpit, and Jason exchanged an amused glance with Tobias as the AI unsealed the door that separated it from the main cabin, and Tobi stalked out, hackles along the ridge of her spine raised.

"Shoulda let you, girl," Jason said affectionately, slapping her side and giving her a brisk rub.

* * * * *

The surveillance hut they'd been directed to was little more than a shack, nestled in a clearing deep within the rainforest. Jason and Tobias had only just managed to camouflage the *Eidolon* before the heavens unleashed a torrent of driving rain. It came down almost horizontally, sheeting against the mismatched prefab walls on its easternmost side, rivulets of water running through cracks and down walls, wearing runnels into the dirt floor.

<***Now** I know why they named this system Little River,*> Jason heard Tobi grouch, her ears flattened.

The big cat lay on the single, soiled mattress that Jason was certain hadn't originally been a mossy green in color, given its musty smell. Tobi's eyes were slitted in disgust at the swirling eddy that bisected their shelter.

<*Should have headed into the trees.*>

Jason chuckled as the big cat voiced what they all thought. It was ironic that the jungle's forest floor, protected by its thick, interleaved canopy layer, was surely much drier than the shelter in which they currently crouched.

Thunder rolled in waves, coming from the east in the direction of the Gehenna penal colony. A lightning strike a few kilometers beyond, near the New Pejeta Equatorial elevator, illuminated the multilayered rainforest outside their door before plunging the hut into semi-darkness once more.

The moment the deluge let up, the cat would slip out to scout the perimeter of the prison camp and then report back to them. Tobias had left it up to Tobi to decide whether or not it was safe enough to make contact with Calista, after having pressed upon the cat the importance of not being caught.

Jason chanced another quick glance out the hut's entrance toward the east, noting a lightening of the sky in that direction. "I think you'll be on the move here shortly, Tobi," he murmured, glancing back at her.

As if to emphasize his point, the rain suddenly lessened, transitioning from a downpour into a gentle rainfall, and then, shortly thereafter, a misty drizzle. The sun broke through the cloud cover, bringing with it a steamy and oppressive humidity.

<*Ugh, wet grasses,*> the Proxima cat complained, but leapt down from the mattress all the same and high-stepped daintily through the mud-patterned floor to where he stood, looking out. She sighed heavily, but with a full-body shake, nosed her way past him and out into the waterlogged clearing.

An overlay appeared on Jason's HUD, and he knew Tobi had received the same, as Tobias, who had chosen to remain with the shuttle, sent her directions to the prison camp.

<*Don't get caught,*> Jason warned.

She shot him a look of utter disdain from gold-green eyes, as Tobias added, <*And don't take on any of your larger cousins. You may be smarter and faster, but there's a reason they're called the king of the jungle.*>

Jason snorted a laugh as the cat walked away from them, stiff-legged in her affront. He watched until she disappeared into the rainforest, swallowed up by the dense canopy and undergrowth that separated them from the two-kilometer swath of savannah encircling Gehenna.

* * * * *

Calista had spent a wary, wakeful night, huddled against an outer wall within one of the structures, next to the stranger who had insisted on befriending her the evening before. He'd come in on a different shuttle, dropped exactly as she had been—albeit without the swirling clouds of dust that had heralded her own arrival.

The man had wandered in her general direction the moment he'd landed, stumbling in the heat and casting his eyes about as he cautiously assessed his whereabouts. She'd watched as the grizzled blonde woman approached him; the gestures she'd made toward her canteen told Calista the newcomer was being given the same spiel she'd received hours earlier.

The man had responded haltingly to the blonde's query, then they had both turned as the woman pointed in her direction. He nodded, and the blonde left after giving him a long, assessing look. Calista suspected this one was a political prisoner, given how the man moved and the way blondie had dismissed him.

Some sort of prison hierarchy, she supposed, *with her as the leader. I guess it could be worse; we could have been subjected to a shakedown, stripped of our kits and the clothes off our backs.*

Although she knew such was not tolerated. Blondie had told her earlier that any conflicts that arose were treated with extreme prejudice when noticed by the guards. Conflicts were dealt with expediently, and both parties executed.

She turned and inspected the man slumped against the plascrete wall, head pillowed in crossed arms that rested against his knees. Tigan, the man had said his name was, although she could tell by the glint in his eyes that it wasn't his real name.

She shrugged mentally. What did she care if he offered up a nom du guerre instead of his real moniker? As if either would mean anything to her, an outsider.

Calista rose on silent feet, hating to admit what that silence cost her as she bit off a groan in response to the pain she could no longer neutralize with mednano.

Stretching muscles stiff from a night spent on the hardened ground, she took her first few shuffling steps away from the inert form leaning against the wall next to her. Without the mods to blunt the discomfort or lubricate joints now stiff from disuse, she would have to work at staying limber.

She shambled toward the hut's entrance and out into the prison yard. The darkness of night was giving way to a rosy glow at the edge of the horizon, where the silver strand of a space elevator could barely be seen. The man behind her never stirred.

Well, if that doesn't prove that he's not military, she thought with a fleeting black humor, *I don't know what does. Don't think anyone in the service would have missed such a clumsy departure, even sound asleep.*

She gained a bit more grace as she walked, her head tracking back and forth, compensating for her lost eye. Reaching up, she adjusted the eyepatch Blondie had given her just after sunset the night before. It looked like it had been cobbled together from some of the cording off an old prison uniform. With it came a fold of fabric to tuck into place over her eye—and a bit of advice.

"You'll want to be keeping that covered, especially during dust storms, or you'll be fighting infection as well as incarceration," the woman had advised gruffly. Calista had taken it from her with a nod of thanks and affixed it over her head, pirate-style. It felt odd.

But not any more so than the rest of my body, at this point, she mused as she strolled toward the perimeter and began walking along its length. *Savannah, as far as the eye can see, to the east,* she concluded. *Possibly forest a few clicks to the west.*

Noting that others were making their way out of the huts, some beginning morning calisthenics, she dropped where she stood and did the same.

It is the duty of every soldier to resist to the utmost of their ability. To remain in the best possible shape in order to take advantage of every opportunity.

* * * * *

<*Found her!*> Tobi's mental call was triumphant, fierce, and filled with anger.

Tobias accessed the big cat's feed and sent it on to Jason, who drew in a sharp breath at the sight of the battered woman pacing the perimeter of the camp.

<*Stars, Tobe.*> He swallowed hard, taking in her shuffling gait and the way she cradled one arm. <*It's a good two kilometers to the edge of the rainforest. It's going to be a challenge for her to make it that far, especially if we have to maintain cover….*>

<*I know, boyo,*> the AI's tone was grim. <*'Tis a good thing we're planning to wait until nightfall. We'll need every advantage we can get. In the meantime,*> the Weapon Born focused his attention on Tobi, the AI's mental tone stern and commanding, <*observe but do not approach. Keep the feed open so we can study it. Let's see if we can spot any weaknesses, or patterns we can exploit.*>

<*And keep an eye on your surroundings,*> Jason reminded her.

<*Now I know why Beck said, 'not the mama',*> Tobi muttered under her breath while baring her teeth at him with a small growl. <*You say that like I didn't hear you the last time.*>

<*Just…be careful,*> Jason admonished, the cat's unintended humor bringing a brief smile before he returned to his scrutiny of the prison camp and the woman they'd been sent to retrieve.

PART SIX: EXECUTION

DELICATE PROCESS

STELLAR DATE: 03.14.3272 (Adjusted Gregorian)
LOCATION: Key warehouses and farms
REGION: Godel, Little River

The Godel warehouse that Phantom Blade had dubbed 'Target Three' was nestled inside a hollowed-out series of rolling hills, covered in soft green foliage and dotted with trees. A park with a small lake was located across from the entrance, a public magline station two dozen meters from its edge. Jonesy exited the maglev car, hopped down off the platform, and began to stroll along the border that delineated the warehouse perimeter and the park proper.

He pulled the collar of his jacket up around his neck to ward off the spring chill in the air as he nodded politely to two women walking a dog between them. As he approached a sign declaring 'Kilmorran Loading Dock 3C', he checked his chrono. Slowing to time his arrival with the blackout Simone had prearranged, Jonesy glanced around. Seeing no one, he stepped behind the sign, shrugged quickly out of his jacket, reversed it, and slid it back on.

Activating the ident embedded in the Kilmorran Warehouse uniform he now wore, Jonesy strode confidently back up the street and turned toward the dock entrance. The security drone operating it passed Jonesy through with nary a beep.

At the same time, nine hundred kilometers away, an airtruck descended through a snowstorm to the roof of a warehouse, where it landed and disgorged a small, automated maglev cart filled with a shipment of supplies. The truck driver passed his token to the security drone at the dock, which accepted it and allowed the AI and his cart to enter.

He unloaded his shipment on one of the pallets that was set aside for incoming packages, except for a service bot that remained onboard. He then pushed his cart over by a row of empty carts of similar make, and then paused to access the warehouse's database to exchange his token for the bill of lading.

It wasn't happenstance that his location was in front of the nearest warehouse node. After adding his shipment to the day's entries, the AI casually laid a hand against the plascrete wall behind him and dropped a passel of nano onto its surface.

Then he approached the row of carts and, ignoring the cart with the bot on it, grabbed the empty cart next to it and then left.

No one heard the private message sent by the service bot as the AI gave it a swift pat.

<Not a puppy, Landon.>

A quiet chuckle and a *<Woof,>* was the AI's reply before Landon left to drop Charley off at the next location.

For this op, each of the AIs would be inserted inside a frame that looked like a service bot but was not. Once the DBC unit was identified, each could shed their faux shell casing, revealing a compact stealth frame that Shannon had devised for infiltrations back in Alpha Centauri. Its articulated limbs, supply of reconnaissance drones, and access to nanotransfection units and a healthy supply of formation material made it ideal for disabling threats like this.

Five minutes later, the nano had done its work. After confirming that the sensors monitoring the dock were offline, Logan moved inside Target Two's food storage area to begin his search.

The process was repeated at a warehouse built into sun-bleached cliffs looming tall above brilliant blue waters. The cliffs overlooked stucco villas with colorfully tiled roofs dotting the coastline of an archipelago of islands just off the equator. This was Target Four, Charley's responsibility.

Then it was Landon's turn. Terrance dropped him off at Target One, just outside the Outer Belt maglev line that ringed the bustling metropolis of New Kells. As the executive passed by the cart inside which the AI was embedded, he reached out to give it a pat.

<*Touch it, and I'll tell Khela what Beck did to her new combat boots,*> Landon warned the exec.

Kodi snickered inside Terrance's head. <*Told you not to take that last ping from Logan,*> his partner smirked over their private connection.

Terrance just shook his head and exited the warehouse, bent on his own destination, Target Six. As he did, he reached out to Shannon.

<*How goes it?*> he asked the *Vale*'s AI and was treated to a glare.

<*When I said I'd be willing to leave the* Vale *and wear a frame for this op, 'cleaning bot' was not what I had in mind, Terrance.*>

He grinned. <*I hear it's what all the AIs are wearing these days,*> he teased. <*Well, at least the AIs of Phantom Blade. Besides, it's your design, isn't it? The same stealth frame you created for Landon to use when we rescued the AIs back in Alpha Centauri?*>

<*Yes, but I never thought **I'd** be stuck inside one.*> Then, grudgingly, she added, <*I think I've found it.*>

She switched over to the encrypted combat net and shared what she'd found with the rest of the teams.

<*Up in the rafters. See it?*>

Highlighting a small device nestled against one of the beams, she used the warehouse's nearest optics to access a closer image.

Terrance heard Jonesy whistle. <*Yeah, same here. Going to be a bit difficult to get to,*> the engineer murmured. <*But someone got it up there without being caught, so we should be able to get it down the same way. Just have to figure out how it was done.*>

<*Looks like the warehouse DBCs are all installed in the same spot. Makes sense,*> Landon mused. <*Releasing from above pretty much guarantees that the airflow will carry the contaminant throughout the*

buildings' contents.> He showed an overlay animation of the interstitial air pressure fields and the direction of airflow inside Target One.

<*I think I've found our access point,*> Charley sent, tossing an image siphoned from the optics along the far wall. He highlighted a ladder attached to the plascrete, tracing it upward. <*We'll have to jam the sensors in this area first before we transition out of these maintenance bots into our stealth frames—but we knew that going in. Terrance, you and Jonesy are going to have to free climb it. You up for that?*>

<*Ooo-rah,*> Jonesy said, causing Terrance to grin at Kodi's reaction.

<*I knew he'd been spending too much time down in the Vale's Marine sector….*>

* * * * *

From her position at the edge of Farm Target One, Khela stared at the tidy rows of plants, green stalks tipped with shocks of gold and swaying in the fall of a summer rain. She turned in a slow circle, gentle drops pattering on her face as the small, grey-white cloud in an otherwise blue sky passed directly overhead. The rain glinted in the sunlight as it lightly coated the clusters of grain topping each plant.

<*Beautiful sight,*> she commented to Lena as she shared the imagery with her second-in-command. The other Marine sent her a smile of agreement.

Lena highlighted a small bot traveling between two rows. <*If I had to guess, that's one of two possible places our DBC might have been planted—pardon the pun, ma'am,*> she said.

<*Kind of what I figured, after studying the list of equipment,*> she responded absently as she began to pick her way down one of the rows toward the little machine. <*The banks of storage silos are the*

other, correct?>

Lena sent her a nod. <*They would be my choice, if I wanted to wreak the most havoc. Their contents could be considered volatile, under certain conditions.*>

<*Understood. But while I'm here, I might as well give this little guy the once-over. What's it doing?*> Khela asked curiously.

The lieutenant laughed. <*Oh, a little of this, a little of that. Those bots are responsible for tilling and amending the soil, balancing its pH, and then planting the seeds,*> Lena responded. <*They ensure the sprouts are adequately fed and receive exactly the right amount of moisture for optimum growth.*>

<*Next, you're going to tell us it changes their nappies and reads them bedtime stories after tucking them in each night,*> Tama added drolly, then laughed as Lena shot her partner a mental eyeroll.

Ramon snickered. <*Well, we'll just make sure mama-bot doesn't have any surprises for her little minions under the hood,*> he said, sending them a feed from his location.

Unlike the farm where Khela stood, his assigned location encompassed vines of various types, both fruits and vegetables, planted along sloping hills. From his feed, it appeared as though he was standing at the mouth of a steep valley, rows of trellised plants rising on either side of him.

<*How many bots would you say tend one of these farms, anyway?*> he asked Lena, and Khela halted her approach as she awaited the woman's response. But it was Tama who replied, the AI sending them a derisive sound as she made a clucking sound.

<*Didn't you access the files you were given on your location, Ramon? Sloppy work,*> she scolded. <*Oh, and your target's not a farm, soldier, it's a vineyard.*>

<*Farm, vineyard, you say 'tomato',*> Ramon said, and Tama's expression turned quizzical.

<*Well, yes, tomatoes do grow on vines, but what….*>

Ramon's avatar waved her query away. <*Nevermind, was something my ma used to always say. So, these bots…?*>

<Only two. They're efficient things and can cover hundreds of square kilometers in very little time. You'll have one on each side,> Lena informed him, and he nodded before beginning his trek up the nearest hillside.

Five minutes later, Khela had ruled out her two bots and was headed toward the farm's silos when Tama reported back in.

<This hydroponics farm is different from both yours and the vineyard Ramon is covering. Looks like their approach is similar to the one they chose for the warehouses.> The AI embedded in Lena sent an image of the DBC, attached to the system's network of watering lines. *<Except that this one appears to have tapped into the irrigation system. Standing by; we'll be ready to disengage once you and Ramon have a positive ID, too.>*

<Ahhh, good thinking,> Ramon sent, and after another few minutes, she heard a *<Bingo!>* from him as well.

That left all the strike teams waiting on Khela to identify the final threat. She double-timed her approach to the silos.

A CONVENIENT LITTLE RIOT

STELLAR DATE: 03.14.3272 (Adjusted Gregorian)
LOCATION: Verdant Mining Platform
REGION: Inner Asteroid Belt, Little River

The two operatives inserted by Giovanni's office onto the Verdant mining platform two weeks before had heard through secured transmissions that there had been a leadership change at the top. Both had speculated how quickly that change would bring about the sabotage of the platform. Neither of the men questioned that the escalation would occur; General Jones's hawkish reputation was well known.

They'd been furnished with spent air filters prior to their arrival, ones well past their useful life. The platform's air filter sensors had been bypassed early on, just after they'd arrived. All that remained was to arrange for a swap and sound the alarm.

Given Jones's reputation, the two men had thought a good career move might be to show a bit of initiative, so they'd done a bit of extra work on the water reclamation plant and hydroponics bays, as well. When the order had come to 'expose the deplorable working conditions' to the platform's inhabitants, its wording had emphasized the need to escalate the situation rapidly.

<Conditions on Verdant need to be desperate, with people rioting, by the morning of the fifteenth,> the missive had instructed. *<Escalate to include loss of life by then. Make it good.>*

Myron had slapped his partner, Lonnie, gleefully on the back. "We'll give 'em an Ides of March they'll never forget," he sniggered, rubbing his hands together before sending the execute codes to each of the small packets of nano they'd emplaced for their sabotage.

Lonnie had just eyed him warily. Myron's tendency to quote obscure things was just weird sometimes.

*****

Mo Chaudry pocketed his hand pulser and stuck his head carefully out the entrance to the water reclamation facility where he worked, looking both ways before exiting. Distant shouts reached him, and he flinched, reversing his course and opting to head for his quarters via a more circuitous route.

The engineer was profoundly glad he'd sent his daughters back to Godel on that courier ship—although he wished Molly would send him more than a smilingly vague 'we're all fine' response to his queries. He knew her government job kept her busy, but those were his girls, dammit.

When he got back to his quarters, he'd message her and ask to speak with the girls, despite the four-minute lag. He wanted to reassure himself that Lindy was handling the displacement without issues; he knew his youngest tended to have trouble sleeping in new environments.

Slipping behind the water reclamation plant, he stopped in surprise at the sight of two repairmen working on the sewage intake valve. Concerned, he started forward.

"That's funny; I don't recall seeing any maintenance on the sched—"

He ground to a halt as one of the men rose and he came face-to-face with a pulser.

*****

Deep within the Presidium, Rachelle Feretti smiled in satisfaction at those seated around the Council table, as General Jones brought up the inner-system public news feeds. Breaking news filtering in from numerous sources featured panicked messages from individuals trapped on the Verdant platform, their optics showing company police being overwhelmed, and executives being dragged from their offices.

Reporters, piecing together the story from different on-site sources, told a tale of catastrophic environmental failure, corporate neglect, and a rising number of fatalities. Interspersed among these were plaintive cries for help.

"Well now," Feretti murmured, her eyes gleaming with avarice. "We can't very well stand by and see helpless people fall victim to corporate greed, can we?"

General Jones's predatory expression rivaled her own. "Our cruiser is on its way," she announced. "ETA, oh-two-hundred local tomorrow, the fifteenth."

Feretti looked off into space, one finger tapping her blood red lips as she mentally calculated the time differential. Her gaze dropped back to the general. "And Godel's response?"

"They've warned us away," Jones admitted. "Threatened to stop the cruiser with deadly force if necessary."

The premier's brow rose.

"And are you ready with our response to that?" she queried.

Jones bared her teeth in a rapacious grin. "How many warehouses and farms would you like destroyed, Madam Premier?"

She turned to the Council chambers' holo and brought up a representation of Godel, with icons over each of the warehouses and the three farms. They were glowing green in readiness.

"And the stasis tech is within our reach?"

Feretti's sharp question punctuated the tense anticipation that had built around the table. She saw with amusement the startled look exchanged between Coletti and Savin as they realized that the Office of Finance and the Guard had no knowledge of this separate, covert operation.

Jones nodded in satisfaction. "It is indeed. The trap will be sprung at sunset," she responded, her tone one of confidence.

Feretti clapped her hands once, sharply, causing Coletti to

jump.

Her lip curled in an anticipatory smile as she ordered, "Then take them out. Take them all out."

All across the image on the holo, green icons abruptly switched to a blinking red.

EVENING EXFIL

STELLAR DATE: 03.14.3272 (Adjusted Gregorian)
LOCATION: outside Gehenna prison camp, equatorial region
REGION: Barat, Little River

This was Calista's seventh circuit of the camp's perimeter. She caught movement out of the side of her eye and turned to see Tigan making his way toward her, his expression one of concern.

"You didn't stop to eat?"

She held up a half-eaten ration bar by way of reply as he fell into step with her. After a moment of silent walking, he tried again.

"It does you no good to wear yourself out in this heat, you know," he said, shoving his hands into his pockets and glancing over his shoulder at the guard station in the distance behind them. "It's not like they're going to care or intervene if you drop from heat exhaustion."

She shrugged silently and continued her measured pace.

"At least tell me you're drinking enough to keep yourself from collapse."

In response, she jangled the canteen attached to a belt loop, not breaking stride as he huffed an annoyed breath at her reticence. She didn't much care that he found her conversational skills lacking. Sadly, they weren't off-putting enough to deter him, for he continued to keep pace with her.

Outside the camp on her left, the shorn ground cover gave way to meter-tall savannah grasses. Here, the veldt had been allowed to grow practically to the edge of the wire fence that marked its boundaries, and the ES field that reinforced it.

Up ahead, the grasses parted around a mound of boulders that rose chest-high. A rustling motion near the base of one of them—something the winds could not account for—caught her eye.

Her training had her automatically reaching for nonexistent augmentation to scan the area for threats; she made an aggravated noise deep in her throat at the futility of the action.

Tigan turned a questioning look her way at the sound, but she didn't bother to explain.

Her attention arrested by the unexplained movement, she slowed, her eye trained on the spot where she'd sensed movement.

The man beside her noticed, and his gaze followed hers to the pile of rock. His brow furrowed, and he began to turn to ask what she'd seen, when she expelled a soft breath in surprise. She schooled her expression so as to give no indication of what she'd just seen, but it was too late.

Tigan turned, eyes widening in shock at the tawny figure that crouched beside the boulder, golden eyes focused unwaveringly on the two humans.

"Easy," she murmured as the man flinched. "There's an ES field separating us, you know."

"Dangerous, vicious creatures," the man muttered, and she broke away from the welcome sight of Tobi to send an appraising glance at Tigan. The man's eyes were dilated in fear, his hands clenched at his sides.

No uplifted animals here in Little River, she reminded herself, just as the suppressor they'd embedded to ward against unauthorized use of her Link tingled a warning.

She shot Tobi a glance and gave a quick shake of her head as the Proxima cat attempted to contact her again.

Ignoring the pain, she drew to a stop in front of the boulders. "Think I'll stop here for a rest," she told Tigan. "Don't stay on my account, if my friend makes you uncomfortable." She couldn't keep the thread of humor from her voice; knowing he couldn't possibly know the truth of her statement, she didn't even try.

Lowering herself carefully to the ground, she sat cross-legged facing the big cat.

Tigan hesitated, then with a sound of frustration, joined her.

"You're as bad as the premier," he grumbled, and her eyebrow shot up, above her eyepatch.

"Feretti, isn't it? Sounds like you're speaking from personal experience," she observed, then saw him flinch and look furtively around before shrugging noncommittally.

She didn't pursue the subject, although she wanted to. Something was nagging her about this man. Something about his actions wasn't adding up, but she couldn't quite put a finger on why just yet.

Dammit. My thoughts—it's like straining to see through clouded plas! she raged helplessly. *No mental clarity at all, with my augments fried like this.*

Resting her cast on one knee, she reached for a few loose pebbles on the ground before her. Tossing them one by one at the ES field, she watched as it sparked blue at each tiny impact.

She sent a meaningful look Tobi's way and saw the cat nod.

Message received.

Calista then turned to the only source of information she had—one she suspected knew more than he intimated.

"Know anything about these suppressors they implanted in us? They're equipped with trackers, I suppose," she said, her one eye intent upon his face.

"What?" Tigan jerked his gaze from the unblinking stare of the big cat to regard Calista with surprise. "Of course they are. Passive, though. They're only programmed to respond if pinged."

Calista nodded slowly, holding his gaze. "What if we try to use our Links to contact someone on the outside?"

"Link? You mean your implant?" Tigan asked, startled at the unfamiliar term. "Well, for one, you're blocked from the world net. Second, any comm signal strong enough to reach you across that wasteland," he gestured out toward the savannah, "would be picked up by the guard monitoring comms inside the bunker."

"But if you and I wanted to communicate privately, across the prison yard?"

He laughed, a short, bitter thing. "Give you a hell of a headache, but no, they wouldn't trace it. Wouldn't do you any good, either, and they know it." He eyed her with suspicion. "Unless you're thinking about trading in contraband. And then the guards would expect a cut of it."

It was all she needed to hear.

<*Tobi?*> she sent, and nearly doubled over from the shaft of pain that lanced through her brain as she accessed her Link.

Faintly, she heard the cat's response. <*Jason is coming, tonight. Be right here,*> Tobi reached out a paw, claws extended, and scraped the ground in front of her, <*just after dark.*>

Tigan backpedaled quickly at the Proxima cat's movement, but Calista hardly noticed. The pain triggered by Tobi's response was blinding, and she gasped, gripping her head with her good hand.

<*I'll be here,*> she managed, then she saw the big cat slip away.

* * * * *

Tobias handed Jason the kit that would replenish Calista's mednano and crack the suppressor embedded in her skull. Jason stashed it in the small pack, along with the chameleon cloak that would hide her from scan, and a pulse pistol keyed to her bio signature.

Slinging the pack over his shoulder, Jason refreshed the nano inside the fabric Elastene bands encasing each wrist, then reached for an E-SCAR rifle and a bandolier of spare power packs.

"Sun sets at oh-seven-twenty," the Weapon Born reminded him. "The disturbance our friendly agent has arranged is going to begin at oh-seven-forty. The glitch will occur thirty seconds after." Jason nodded as Tobias continued. "You'll have fifteen seconds to get her through the field, no more. Got it?"

"Won't be a problem, Tobe," he assured the AI, slapping his old friend on the shoulder and giving Tobi a scratch behind the ears. "I can carry her if I need to, no sweat."

<I can come with you if you'd like,> the big cat suggested. *<Scare off any sentries that approach.>*

"No need, Tobi, I'll be fine." He stepped toward the hatch of the shuttle, then paused. "If they don't come through for us with that airfoil…."

"No worries, boyo. Tobi and I will be aloft by then. If need be, I can fly *Eidolon* all the way in." The battleframe shifted as Tobias approximated a shrug. "We run a much higher risk of detection, so it's not ideal, but we'll have her back, and that's all that matters."

Jason crooked the AI a half grin, sending him a sloppy salute before triggering the hatch open and fading into the rainforest.

TOO LITTLE, TOO LATE

STELLAR DATE: 03.14.3272 (Adjusted Gregorian)
LOCATION: Key warehouses and farms
REGION: Godel, Little River

Shannon had been the first to raise a concern about timing, during their briefing back on the *Vale*.

"If the DBC units are connected to each other, as well as to the master control on Barat," she'd warned the rest, "then the first unit to be decommissioned could trigger a warning to the rest."

"So the question isn't just when the instructions for a biological agent will be sent to each converter to print," Jonesy had mused, following her train of thought, "it's whether or not tampering with one will trigger an automatic execution order in the rest."

"And, no offense to you humans," the silver-eyed AI said, slanting a pointed look toward Khela's Marines, "but even your augmented reaction times are too slow to prevent it from happening."

It had been Charley who came up with the solution. It was the same one he was poised to implement as he clung to the rafters inside Target Four.

His brain processed the skirling of seagulls, calling to one another as they wheeled above the cliffs ringing either side of the warehouse. His optics captured the motes of dust that danced through the lone sunbeam slanting down from the single transom window to the left of his frame.

But most of his attention was focused on the small, disc-shaped object affixed to the beam, twenty centimeters from his torso.

<*Ready?*> he asked the others, and received affirmatives from everyone but Khela.

After a beat, Charley heard Terrance's voice prodding her.

<*Khela?*> the exec queried, inserting a note of humor that was

almost convincing, if one ignored the strain behind it. <*Hurry up, love. I'm hanging from a rafter over here. Literally….*>

<*Ten seconds,*> she responded finally, and Charley could hear her quiet panting as she scaled the inside of the silo where she'd spotted the last device. <*Five…. Okay, I'm here.*>

<*Interfacing with DBC at Target Four…now,*> he said, reaching forward and dropping nano on the little unit.

Inserting himself into the connection, he shunted its auto-response to always return positive. Satisfied he'd successfully neutralized the danger, he sent the 'go' signal for each team member to begin the DBCs' shut-down sequence.

<*Target Two is neutralized.*>

<*Three's down.*>

<*Vineyard bot's dead,*> Ramon informed them, echoed by a call from Tama at the hydroponics farm.

<*I've got Six,*> Terrance's breathless voice came across. <*Damn, that's one helluva climb down….*>

<*Five is outta here,*> Shannon's sassy tone came over the net next, as her avatar mimed drop-kicking the little disc into oblivion.

<*One is neutralized,*> Landon said, then, in a warning tone, <*Stay sharp. You still need to make it out of your respective locations without being—*>

<*Shit!*> Khela's voice was tense, and she sounded winded, as if she were sprinting. <*I just checked the first three silos, and there's one in each of them! First one's down, I'm headed to number two. Hang on….*>

Charley neutralized the unit before him and began the long climb back down to the warehouse floor when Khela broke in again.

<*Okay, I'm at the second one. Deacti—* ***Shit!***>

Charley began racing for the exit, spurred by the urgency he heard in her voice.

<*Guys, mine just started blinking rapidly. It's not taking my nano. It just released a cloud of something—*>

<*Khela, get out of there!*> Terrance's voice cut in urgently, but his order was met with silence from the other end.

Charley increased his speed. He burst from the warehouse out into the warm coastal sunlight, angling for the nearest aircar in employee parking. He slapped breaching nano onto its frame, hacking its controls. Seconds later, he was airborne, banking over sparkling blue seas to head inland at the craft's best speed.

Khela's voice came back over the net. <*It's okay, I think I can—*>

The sound of an explosion abruptly cut her transmission.

<*Someone get me down there!*> Marta's voice cracked like a whip. <*I'm on my way to the shuttle bay now!*>

Charley sent the ship's doctor a swift response as he reached mentally for the controls of the shuttle cradled in the *Avon Vale*'s amidships hold. He knew that the vessel, like its sister ship, now had a portable autodoc and a stasis pod for triage. Bypassing the lockdown code and startling the bridge crew, he shut down the starboard dock's ES field and opened its bay doors. Releasing the clamps, he dumped the fighter out into nearspace and activated the vessel's thrusters.

<*Scrambling* Sable Wind,> Charley said tersely as Simone's voice came online, informing them that the doctor was on her way from State House in their fastest vehicle.

<*Simone,*> he ordered the Godel AI, <*Send me a satellite feed of the silos at Khela's location.*>

<*Th…They're gone,*> she said brokenly. <*The storage silos have been obliterated. All of them—all across the whole planet.*>

A stunned silence carried across the combat net, broken briefly by Terrance's anguished cry.

<*Khela! No!*>

*****

Khela was just reaching for the DBC unit, when she caught sight of the unmistakable shape of explosives, tucked high in an adjacent rafter. She pulled a small aerosol canister of colloidene nano from her kit and sprayed a stream of light-as-air particles at the package just beyond her reach. The nano clung to the surface of the explosives, its analysis causing her lips to tighten.

She instructed the nano to trace the line that led up to the bomb, and sucked in a sharp breath as she realized the extent to which this silo had been rigged. Telemetry from the nano suggested that the entire complex, stretching kilometers in length, was wired to blow.

She suspected she had mere seconds to act. Snapping a line to the rafter above her head, she fast-roped to the silo's floor seventy meters below and hit the ground running.

She had no idea how quickly the substance would spread, nor did she have any way of knowing how much of a concentration would be required before there was enough to spark a conflagration.

One thing she was sure of: the little unit that was printing its biological material would most certainly have the ability to generate a spark, once that threshold had been met.

Khela's top speed was twenty-four meters per second, thanks to the augmentation she'd received when joining Phantom Blade. Her Marine training had taught her that the rapidly expanding gases in a primary blast could reach an excess of eight thousand meters per second, depending on its yield. She was no physicist, but even she could do the math for that calculation.

She was the daughter of a physicist, though, and had been around him enough to absorb certain concepts, like the inverse square law. Which meant the farther away she was, the better her chances were of survival—although any Marine with a shred of self-preservation could also have told her that.

She activated her flowmetal synth-armor as she went, racing away at her top augmented speed.

The explosion followed fast on her heels, the leading shockwave lifting her and sending her body cartwheeling through the air. Shrapnel from the shredded silo overtook her, debris that would surely have impaled her but for the hardening of her armor. The rarefaction wave that followed sent her tumbling back, along with the wreckage that had flown out to meet her.

The world around her was one great conflagration; superheated air searing her lungs, despite the armor's heat sink features. She barely registered the broken tree trunk that abruptly stopped her as her body slammed into it. She lost consciousness before her body hit the ground.

She came to with an agonized groan as something heavy was lifted off her. She ordered her mednano to perform a diagnostic assessment of her injuries as her armor unlocked. She instantly regretted it as she realized it had been holding her injured body immobile.

Definitely a few cracked ribs, she thought, and then, *Terrance is going to kill me….*

A mechanical frame came into focus, peering down at her as Charley asked, voice tinged with concern, "Captain, can you hear me?"

She nodded weakly. "Thank stars for armor," she gasped, mentally adding 'punctured lung' to her tabulation of her wounds. "Muted the sound of the explosion."

He nodded, then bent lower. "Can you reengage your flowmetal again, so that I can lift you without harm?"

She laid her head back down and, a moment later, felt herself being lifted by the powerful AI and carried over to where *Sable Wind* sat amid a field of debris.

<*Charley has her,*> she heard Marta call out over the combat net, and then Terrance established a private connection with her, his concern flowing into her to the exclusion of all else.

<*I'm fine,*> she assured him, <*just a little bent.*>

<*Thought you said Marines were tougher than that,*> he teased gently. <*Be there in five. Oh, and one more thing….*>

She sent the essence of a weary query his way.

<*Don't you* **ever** *get yourself blown up again. Hear me?*>

*****

The ride back to State House in the city of New Kells was somber, with the *Sable Wind* given clearance to land on the lawn outside the east entrance—although tensions were clearly elevated, and security on high alert.

Marta had assured Terrance that Khela would be fine with a brief stint in one of *Avon Vale*'s autodocs, so he had reluctantly disembarked with Logan, who had exchanged his maintenance bot frame for a humanoid one while en route.

After dropping them off, Charley quietly lifted off to round up the rest of the team and deliver them back to the ship.

Terrance and Logan were met at the entrance by a subdued Simone, who ushered them through security and into the president's main briefing room. The security detail at the entrance had been doubled—and it didn't consist of the same guards who had been present during their lunch, he noted.

Edouard Zola turned as they entered, and Terrance could see the strain bracketing his mouth as he nodded quietly before returning to the holo and the reports of devastation filtering in from across Godel.

"Your wife?" Edouard asked quietly, his eyes still trained on the holo.

"Marta says she'll be fine," Terrance assured him. "What's the damage?"

"Extensive," Celia admitted, stepping forward to greet the two. "Evidently, the DBCs were merely part of their plan. Either that, or they were a distraction, deliberately leaked to pull our attention away from the true threat."

Edouard shook his head, glancing wearily over at Celia. "No, there's no doubt that the spread of the spores would have dealt a heavier blow. They would have killed off all currently growing crops, possibly contaminating the soil and requiring remediation before we could begin to grow again."

"So Barat's goal was to inflict maximum damage," Terrance murmured thoughtfully as he approached the seating area Edouard indicated and lowered himself into a chair. "Take out existing food stores with the explosions. Inhibit future food growth through the spread of the spores."

Logan nodded as he joined them. "The spores were a precision-engineered form of an old nemesis to a farmer's crops, *teliomycetes caries*," he informed the humans. "Our doctor found traces of it within Captain Sakai's lungs."

Terrance experienced a shaft of alarm; it must have showed on his face, because the profiler sent him an inscrutable look.

"The spores have been removed," the AI informed him. "She was not harmed."

At that moment, Terrance didn't know whether to thank Logan or to punch him. He settled for shooting him a dirty look before turning back to Zola and Mastai.

"I assume by now that Barat has to know that at least part of their plan was foiled," he commented, one brow raised.

Edouard nodded, settling into an upholstered chair across from him. "Unfortunately, it doesn't matter. The destruction of our current food supply accomplished what they set out to do all too well, I'm afraid. We have a major crisis at home to deal with right now. No one cares about Verdant mining anymore."

"The vein of pure crystal silica you mentioned, in the asteroid at your inner belt." Logan's words were met with nods of confirmation.

"It's not just the silica we're concerned about," Celia told them, crossing one leg over the other, hands automatically reaching out to smooth the hem of her dress. She plucked at it, toying at it with nervous fingers; her only sign of agitation in an otherwise placid face. "We have a few thousand Godel citizens on that mining platform. The WaNei asteroid is a Godel-held territory in the inner belt—its people expect protection from us. As well they should."

Terrance looked from one to the other, then leant forward in his chair. "Why do I hear a 'but' coming?"

"Because there is," the president admitted. "We received news a few hours ago that Barat has renewed their harassment of the shipping lanes. They also began to adjust the trajectories of several of their military ships. Their new headings have them pointed directly at several of our other mining interests."

At Terrance's questioning look, he explained, "Barat played us well. We thought we had the situation here on Godel secured, so we redirected our home fleet to address the shipping lanes and to provide cover for the other mining concerns. We had to protect our people, and they knew it." He spread his hands and then let them fall. "We knew what they were doing, but it didn't matter, we couldn't do much else. Such actions couldn't go unanswered."

"Which left you vulnerable here on Godel," Logan prompted, and Celia nodded.

"Even though the farms and some of the storehouses were saved, the planetwide loss from the explosions was significant," she explained. "Our congress has enacted a state of emergency, and our Planetary Disaster Agency has drafted all available military for assistance in managing the crisis. This means we've had to recall the remaining military to help with emergency management here at home."

Edouard ran a hand down the chair's upholstered arm, then raised it in a small shrug. "And that means recalling any ships that might have been in a position to offer protection to Verdant."

At Terrance's grim expression, Celia nodded.

"So, you see, even if we could make it to Verdant in time, there would be an outcry if we pulled soldiers away from the very visible relief efforts here at home to do so."

He was interrupted by a ping from Landon, marked urgent. Raising his hand toward the president, he asked, "Will you excuse me a moment? I'm getting an urgent call…."

The connection wasn't private; Logan, Charley, and Shannon had been included as well.

<*I have an idea,*> the *Vale*'s current acting captain informed the three. <*But we'll have to act quickly if it's going to work. The stasis pods we've used for long transit times between systems can also protect a company of soldiers from a hard burn.*>

<*And tell them we'll take all the weaponized drones they'd like to throw at us,*> Charley supplied. <*No need for personnel to control them; we'll run out of cargo space before I run out of capacity.*>

Terrance sat up straight, his gaze seeking Logan's, the question within them burning bright.

The profiler sent his agreement. <*It's only the human soldiers who would need stasis. We can line up the battleframes for any AI troops they can spare along our corridors, if need be.*>

<*How quickly can we make it out there?*> he asked his team.

<*Pretty damn fast,*> Shannon assured him. <*With the upgrades we made to the* Vale *before we left Tau Ceti, and with my AP drive deployed, I can make it to Verdant in four hours if I accelerate at fifty gs.*>

Terrance whistled mentally.

<*The Barat cruiser that's been closing on the asteroid for the past ten hours has a burn of one-point-five gs,*> Landon contributed. <*At that rate, it'll take them another twelve to make it there. If Godel has a supply of hydrogen to top off our tanks…?*>

Snapping his head around to Edouard and Celia, a huge grin breaking out on his face, Terrance stated, "I believe we might have a solution to your problem, Mister President."

LITTLE BIRD

STELLAR DATE: 03.14.3272 (Adjusted Gregorian)
LOCATION: New Pejeta Veldt, just outside Gehenna
REGION: Barat, Little River

Tigan reappeared by Calista's side just as the sun set and she was once again walking the perimeter.

"Go away." Her voice was toneless, her one good eye trained on the savannah grasses on the other side of the ES field. "I'm not in the mood for company right now."

The man just kept walking by her side, easily keeping pace with her own irregular cadence. She continued to ignore him, casting about for a way to rid herself of his presence. But then she mentally shrugged. If he wanted to take the opportunity to escape, what was it to her?

After a moment, he broke the silence.

"That cat you saw earlier," he murmured. "You recognized it, didn't you? Someone's pet, maybe? Owned by a friend."

She sent him a jaded look. "That's one hell of an imagination you have there. What, because I wasn't afraid of something on the other side of an ES field and you were?"

He shot her an irritated look. "Don't be a fool. Someone's planning to spring you from this hellhole, and I want to help."

She stopped abruptly three meters from the pile of boulders and stared at him, her uncovered eye narrowing. "Let's pretend for a moment that you're not a raving lunatic. What in the stars would possibly motivate you to want to help a complete stranger do something idiotic like try to escape?"

His eyes bored into her. "Because I'm the reason you're here."

She reeled back as if he'd struck her, her eye widening in shock. Then it narrowed again, and she shook her head once, turned, and resumed walking.

"You don't believe me," he said quietly, "but it's true. I'm the one who ordered you arrested on Phaethon."

There was a pause.

"So, you know where I was arrested. Well, bully for you." Her tone was hushed so that it wouldn't carry, but the sarcasm was clear.

"You weren't supposed to be interrogated," he muttered. "It should have been a simple exchange—the stasis tech for you. They went behind my back."

She inhaled sharply, and he continued.

"I'm also the one who leaked the information to Godel about where you'd be taken, and how best to get you out of here." He stopped as they drew abreast of the boulders. "I was imprisoned because they discovered what I had done." His next words removed all doubt. "Captain Rhinehart of the *Avon Vale*...I'm Giovani Perelman, former head of Information here on Barat. And I'm in here because of you."

He stopped as she turned abruptly, crowding him. She grabbed the front of his coveralls and jerked him forward until their faces were centimeters apart, the material bunched in her fisted hand, her anger a palpable thing.

"Believe me now?" he asked quietly, and then, with a flick of his eyes back toward the main camp, added, "You might want to let me go before you draw unwanted attention to this area."

She released her fist and gave him a small shove, then turned to face the expanse of savannah that stretched as far as the eye could see.

"You bastard," she breathed. "Your people too. Bastards, all of them."

"We might seem that way to you," he agreed, stepping up next to her. "But it's the only way of life we know."

* * * * *

Calista wasn't alone. Jason lay prone, his camouflaged form buried in the grasses next to the boulder, digesting the scene playing out before him. He had a decision to make—trust the man, or neutralize him.

After what he'd heard, he sorely wanted to choose the latter. But then his appraising glance took in Calista's wrapped arm, her obvious limp, the eyepatch. The man could be of use, helping him get her clear.

There was no way the man could be left behind now. He wasn't going to leave Calista alone, that much was obvious. Jason shrugged mentally. He could always kill the man later.

At the appointed time, as promised, a shout rang out from the other side of the prison. Jason watched the ES field carefully, and when it gave a telltale flicker, he surged to his feet, racing toward the camp. He reached the fence in seconds, his CNT knife slashing through the wire.

Calista stood to one side, her eyes doing a quick scan of the area before she ducked through the opening.

The Baratian seemed unsurprised at Jason's sudden appearance. Suspicion flared inside him at that, but he didn't have the time to waste on stopping—or silencing—the man at that moment. He crowded Calista, pushing through the hole in the fence immediately after her.

Jason gave each a gentle shove and pointed toward the boulders.

"Get into the grasses behind the rocks," he directed. "Quickly!"

Trusting them to do as ordered, he whirled, holding the fence together with one hand at the top while the other held the seam together midway down. Nano mended the tear in both locations.

Won't stand up to close scrutiny, but it'll do.

Ticking the seconds off in his mind, he raced back through to the other side of the ES field just before it snapped back into existence.

Crouching beside Calista, he held her face in his hands.

"Hey, ESF," he murmured, rubbing a thumb over the brow of her dead eye. "You call for a taxi?"

"Took you long enough, flyboy." A lopsided grin appeared as she gripped the hands that held her face. "Just so you know, that'll affect your tip."

He kissed her hard and fast, then turned to reach into his pack. Pulling out a chameleon suit, he tossed it to Calista, then handed a backup camouflage cloak to the man.

"Wasn't expecting company, so that'll have to do," Jason whispered to him while tilting Calista's head forward.

Once the base of her skull was exposed, he injected nano containing the antidote for the suppression code. As she flipped her hair back, he injected her with a fresh batch of mednano.

<*You back with me now?*> he sent, cocking a brow at her as he sealed his pack and shouldered it.

<*Five by five, flyboy,*> came the welcome response.

He nodded, indicating the man with her. <*Your call. Unlock his suppression, or withhold? Do you trust him?*>

He sensed a flash of hot anger from her. <*No.*> Her voice was uncharacteristically bitter. <*He's a spook. The whole takedown on Phaethon was his idea.*> She paused a beat, then added grudgingly, <*But it'd be safer to communicate this way, I think, so go ahead and do it.*>

<*You just give the word, ESF, and he's a dead man.*> Jason heard the bite in his own mental tone, but refused to back off.

She shot him a smile before giving him a brief shake of her head.

<*Might take you up on that later, though,*> she responded.

Gesturing to the man to bend forward, Jason repeated the process, adding a token inviting him to join a close three-way network.

As the man shrugged into the camouflage cloak, Jason slung one of Calista's arms about his neck. <*Grab her other arm,*> he instructed the man. <*We'll support her between us.*>

He knew she was soldier enough to realize the wisdom of this, and was relieved when she didn't protest. Gripping the back of her belt firmly in one hand, he wrapped the other around her arm, just above her cast. Flipping the hood of his chameleon suit up over his head, Jason stood and glanced over at the man to ascertain his readiness. The man nodded back at him, coiled and ready.

Just before Jason stood, he launched a passel of microdrones—scatterbots and jammers—programmed to follow in their wake. Gathering himself into a crouch, he gave Calista's arm a quick squeeze.

<*Go!*> he sent, then launched them forward into a ground-eating run.

They sprinted through the savannah grasses, their destination being the rainforest two kilometers away. Calista was half-running and half-carried, her breaths coming in short, soft grunts from the strain of assisting as much as she could.

Jason kept an eye on the feed from the microdrones, noting when and how often they were pinged by active scans from the prison. He relaxed slightly as he realized the scans were lessening in intensity.

It appeared as if their departure had gone unnoticed, and the disappearance of two prisoners unremarked—at least so far. Jason knew better than to assume this would hold true for very long.

They were highly dependent on the microdrones' ability to spoof Gehenna's scans. Certainly, the cloaking tech they wore would do nothing to hide the disturbance in the grasses. Their track would provide clear indication of their destination for any pursuing them, the moment the prisoners' disappearance was noticed.

He'd breathe easier after they made it to the concealment provided under the forest canopy; once there, he'd contact Tobias to set a rendezvous time.

They made it to the tree line without incident, and the two

collapsed, winded. Jason crouched next to Calista for a quick examination before scouting the area.

"You with me, ESF?" he asked with a quick grin and an arched brow as she worked to catch her breath—an act he knew she'd never need if she'd had access to her mods.

"Wait'll we get home, flyboy," she said on a deep inhale. "I'll have you breathing my exhaust fumes again in no time."

"Think you've got that backward, lady," he drawled, tweaking her eyepatch back in place. "Don't worry. Marta had Landon squeeze in a portable autodoc next to the stasis pod in the *Eidolon*.... You'll be ready to take over your captain's duties by the time we get back to the *Vale*."

She sent him a crooked grin, neither of them catching the sudden surprised look that passed across the face of the man with them.

Jason pulled his pulse pistol out of his holster, checked its charge, and handed it to Calista. Then he swung his E-SCAR around and pointed it at the man's chest.

"Okay, asshole. Give me one good reason I shouldn't kill you right now."

The man stared back at him without flinching.

Guy's got a pair, I'll give him that.

"The name's Giovanni. And I never intended for them to torture—"

"I don't give a shit!" Jason brought the stock of the E-SCAR up to his shoulder.

"I want to defect," the man blurted out, looking in panic from one to the other. "I have critical information for Godel that could save millions—*billions*—of lives!"

Jason stared down the sight of his rifle for two long seconds as Giovanni held his breath and stared back at him.

He bit off a curse and lowered his weapon.

"Fine," he growled. "But give me any excuse, buddy, and your ass is mine."

He stood, holding out a hand to Calista. Pulling her up, he nodded out at the savannah.

"Be back in a few," he said. "I've got to get this airframe assembled, but I'll do it real fast." He emphasized that last with a shift of his eyes to indicate Giovanni.

She followed his glance, then nodded.

Message received; she'd keep the man's attention away from Jason so that he could use his full capabilities to speed the process along.

With a wink, he stood, and then glanced over at Giovanni. Nodding back toward the camp, he admonished, "Keep an eye out. If you see any indication we're being followed, let me know."

The other man nodded and moved to crouch next to Calista, his eyes on the savannah they'd just crossed.

Jason didn't wait. He stepped deeper under the canopy, placing several thick trees between him and the Baratian before pivoting and breaking into a run. He leapt over fallen logs, weaving around brush, feet treading so lightly upon the jungle floor as to hardly be heard, his heading two hundred meters north and a few dozen meters toward the interior.

There, an airframe rested. It was compact, easily transported, and its design simplicity lent itself to swift assembly. The instructions to do so had been pushed to him by the operative just before they'd departed the maglev yard.

It was exactly where they'd said it would be, and Jason analyzed its specs as he divested it of its covering. It reminded him a bit of the reproduction MH-6M Little Bird he'd once flown over a century ago in Proxima.

One clear, plas, domed bubble enclosed a single seat. Folded back and pinned into place for transport were a boom and seven blades—five attached to a whisper-quiet rotor above the dome, two on the antitorque rotor at the end of the boom.

Jason caught it by its skids and pulled it out toward the rainforest's edge, then began rapid assembly, his hands moving in a blur that only someone with L2 reflexes could match. He swung the boom out, pinning the extension in place before doing the same to each fully articulated blade. A bench on either side folded down with attached lanyards to secure cargo—or, if needed, hold additional personnel.

Ducking inside, his eyes quickly scanned the basic, low-tech avionics inside the cockpit. They were minimal, but that was just fine by him. He'd been flying aircraft his entire life; he could do this blindfolded.

It was time.

He raced back toward where he'd left Calista, only slowing as he approached. A few meters out, he deliberately stepped on a patch of dried leaves, the rustling sound carrying toward the two crouched along the rainforest's edge.

Giovanni turned at the noise, as Jason knew he would.

"No followers, so far," the man said, his voice terse.

Jason just nodded as he bent and lifted Calista to a standing position.

"Ready?" he asked, and she nodded.

"Never been readier."

He hesitated. "It'll go more smoothly if I carry you," he began, but stopped as a warning glimmer flashed in her good eye. Then she sighed resignedly.

"Faster too, I suppose."

She reached up and wound her hands around his neck, and he lifted her up, nodded once more to Giovanni to follow, and then led the way back to the rotorcraft.

"Interesting," she murmured as they approached, her eye appraising the little plas bubble with its single seat, two benches, and main and tail rotor systems.

"Let me get our friend clipped in first," he advised, leading Calista to where she would sit, on the bench just to the right of the bubble.

She nodded, then sat as he rounded the nose of the craft and began hooking Giovanni into position.

"It could get windy," he warned, "and a bit bumpy, depending on winds aloft."

"Don't worry about me," the Baratian man said tersely. "Anything's better than another day inside that hellhole."

Jason shot him a look but refrained from commenting. He reached up to test the connection, limiting himself to a brief, "We'll be airborne shortly."

The little craft was nimble, and surprisingly quiet when he spun up its rotors. With his two charges seated sideways, feet planted on its skids, he pulled up on the cyclic, and the Little Bird rose almost silently into the humid, night air.

Slowly, he wound up on the throttle in his left hand and, with the collective up, pushed the cyclic forward, tilting the craft's nose headfirst. And then they were skimming along, just five meters above the surface of the grassy veldt, at a kilometer-eating clip toward the rendezvous point where the team awaited them.

*****

As Jason and the two liberated prisoners were cutting a swath through the veldt, Tobias brought a cloaked and silent Eidolon to a hover just above the clearing that had been their hideout, twenty kilometers away. His passive sensors registered the flickering of energy as the ES field at Gehenna cut out. Shortly thereafter, the shuttle's optics showed a track of disturbance leading from the camp toward the rainforest.

So far, so good….

Surprisingly, an alarm had not yet been sounded, although he knew their luck would not hold for much longer. He and Jason had agreed to maintain comm silence until he reached the rainforest's edge, just in case the guards were monitoring for indications of stray transmissions, encrypted or otherwise.

The ribbon of disturbed grasses that indicated Jason's progress was wide—wider than he expected two humans to make. It puzzled him until it reached the tall canopy of trees beneath him, and his readings informed him that there were not two, but three individuals down there.

Who is that with them?

He saw Jason leave the two and race toward the coordinates they'd been given, where the Godel undercover operatives had said they would deliver the escape craft.

<Assembling the rotorcraft now,> he heard and was relieved to see through the feed Jason sent that there was indeed an airframe. Two clicks were all he risked from his altitude and distance.

His tension lowered a notch when he saw the craft rise and begin its flight along the edge of the trees, leading north, away from Gehenna. As agreed, Jason flew nap-of-the-earth, his flight course hugging the terrain to avoid detection. This was standard in a high-threat situation like this, but it required skill and concentration—and superb reflexes.

At the prearranged coordinates, the little craft rose above the triple-canopied jungle and turned on a heading that would bring him to the clearing where they had staged this operation.

Suddenly, the shuttle's threat detection system went crazy as the area was painted by active scan. Tobias was confident that *Eidolon* had evaded detection; he could not say the same for the little craft approaching him.

In the next moment, scan confirmed the launch of a missile, tracking toward the small airborne vessel.

CRASH AND BURN

STELLAR DATE: 03.14.3272 (Adjusted Gregorian)
LOCATION: New Pejeta Veldt, just outside Gehenna
REGION: Barat, Little River

Calista, seated on Jason's right, saw it first.

<*Heads up!*> her voice sounded in his head. <*Tango incoming, eight o'clock.*>

<*Tobe?*> Jason's terse voice reached out toward the shuttle, hovering to the west by several klicks.

<*I see it,*> came the reply. <*Acquiring a targeting lock now.*>

It was going to be close. Missiles like the one hurtling toward the airframe typically had terminal speeds of up to five kilometers per second; Jason's craft had just reached that very distance from the prison, and the missile was rapidly gaining on them.

<*Hold on!*> Jason sent a mental shout to his two passengers as he slewed to the right, the Little Bird flying sideways as he willed the small craft to bend to his command.

Straightening after they were once more above the savannah, he hammered the collective down, using it to adjust the rotor blades into a position of negative lift that sent the aircraft plummeting.

He ignored the curses of the man on his left and the thump on his right as he leveled out, his eyes on the little craft's readouts as Tobias fed the missile data to his HUD.

<*Looks like a targeted EMP,* > Tobias sent. <*Can't get a good read on it. Depending on its yield, you'll likely lose Link until your nano reserves can repair your unshielded interfaces. Ride's going to get rough for a bit, boyo. Do what you need to do to land; I'm coming in and will be right behind you. Taking it out—now.*>

He sent a quick acknowledgement as he shouted to his passengers, <*Cover your eyes!*> He didn't dare do the same.

The explosion came, near enough that the targeted EMP fried every speck of unprotected nano, and took out every electronic device inside the Little Bird. Including his optics. The close proximity of the blast felt like runaway thermite, and a blistering whiteness seared Jason's eyes.

His eyes felt as if acid were etching its way into his brain through his eye sockets, and the whiteness gave way to an impenetrable red that faded to black.

He realized the explosion hadn't just damaged his optics…. The flash itself, at such close proximity, had rendered him temporarily sightless. He was, quite literally, flying blind, and the airframe had been hit hard, buffeted by the blast wave.

"Dammit!" he swore, gritting his teeth against the pain and trying to ride the turbulence by the feel of it in the seat of his pants. "Calista! You with me?"

Nothing.

"Buddy, you'd better be awake, or we're going to be very dead, very soon," he yelled over his left shoulder, every move his head made pounding into him as if a red-hot poker was stabbing into him from where his eyes once were. "I need your help!"

"Help! How?" The voice was threaded with panic.

"What's my angle of attack?"

"Your…wha—?"

"Am I upright, dammit!" Jason demanded. "I can't see a thing, so you're going to have to help me get this bird down."

"Shit! Okay, you're, uh, leaning too far my direction. Too much! Too much! Right, yeah that's good," the man said, his voice shaken but resolute.

"Okay, how's my nose?"

There was a pause.

"The nose of the *aircraft*, dammit! Am I tilted up or down?"

"Uh, you're tilted up a bit." The man must be leaning into the cockpit; his voice was right next to Jason's left ear, but it still sounded muffled and distant—another factor of the blast.

"Level now?"

"A little more.... Shit! Too far! Too far!" The man's voice sounded freaked.

"Okay, you're, uh, upright, and the nose is level, but you're kind of...." The voice dropped off as if the man was searching for the right words to use. "You're flying sideways. I didn't know a craft like this could do that."

Jason eased up on the left foot pedal and felt the uncoordinated turn he'd barely registered ease into proper alignment.

"Yeah." The voice sounded amazed. "Okay, you're straight now, and uh, maybe ten meters from the grass."

"Good," Jason encouraged, gritting his teeth against a ringing in his ears that had decided to join the party. "That's good. Keep talking me down."

The Little Bird was a trooper; with the combined direction of Tobias and Calista's jailbird friend, he made it to the ground, though he hammered the landing.

He heard the shuttle approaching above the trees to the west, and he fumbled for the restraints, releasing them before reaching around for the pack he'd tossed behind his seat.

He rummaged around inside using only his sense of touch, until his hand collided with the mednano injector. Seizing it, he dialed in another dose and injected it straight into his eye, and...nothing happened.

Dead, just like every other bit of tech around him.

"I'll unstrap her," the man's voice said to his left, and he heard the crashing noise of feet tromping through grass, followed by the snick of a clasp being undone. A groan from Calista informed him she was coming around.

"How's the eyesight, ESF?" he asked, and heard her draw in a sharp breath, then expel it.

"Seeing afterimages a bit," she said finally, "but it could be worse. I think I knocked my head pretty good on that last maneuver."

More rustling, and her voice returned, annoyed. "I can manage, thanks. I don't need your—"

Her voice cut off with a strangled yelp, and Jason heard a brief scuffle as the man dragged Callista away from the downed Little Bird.

Jason lunged for his E-SCAR only to freeze when the man warned, "Try it, and she's dead." A short laugh. "Most likely by you, pilot, since you couldn't see what you're shooting at anyway."

"What do you want, Giovanni?" Calista's voice dripped with scorn. "Freedom? You've got it. Now leave."

The man laughed. "I want what I've always wanted—your stasis tech. And you two are going to help me get it."

The sound of a rapidly approaching hovercraft cut through the night. Its audio signature told Jason it would arrive before Tobias.

Jason turned his head from side to side, the movement fairly splitting his skull, as he blindly tried to isolate the sounds that would tell him the exact location where the man stood. Bracing himself, he planted his feet on the plas frame of the bubble and prepared to move.

A soft cry arrested his plans.

"Don't try it," the voice warned. "You move, and I snap her neck."

"You weren't really ever a prisoner, were you?"

Calista's strained voice caused Jason's temper to flash. He forcibly stomped on it; now was not the time to go cowboy.

Giovanni laughed, the sound harsh. "Smart woman," his voice approved. "No, my incarceration was my one chance to redeem myself. Which should concern you both, since it means I have nothing to lose if I fail."

The hovercraft stopped, and the sound of soldiers disembarking met Jason's ears.

Three, plus one still at the controls, he mentally counted as one approached and hauled him roughly from the downed bird, pressing a pistol up under his chin.

"I'm sure your partner won't have come all this way just to see you both die," Giovanni continued conversationally. "So we'll just wait for him to land and show himself. And then we'll close our deal."

Jason could hear the shuttle on final approach, the sound coming from above and behind him. At the same time, the welcome voice of the Weapon Born filled his mind.

Their Links had just reset.

<*Sending you a visual, boyo, but it'll be off-axis by about thirty degrees after I land,*> Tobias informed him. The feed from the shuttle's sensors came online; it was an aerial view, but good enough to confirm his initial count.

It took a moment for Jason to adjust to the perspective, given that he was unused to seeing himself from a third-person view. But he adapted to it, wincing as the soldier whose weapon was trained on him prodded him forward.

Calista's mental voice joined in as she, too, received the feed. <*Looks like it's a standard pulse pistol he has jammed at the base of your skull,*> she informed him as he began to make his way haltingly toward them.

He caught a glimpse of the weapon Giovanni had trained on Calista and groaned a mental laugh in her direction. <*Guess I don't rate like you do,*> he joked. <*He's got you dead-to-rights with a nasty little piece of work.*>

He highlighted the plasma rifle on the feed, a weapon his soldiers had obviously supplied; the man sure as hell hadn't had it on him before they'd landed.

<*Well don't I feel all kinds of special,*> came her sour reply.

He would have laughed if he'd been in any condition to. But each step forced upon him was agony, his inability to see the ground at his feet adding a jarring quality to his movements.

"How'd you get your soldiers here so fast?" he asked, stalling for time as he cast about mentally for a way he and Calista could overcome their captors. "You couldn't have known where we'd end up."

Through *Eidolon*'s sensors, he saw the man smirk. "I couldn't, but your supplier could."

Giovanni nodded to the remaining soldier on the hovercraft, and the woman propped up the battered form of the Godel operative who'd provided them information and supplies the day before. By the UV data from the sensors, the man had been killed recently; the body was still warm.

Well, shit. He may have been an asshole, but he didn't deserve that.

Giovanni's smirk widened as he realized Jason couldn't see who he was indicating, but didn't bother to correct the problem.

The soldier marching Jason forward yanked him up short at the sound of the shuttle's approach. He ground to a halt as *Eidolon* landed, its thrusters kicking up loose particulates in the grass and hitting them all in the face, though Jason barely felt the sting for the unrelenting fire burrowing into his brain.

<Tobe, I'm not in the best condition right now,> he warned the AI on a private channel. *<And neither is Calista.>*

<I know, boyo. I'm thinking.>

As the shuttle powered down, Giovanni called out. "I know you're in there, and I know you can hear me. Get that stasis unit unloaded if you want your people back alive."

There was a pause, and then Tobias's voice projected from within the shuttle. "It'll take me a moment to get it ready."

"Don't take too long." Giovanni's smirk grew ugly. "The longer you wait, the worse shape they'll be in when you get them back." He nodded at the soldier holding Jason.

Through the feed, Jason could see the man's hand pull back, and caught the glint of a knife as it drove forward toward his thigh. He had a split second to shift the slightest bit and lead the blade, although he didn't dare reveal he could avoid the strike altogether. He did what he could to mitigate its impact before the blade slid home, but it still hurt like a mother.

He allowed a groan to escape his lips and bent forward, gripping his bloodied leg.

* * * * *

Calista drew in a sharp breath as she caught the glint of a CNT blade in the soldier's hand. With a quick thrust, the Baratian's weapon sliced through Jason's chameleon suit, past his base layer, and deep into his thigh.

She thought she saw Jason shift minutely right before the blade struck home, but she couldn't be certain. If he did, it hadn't been enough to avoid the blow altogether. The EMP had deactivated the nano woven into his chameleon suit, and she could clearly see the red stain that darkened the desert camo pattern of his fatigues as it spread.

Jason shouted in pain as the soldier pulled the knife out. His hand gripped the wound reflexively, blood welling up to drip down his fingers onto the grass beneath him.

<Jason—>

<I'm fine,> he interrupted, but she knew by the strain in his voice that he was far from all right.

A sound from the shuttle had her turning just as the ramp began to extend.

"Enough! I'm coming out!" Tobias called sharply from inside the ship. "But this equipment is delicate and heavy. I need to load it on a skid in order to get it down to you."

The AI's reference to delicate equipment caused a distant memory to surface. Calista shut out the scene before her as she chased the maddeningly elusive thought. Frustration mounted as the quagmire her captors had induced in her mind refused to relinquish the details of the event.

It's important, dammit. It concerns the stasis tech. Something about an erratic and temperamental relay….

Her eyes snapped open, and she straightened. *<Tobias—the*

stasis pod. It's one of our standard portable units, isn't it? The kind we used back on the C-47 in Proxima?>

<*Aye, lass, it is,*> the AI confirmed.

<*Then it's powered by one of our modified MFRs.*>

Excitement coursed through her as the memory solidified. The MFRs—Matchbox Fusion Reactors—powered everything aboard the *Avon Vale,* including the ship's battery of eight engines. And she'd been in charge of their design.

<*We invented those at Enfield Aerospace, remember?*> Calista reminded him. <*Me and Shannon and our TechDev team. Shannon had a little trouble stabilizing the Localized Micro-Plasma relay at first, but I know how she fixed it! A little tampering in just the right spot can cause it to go critical—*>

<*Ah, lass, Jonesy beat you to it,*> Tobias cut her off, his tone warm and reassuring. <*He's turned it into a tidy little bomb. All it needs to self-destruct is this command code.*>

Calista felt a smile tugging at her lips.

Good old Jonesy. Of course he did. Best thing I ever did was steal him away from the Space Force....

The code appeared on her HUD, and she considered it a moment. Clever but uncomplicated—and set up in such a way that it was impossible to trigger accidentally.

She connected with the pod and began an assessing probe. After a quick review of Jonesy's modifications, she was ready to pronounce it fit for duty.

<*Oh, yes.*> Satisfaction colored her words. <*That'll do. That'll do quite nicely.*>

The hatch on the shuttle cycled, and she saw Tobias exit, clad in an organic frame that she knew should pass as human. She watched as he maneuvered a lightweight, self-contained maglev frame down the ramp. Inside the frame rested the stasis pod.

"That's far enough!" Giovanni's voice rang out, and Tobias stopped the pod's advance. The Baratian's hand tightened on her arm as he motioned two of his soldiers forward. When the one guarding Jason hesitated, he waved the man onward impatiently. "He's completely blind, you ass. Now bring that thing here."

"He saved your worthless life, you *ass,*" she retorted before she could censor herself.

She knew her barb struck home when he gave the arm he held behind her a vicious twist.

"You'll shut up if you know what's good for you," Giovanni snarled. She went up on her toes to relieve the pain, breathing through it until he released her with a shove.

The soldiers approached the pod with an abundance of caution, and this seemed to anger Giovanni. He snapped at them to hurry. They did, double-timing their payload to the man's side.

He leant in to examine it more closely, and then with an abrupt motion, gestured them toward the waiting hovercraft.

*****

Jason used the diversion to palm the CNT blade he'd used on the prison fence. He closed his eyes, readying himself, willing the pain in his head to recede as he performed a quick internal evaluation. He'd need to compensate for the spatial difference between *Eidolon*'s visuals and the inputs from his own optics. His leg was inconsequential; the wound burned, but didn't impede his abilities.

Now all he needed was an opportunity to move against the man who held Calista.

He noted with dismay the growing distance between them as Giovanni motioned his soldiers to bring the stasis pod to rest near the hovercraft. He stopped them from loading it with a wave of his free hand. The other still held the plasma rifle, trained unerringly on Calista's back.

Giovanni glanced skyward and Jason tensed, bloodied hand tightening around the blade hidden by his side. His head turned blindly and his ears strained for a clue to what the man was expecting, while he searched the shuttle's feed for approaching vessels.

<*Tobe, something's going down,*> he warned, as the shuttle's scan flagged a vessel of some sort coming in low and fast.

It was a gunship, bristling with chainguns and missile launchers. Jason turned toward the threat in consternation, the movement spawning a shaft of pain and vertigo in his head that caused him to stagger. Tobias stepped over to steady him, ignoring Giovanni's growled warning.

Through *Eidolon*'s feed, Jason saw the gunship take a position directly above Calista and the group gathered around the stasis pod. He waited tensely to see what Giovanni's next move was going to be. The man seemed wound tightly—too tightly—and through the searing pain in Jason's head, warning bells were going off….

* * * * *

Calista's alarm mounted at the growing distance between the Baratian who held her hostage and the shuttle. She pulled against Giovanni's grip, but the man refused to relax his hold, his breaths growing harsher in his haste as he propelled her forward.

"You have what you want, lad, now let her go." Tobias's voice, calm and persuasive, reached them as she stumbled over a hillock hidden by the rangy sward.

The Baratian's grasp tightened further as he swung around to face the Weapon Born. Tobias's words proved to be a catalyst for the rage bottled within him.

"What I want? *What I want?*" The man's face was apoplectic. "What I want is the tech you *should* have agreed to trade us when we approached you in the first place."

He tilted his head up to regard the hovering gunship, and Calista could tell the man was communicating with the pilot as it descended. Giovanni grinned suddenly as the craft rotated, and Calista's eyes widened in dread as she realized what the Baratian had done.

The gunship's weapons were now aimed directly at Jason and Tobias.

Giovanni's eyes took on a maniacal cast as he whipped around to face them again. "You cost me my *career*," the man snarled. "It was because of *you* that I was sent to that stars-forsaken prison camp."

She gasped as he planted a hand in the middle of her back and shoved her, hard. She went down on her knees, thrusting her good hand out to brace her fall.

The Baratian's voice cut viciously, his words slicing through her as fear for Jason tightened like bands around her heart.

"You want your precious captain back? Fine. You can *buy* her freedom…with that shuttle of yours." His head lowered menacingly as he raised his hand. "And your life."

Horror washed through her at his words.

"No!" she growled, lurching to her feet and shoving Giovanni back with a strength she didn't even recognize within herself. Raw determination burned inside her as she turned toward the stasis pod.

You. Will. ***Not!***

From the corner of her eye, she saw Jason's hand snap up, saw something slice through the air at an incredible speed, but her attention was fully focused on what she knew she had to do.

She reached mentally for the self-destruct as, all around her, confusion reigned. The numbers on her HUD flashed as they began to count down the five seconds until the fusion reactor failed.

Five seconds. Regret washed over her as she saw the realization of what she'd done register on Jason's face, and he began racing toward her. <*No, Jason!*> she called urgently to him. <*There's no time.*>

She knew she was far too near to the pod, and as far away as the shuttle was, it was still dangerously close.

Instead, she stood defiantly, spending those last, precious seconds pouring everything she felt for Jason Andrews through her connection to him. Bundling a lifetime's worth of love, regret, tenderness, agony and despair into a single, impassioned, emotive burst.

<I love you, Jason. Tell Shannon I'm sorry. I love yo—>

*****

At Calista's shouted "No!" something inside Jason's heart froze, and he realized what she intended to do.

<Stars, Tobe, she's going to use the stasis pod to take out the gunship!>

The world around him slowed as he saw Giovanni swing the rifle toward her. Plunging deeply into his L2 state, he snapped his arm up and let the blade in his hand fly.

It rocketed through the air at an incredible speed, embedding itself into the man's throat—but Jason had known that it would, and dismissed him as a neutralized threat. He was already on the move, reality tunneling down to a single, critical mission.

He had to remove Calista from the blast radius of the stasis pod.

She's too close. Stars, she's too—

He leapt forward as Giovanni's soldiers began to raise their weapons—some aimed at Calista, others pointed toward the shuttle. In the confusion, the gunship rotated, seeking multiple targets before firing, but he knew that indecision wouldn't last long. He just hoped his augmented speed was enough to beat it.

Through the feed, he saw the shuttle's hatch open and Tobias's battleframe emerge as the AI's more fragile, organic frame sought cover. The battleframe, under the Weapon Born's remote guidance, raced forward, and Jason could tell that its trajectory would intersect with his own.

I'm not going to make it!

The thought filled him with despair as the self-destruct countdown flashed to zero on his HUD, and the massive battleframe hit him from behind, covering him as best it could.

The last thing he recalled seeing was the telemetry from *Eidolon* updating with firing solutions for the Baratian gunship, as the world exploded in a maelstrom of white-hot agony—only this time it seared him both inside and out.

MARINES ON ICE

STELLAR DATE: 03.15.3272 (Adjusted Gregorian)
LOCATION: *ESS Avon Vale,* en route, Verdant Mining Platform
REGION: Inner Asteroid Belt, Little River

The *Avon Vale* came screaming in, pulling fifty gravities as it braked on an intercept vector with Verdant Mining and the approaching Barat cruiser.

As Shannon feathered their approach, and the *Vale*'s apparent gravity neared a more tolerable five *g*s, she deactivated the stasis units and sent the awakening humans—those from Godel, along with Terrance, Khela, and Jonesy—a status update.

<*We'll be arriving at Verdant in an hour,*> she informed them all, then reached out to address the Godel faction. <*Your AI counterparts are set up at the midship port airlock, and we're preparing your combat drones to interface with our systems now.*>

While the *Vale*'s humans struck out for the command deck, the rest followed an AI noncom waiting to escort them amidships.

Once they arrived, they fell in by platoon, and Major Fletcher, the Godel AI commanding the company of soldiers assigned to this mission, addressed them.

<*Rules of engagement as discussed,*> the major announced over the Godel team's combat net. <*Our primary goal on the platform is the protection of its inhabitants. Use any non-lethal means at your disposal to suppress those rioters.*>

A dozen of the soldiers were technical specialists, brought along specifically to repair environmental, structural, and stabilization systems onboard the platform. Those petty officers stood aside as Fletcher addressed the rest.

<*Priority one is to get this bucket of bolts repaired. You,*> Fletcher instructed, tagging his company's first platoon. <*Clear the route so these folks can get to work on repairs. Your only responsibility is to keep*

them safe and get them where they need to go. As for the rest, Captain Janel has your assignments. I want the Baratian bastards who started this thing rounded up, and order restored to this platform by the end of next watch. Any questions?>

There were none, and an hour later, Shannon had matched v with the station. The STC hadn't responded to her requests for a berth, but the Godel AIs used a backdoor into the station's networks and disabled the automated defenses.

<*Damn, I wish we were going with them,*> Khela told Shannon as she watched the Godel Marines move out through the umbilical. <*I really feel like kicking some Baratian ass.*>

<*Well, we still have our own prey to hunt,*> Shannon replied. <*Can't very well go hunting a cruiser without a breach team.*>

<*Don't worry.*> Khela returned Fletcher's nod with a grim one of her own before he strode off the ship and onto the station. <*My team will be ready.*>

* * * * *

Mo Chaudry pressed his back against the bulkhead, gasping for breath, wondering when the hell he was stuck in would finally come to an end.

His left arm was tingling again, and he slapped the palm of his hand against his thigh, trying to wake it up.

The pulse shot the Baratian saboteurs hit him with had ruptured one of the veins in his arm and, though his mednano had staunched the internal bleeding, the trauma had temporarily damaged nerves, causing his hand to go numb.

"Fucking Barat," he muttered, massaging his hand as he peered carefully back around the corner. "I *knew* things hadn't fallen that far into the crapper here."

He spotted a trio of teens running by with boxes of stolen sim-gear. He had half a mind to stop them, but knew his pursuers weren't far behind.

They had done their job all too well, the station fallen to riots and ruin, but still they were after him. He supposed it was because his ocular implants had recorded their final act of sabotage. If he could broadcast it, the vid would prove that Barat was behind the worsening conditions on the Verdant platform.

Stars, Molly. In case I don't make it…I just hope you and the kids are all right.

He drew in a few more gulping breaths and then resumed his loping jog in the station's half-*g*, his goal a relay—any relay—that would allow him to upload the footage to an outside source.

The last two he'd managed to reach had both been destroyed, deliberately sabotaged to limit the flow of information coming from the platform.

His spotty connection to the station's network had indicated that relay 9A1 was still operational, and it had a direct connection to an external array.

A dozen meters ahead, the passage he was moving down intersected a wider concourse. He just had to cross that, work his way down a few maintenance corridors, and he'd be there.

Then maybe the lazy bastards at Godel will send us some damn help.

Just before he reached the concourse, a series of muted *whumps* came from around the corner, and he grabbed a handhold on the bulkhead, arresting his motion and slamming his shoulder into the wall before he came out into the open.

Rubbing his much-abused arm once more, he drew his pulser and carefully walked the last meter to the corner. A quick glance showed a group of Verdant security to his right, crouched behind thick plas barriers.

On the left was a crowd of rioters, a few with pulse pistols, the rest with whatever improvised weapons they could find. The rioters were hurling insults at the security personnel, who were only firing when the crowd moved in too close.

Mo had already learned his lesson about wearing anything with 'Verdant' on it. The very first time he'd managed to lose the

Baratians, a trio of thugs had spotted him and yelled something about 'Verdant scum' and how he was gonna die. A few warning shots from his pulser had sent them running, but that had clued him in that a change was required.

His jacket had been the first to go, but the form-fitting EV suit he wore underneath still clearly broadcast Verdant colors. Not long after, he'd come to a looted clothing store and stripped down, swapping to a pair of black pants and a loose jacket with a gaming logo on the back.

The irony of the thugs singling him out was that he knew one of them from the docks. The woman was a Verdant yardmaster who managed processing and storage of extracted ores.

Damn idiots…everyone who works here works for Verdant.

He knew that half the security guards had families onstation as well; the fact that they were trying to maintain some semblance of order in the face of such chaos was admirable.

As he mulled over his situation, the crowd advanced once more, and the guards fired wide-spread pulse shots, driving the mob back.

Mo decided he wouldn't get a better opportunity, and when the firing stopped, he dashed from his cover, crossing the concourse as quickly as possible.

He'd almost made it to the passageway on the far side when a pulse blast from the mob's side hit his much-abused left arm and spun him around.

The deck came up to meet him, his face mashing into the hard plas. He slid a full two meters before he came to a stop. He stayed down, taking a moment to regain his senses before flopping onto his back, relieved to see that he had made it to the passageway.

Pulse fire had resumed in the concourse, but luckily, no one seemed interested in him—at least not yet.

Getting up was a struggle, as his left arm was completely numb, and his shoulder felt like someone had taken a hammer to it. The combination of pain and numbness made his entire left side feel like it wasn't properly attached to his body.

Suck it up, Mo. Now move.

Steeling himself with the mental admonition, he drew on a reserve of energy and surged to his feet. Stumbling down the passage, he took a right and then a left, finally spotting the comm relay's door.

It was set into a bulkhead that had to be no more than a few meters from the station's hull. He picked up his pace, bracing himself for what he hoped would be his final task before he would hole up somewhere and wait for the madness to be over.

Upon reaching the door, he found that it was locked—a good sign—and manually input his credentials into the access pad to open it. Once inside, he breathed a sigh of relief. The relay appeared to be intact, the column of equipment displaying a row of green status lights down one side.

He was about to Link to it when the station's network went down again. Muttering a curse, he cast about for a hard-Link cable, but froze when a voice came from behind him.

"Nice try, buddy. You almost made it. Now, turn around."

Mo lifted his hands and slowly rotated, wondering why the man didn't just shoot him. Only one of his pursuers was in evidence. He considered charging the man, but the Baratian saboteur must have guessed at his intentions.

"I'd like to keep this relay intact, buddy, but if you give me half a reason, I'll blast you into a bloody soup."

Mo's shoulders slumped. "You're gonna kill me anyway, aren't you?" he asked in a resigned tone.

"Sure, yeah, but there are a lot of ways to die."

Mo swallowed and began to lower his hands. "What if I just—"

What was sure to be a nonsensical plea was interrupted by a voice from the passageway.

"Sage advice, buddy. Drop it, or I'll blow your brains all over the bulkhead."

The Baratian saboteur glanced to his left. A look of

consternation crossed his face and then his eyes narrowed as he swung his pulse pistol toward the unseen speaker.

Without a moment's hesitation, the newcomer fired.

Mo's attacker fell. Seconds later, a Godel Marine swung around the corner, his weapon trained on the hapless engineer.

"You armed?" the Marine demanded.

"Pulser, jacket pocket." Mo's throat worked, and then he spoke. "Stars…I sure am glad to see you."

The Marine nodded. "Pull the weapon out, nice and slow and drop it."

Mo nodded and complied, tossing the weapon out of reach. "I have evidence against Barat, there were three of them—"

"Three?" the Marine asked. "We got two not far back. Do you know if there are more?"

Mo shook his head. "Not that I saw."

"OK. Come on out. We'll take you to the major." The Marine glanced down at the moaning Baratian. "Along with this trash."

*****

Terrance paced quietly behind the captain's chair as Landon broke orbit with the platform and set the *Vale* on an intercept course with the Baratian cruiser. The plot was displayed on the main holo, with time to intercept hovering discreetly beneath it.

He knew it hadn't been necessary that he come along; in fact, Edouard had seemed surprised when Terrance had declared his intentions. But Phantom Blade was his responsibility, and he refused to see them venture into harm's way alone.

<*Besides,*> he'd admitted to Kodi after the AI had called him on it, <*there's something about being in the thick of things that's a bit addicting.*>

His eyes swept across the almost exclusively AI crew complement staffing the bridge. Landon had proven his tactical mettle back in Tau Ceti. He now sat in the captain's seat and would call the plays for the upcoming skirmish, should one erupt.

Logan and Charley sat at Scan and Navigation, respectively. Khela was seated at Security, and Jonesy—the only other human aboard—was running Comm.

<You know, we might want to take a seat and strap in before all the shouting begins,> Kodi warned him privately. *<I have a vested interest in your continued health, you know.>*

Terrance sent a mental chuckle in response before shifting direction and heading toward one of the observational cradles off to one side.

Charley nodded to him as he crossed behind, the AI already interfacing with the three hundred and fifty space combat drones Godel had provided. The amidships bay doors had already been retracted on both sides, with ES fields in place and ready to disengage at a moment's notice.

He glanced over to where Logan was seated at the station nominally known as Scan. From there, the AI could reveal the ship's true capabilities, should they prove to be needed.

Under Logan's control, all of the carefully disguised armament that was the Q-ship *Avon Vale* could be unleashed against Barat—and demonstrate to all that this old girl had teeth. He almost hoped it would be.

It'll certainly come as a surprise to our Godel guest. He smiled to himself as he glanced over at Simone. *We'll assure her our shields are military-grade as well…as is our crew.*

He'd just reached for the webbing to clip himself into his cradle when he heard an audible gasp escape Jonesy's lips from where he sat at Comm. Terrance looked over and caught the stunned look on the man's face, an expression seized by shock and horror.

<Noooooo….>

The sudden, keening wail echoed sharply through the bridge, and it was as if an electric current had discharged, freezing everyone in place for a brief moment in time.

Terrance leapt to his feet, releasing his restraints with a snap.

He stepped toward the main holo, then stopped as the sound was repeated.

<Noooooo, nonononono…>

Shannon's voice moaned again, and Terrance turned in a circle, glancing from pick-up to pick-up, his body whipcord taut, his stare fierce in its intensity.

"Shannon," his voice rang out, "talk to me!"

Pivoting to face Jonesy, his eyes bored into those of the engineer, demanding an answer.

"It's the cap—" Jonesy started, and then broke off. He swallowed, his voice breaking, "—the captain, sir. She's…." His eyes closed in pain, and Terrance abruptly recalled the many years the former ESF ensign had served with Calista.

Jonesy's next words came out in a barely audible whisper. "She's…dead."

* * * * *

An expanse snapped into place. Charley anchored it; Kodi, Logan and Landon populated it, bringing Terrance, Jonesy and Khela along.

They were back on El Dorado, in the anechoic chamber that Shannon had once called home. The place where she had first met Calista, on the day Terrance had introduced her to the company as Enfield Aerospace's new Chief Pilot.

In the center of the ersatz chamber sat Shannon, surrounded by wave-canceling surfaces, a replica of the Elastene-clad fighter hovering before her.

The AI's silver hair fell around her shoulders, strands that would ordinarily dance with a shimmering life laying dull and flat. Her head hung low, her clothing ripped and torn. Shannon hugged her arms tightly about herself as if she could not get warm. As he watched, her body shook, wracked with sobs. A soft threnody filled the expanse as she rocked herself slowly back and forth.

Jonesy approached her first. Tears tracking silently down his dusky cheeks, the engineer folded his legs beneath him and sat, his shoulder touching hers. After a moment, the man reached back and placed a hand between her bowed shoulders, moving it in gentle circles.

Khela's voice sounded inside Terrance's head. *<I…can empathize.>*

Terrance knew his wife was thinking of her own loss of her dearest friend, Hana, the AI with whom she'd been paired for many years. He glanced over from Shannon to meet Khela's dark eyes.

After exchanging a long look with him, she stepped up to the AI's other side and sank down next to her, gripping Shannon's hand tightly in both of her own.

No words were offered, just shared sorrow.

"Is that…really Shannon?" Terrance whispered in a low voice, turning his gaze from the pain-wracked frame of the *Vale*'s AI to Charley's fathomless, sea green eyes. "Is she truly expressing grief as a human would?"

The Tau Ceti AI shook his head, and a connection sprang up between the observers standing on the chamber's edge.

<It's a visual representation. Something that you can relate to, symbolic of the feelings she's expressing to us,> he gestured between himself, Kodi, and the twins, *<and translated into an iconography you would understand.>*

The AI smiled, and there was a sadness to it that touched something deep inside Terrance.

<The reverse is true as well. Her grief is all-consuming right now, and she's unable to fully process the way in which Jonesy and Khela are sharing that grief with her. So I'm translating their unspoken attempts to give solace in a way she can comprehend.>

Terrance shook his head as he absorbed what Charley had just told him. He knew he was holding his own sorrow at bay, held hostage to the imminent danger the *Vale* faced. Looking at the three before them, he hated like hell to yank them from their grief and demand that they return to their stations.

A shaft of anger shot through him as he realized that Barat's greed was robbing them all of the opportunity to mourn, and he cursed the timing that brought the news at such a critical juncture.

He began to step toward them, but Kodi reached out a hand and stopped him.

<*Let them be,*> the AI he was paired with advised. <*Give Shannon her space.*>

<*But the cruiser—*> Terrance began, and Kodi shook his head.

<*First, it's nothing for us to maintain this expanse,*> his partner reminded him. <*It takes a fraction of the processing power that we collectively have.*>

Terrance shot him a hard look. <*Tell me something I don't know.*> He heard the harshness in his own mental voice and reigned himself in, sending Kodi an apologetic thought.

<*Second,*> Charley's voice interjected, his tone calm and reasoned, <*Jonesy and Khela are strapped into their cradles back on the bridge, and will be relatively safe during any maneuvers that may be required of the* Vale.>

<*Third, I can take over for Shannon,*> Landon joined in. He added with a smile, <*Khela's services aren't necessary at the moment, and if it's essential for a meat-suit to be in Engineering, we can always send you.*>

<*Gee, thanks. I think,*> Terrance sent, cocking his brow with a sardonic look. <*Is there a fourth?*>

<*Fourth, I agree,*> Logan said abruptly. <*Leave them to mourn.*>

Terrance saw the profiler's gaze land on his twin, and he realized suddenly that the AI would understand all too well the loss Shannon was experiencing.

He shook his head. *In some ways, this reality they've created here seems as fragile and delicate as an eggshell,* he thought as he looked around in amazement one last time. *But it's one hell of an eggshell. If*

I know Charley, he has these three wrapped in titanium, and warded against the tempest raging outside.

"Okay, then," he spoke aloud. "You've convinced me."

<*Good. Besides,*> Charley added with a twist of humor and an audacious wink, <*I'm more than capable of handling both the drones* ***and*** *the* Vale, *if any of the others get distracted.*>

Landon sent a flash of derision. <*Fine. Flaunt your heritage, why don't you. Oh, and fat chance, my friend.* ***I'm*** *running the* Vale. *And I intend to extract my pound of flesh.*>

<*As do I.*> Logan's thoughts flared with a burning anger. <*Let's go kick some Baratian ass.*>

* * * * *

Landon turned the *Avon Vale* as it closed within fifty thousand kilometers of the Baratian cruiser. He angled the vessel so its engines were not exposed to the enemy, while still allowing him to apply heavy thrust to match velocity.

The vector had him easing ever closer to the enemy ship, but he didn't mind. It also sent a clear message: *You will have to go through us to get to your objective.*

In case the Baratians weren't too bright, Landon was preparing to hail the enemy ship, when a call came in from them.

He accepted the communication and activated full video, letting the enemy see what they were up against.

"Civilian craft approaching Verdant Mining, you are entering an area of—" The Barat officer broke off with a scowl as she realized what she was addressing.

Her tone changed, and she stated flatly, "Get out of our way, or suffer the consequences."

Landon sent the woman a surprised look. "This area is considered inter-system space. It's free to anyone who wants to transit. Why should I get out of your way? Perhaps you should move instead."

The woman's eyes narrowed. "We've been watching you. Your ship just left Verdant, probably to sow more unrest. We, however, are on a *humanitarian* mission," she snarled. "Something your kind wouldn't understand. Now make a hole, or we'll make you *into* one." She bared her teeth, as if the thought of firing upon the *Vale* held great appeal.

Woman, you have no idea how appealing that thought is to me, as well. Just give me an excuse. Please….

Landon's expression didn't change, although he didn't attempt to censor the flare of fury he sent to his brother and the other members of the team.

"If by 'sow unrest', you mean render aid, you'd be correct," he countered, his mild tone revealing none of the rage churning inside him. "In fact, we just ferried a large number of emergency personnel to repair the platform, and Marines to stabilize the situation."

The woman's nostrils flared at his words, and she turned her head to one side. Audio cut out, and Landon was certain she was confirming this with her own communications team. When she returned, her eyes were cold and hard.

"You were warned," was all she said before the feed cut out.

Landon turned to Charley, his expression anticipatory.

"Ready?" he asked, and the Tau Ceti AI nodded, hunger burning in his eyes.

With a satisfied smile, Landon sat back in his seat.

"Release the drones."

* * * * *

The ES fields snapped off, and three hundred and fifty military drones drifted from either side of the *Avon Vale*. They emitted no EM, only being propelled outward by the expulsion of air from the bays.

Charley suspected that if the Baratian cruiser—a stubby,

utilitarian thing named the *Coldfire*—saw the drones, it would think them nothing more than chaff.

Beams lanced out from the *Coldfire*, striking the *Avon Vale* fore and aft, those shots being partially deflected by actual chaff and the Elastene plating on the ship.

Several other shots lanced through the cloud of drones, but Charley was weaving them in an erratic pattern, so none of the beams struck.

He assumed that the humans aboard the enemy ship were attempting to assess whether the drones were powered by sentient beings or if it was artifice, a ploy to deter the cruiser from achieving its goal.

Landon held his course, not even rolling the ship when the enemy attacked, baiting the *Coldfire*'s odious captain into thinking that the *Vale* was all bluster and no substance.

<*Think they'll fall for it?*> Charley asked.

In response, Landon fired the starboard maneuvering thrusters, bringing the *Vale* onto a vector that would see them pass within a dozen kilometers of the Baratian ship.

<*There. They have to deal with us now. No sane captain would let a hostile ship pass that close to their hull.*>

The *Coldfire*'s skipper didn't disappoint. Two dozen missiles belched from its nose, streaking toward the *Vale* on erratic courses as the ship's civilian-grade point defense beams came to life.

<*Going to bring out the big guns?*> Landon asked.

<*Just waiting to see if they'll commit more in their opening salvo,*> Charley responded, carefully recalculating timing on the ship's weapons activation and tracking systems.

With only thirty seconds to spare, a ripple passed along the length of the *Avon Vale* as hull plating slid aside. Twenty-five-centimeter lenses were exposed to the deep black as Charley triggered the port beams and sent collated streams of photons slashing through vacuum to vaporize the missiles.

The somnolent ship was finally revealed for what it truly was: a tiger in disguise.

Ten of the incoming missiles were destroyed in the first few seconds, and another five spun off course moments later. Charley tracked the remaining nine, bringing a group of drones in close to fire on the missiles. The *Vale*'s shorter range ten-centimeter beams came online, adding to the invisible barrage whittling away at the *Coldfire*'s attack.

When the last missile was destroyed a kilometer off the *Vale*'s bow, Landon growled into Charley's mind.

<*You done toying with them now?*>

<*I just wanted it to be clear that they are the aggressors here.*>

<*Point made,*> the acting captain said. <*Now take them out.*>

Charley had been with Phantom Blade long enough to get to know Calista. He respected her. More, he truly liked her. He thought of Jason and Tobias, and what they were going through on Barat, and something deep inside him burned, raw and ugly.

With grim determination, Charley brought the full squadron of drones to life as he sent them charging across the void. At the same time, beams from the *Vale* raked over the *Coldfire,* burning away the Baratian ship's defenses.

The enemy ship deployed its own chaff and a meager number of drones, but Charley swatted them out of the black like so many flies.

His drones were the tiger's claws, long and sharp. They dove in close, their maneuvers unmatchable by any human-controlled tracking system.

You trust your NSAI too little, Charley thought as he watched the *Coldfire* respond too late to one attack after another.

Though the enemy cruiser fired another two hundred missiles in a desperate bid to stay alive, none made it even halfway to the *Avon Vale*. In response, it adjusted course, moving from a vector-matching approach with the Verdant platform to a collision course.

<*Blow it,*> Landon ordered.

<With pleasure.>

Charley brought fifty of his drones in to fire on the *Coldfire*'s port engine, shredding the cowling bell and breaching the plasma chamber.

The enemy ship shuddered, its hull appearing to ripple from stern to bow as the engine blew, the force of the explosion sending the craft veering off course. Then the starboard engine died, and the vessel went dark, a drifting hulk headed nowhere in the endless darkness.

<Let them go,> Landon said. *<Barat can have its own humanitarian crisis for a change.>*

Charley didn't respond for a minute, calculating the risk that the enemy ship posed. He fired a few more shots, disabling its remaining maneuvering thrusters, before recalling the remaining hundred drones.

<Neutered,> he said on the bridge net, noting the satisfied look on Terrance's face.

"Good," the Enfield scion said aloud. "Now let's get to Barat, we have a pickup to make."

STAR LIGHT, STAR BRIGHT

STELLAR DATE: 03.17.3272 (Adjusted Gregorian)
LOCATION: State House, New Kells
REGION: Godel, Little River

The night sky above New Kells was crisp, the air cold. Godel's single moon, Escher, hung low in the sky. As Jason watched, the silvery orb of the moon's own satellite, Bach, was swallowed by the larger disc, as the smaller moon-moon's orbit obscured it from view.

The gravel crunched under his booted feet as he turned away, wandering aimlessly through the gardens of State House. He came across the occasional agent from Edouard's presidential detail making their rounds, but each one had merely nodded and then veered away, understanding his need for solitude.

The previous few days had passed in a dull haze. He recalled numbly the events the night the stasis pod blew, his mind ticking them off, one by one.

Eidolon's hatch opening, the ground shuddering under the weight of a battleframe as it raced to his side. The concussive wave of an explosion rolling over him, a sensation of blistering heat that seared exposed skin. The quiescent shuttle erupting above his head, the acrid after-smell of ozone hitting the back of his throat from the firing of *Eidolon*'s e-beams—like chlorine, and yet not.

The sound of bodies dropping.

He'd still been conscious at that point, though in shock.

He recalled the cool, metal touch of a hand supporting him as a spray of mednano was applied to burns covering neck, hands, and face—everything not protected by his base layer.

The stabbing pain behind his eyes easing as the mednano had begun its work. He'd rolled forward, burying his charred head in blistered hands as his sight began to slowly return. Not wanting to see through newly-healed eyes the blackened crater before him where a vibrant woman once stood.

Stars…Calista….

Jason knew she'd sacrificed herself to save him. It didn't make accepting it any easier.

His awareness of the events that night on Barat felt far more vivid than his current surroundings. He looked up, unseeing, at the night sky above him as the memories played out yet again inside his mind.

His eyes pricked, burning as he gave himself over to the jagged pain that ripped through him at the thought of the woman he'd lost. The woman they'd all lost.

Fuck, it hurts.

Logan told him what Charley had done; the cruiser's missile salvo had been the excuse the powerful AI had craved, releasing some of the rage they'd all felt at the news of their captain's loss.

The profiler had shared the feed from that day with both Jason and Tobias. He'd reviewed the recording, seen the *Avon Vale* throw off her guise as the warship hammered the Republican cruiser, until all that remained was a kilometers-wide debris field.

He'd heard it would take a Godel cleanup crew another few days' worth of dragnet duty to clear the lanes for safe transit.

Jason supposed that someday, once he began to feel something again, he'd be impressed—amazed, even—at the formidable power Phantom Blade had achieved.

But he couldn't really find it in himself to care right now.

He thought about the conversation they'd had with Simone about religion. Well, if a supreme being existed, he bitterly resented the seeming indifference to the fact that a woman as strong, smart, and infinitely talented as Calista had lost her life. Especially in such a senseless way.

A noise from behind warned him that he was no longer alone. He ignored it, willing the presence away.

Whoever it was decided not to take the hint.

"I've been told that your ancestors used to look up and wish upon the stars," Simone's voice cut into his thoughts, as if he'd conjured the AI simply by thinking of her.

"Wasn't why I was looking up." His voice was curt. He turned, facing away from where she stood. "And if you're about to say something religious, forget it. I'm not interested."

"No. At least, not like you think." She stopped next to him, her frame relaxed, head tilted back. "One of your ancients from Old Earth once wrote, 'Talk to me about the truth of religion, and I'll listen gladly. But don't come talking to me about the consolations of religion, or I shall suspect that you don't understand'."

She turned to glance at him. "I understand enough to know that there is no consolation, not at a time like this." Her eyes once more sought the night sky. "Tobias told me that this is the first time you've lost someone truly close to you."

He tensed, angry at what felt like betrayal from an old friend. She must have sensed it. She turned toward Jason.

"Don't blame him. I asked. I was concerned." She hesitated, then continued in a soft voice, "I lost someone too, once."

"It's not the same." His voice was harsh, and yet he couldn't stop it. "I can't bring her back. She doesn't have a system restore point."

The words hung between them. They'd been cruel, he knew, deliberately hurtful. They implied…a lack of sentience. AIs might be able to back up a copy of themselves to immutable crystal storage, true. But most didn't.

Simone turned her face back toward the glittering expanse above them. "I remember looking out there and raging against the unfairness of it all. The death was so unnecessary, a waste."

"So your faith failed you, then." He could hear the bitterness in his voice, the sharp edge, his words continuing to seek a target to hurt.

"On the contrary," she responded, her tone mild. "I don't see where we've been promised anything special or unique." She shrugged. "I've certainly not been visited by an oracle, or told that the people I care for get any form of special dispensation."

Jason's laugh was harsh. "Why are you here, again? Because you're doing a piss-poor job of cheering me up, in case you were wondering."

Simone just stood there quietly. Not speaking. Not moving.

"You're right, Jason. She's gone," she said suddenly, her words harsh, shocking him like an electric current. "And nothing will bring her back."

He eyed her warily for a moment. "Thought your kind believed in life after death and the immortality of the soul."

"*Neshama,* yes," was all she said in response.

The word didn't translate for him.

"Neshama," she said again, then explained, "The breath of the creator, that spark that is in all living things. We believe it is not subject to the dimensions of spacetime as we know it. Or of entropy," she added somewhat incongruously.

Jason turned on her suddenly, irritation sparking in his eyes. "What the fuck does entropy have to do with anything?"

Simone held his angry gaze, her own steady. "Everything in a closed system goes from a state of higher energy to a lesser one, from order to disorder." She gestured to the stars. "You're a pilot, you know this. You have to pump energy into a system to maintain order."

After a long moment, she spoke again, her voice whisper-quiet.

"The same can be said for you. Phantom Blade came into existence to fight against corruption and decay. Your people's actions in Little River worked to restore order where Barat fought to dismantle it." She paused. "Calista pushed energy into a situation unraveling on the Barat plains in order to prevent your loss of life."

Her tone gentled, and she reached out to touch his arm, then withdrew it. "All I'm saying is that, as you work through your grief, don't ignore her sacrifice. Don't let entropy steal her gift away."

Jason's numbed mind didn't take in all the AI said. Possibly, he knew, it never would.

It was a long time before he noticed she'd slipped away.

* * * * *

Terrance lay in the dark, one arm around Khela, her head tucked under his chin and her hand resting on his chest. He could feel the beat of her heart, pressed against his side, and he shuddered inwardly at the thought of what losing her might do to him.

The file he'd reviewed—the one recorded by *Eidolon,* of the flight, the sudden betrayal, and Calista's final sacrifice—was one he'd asked Charley to send to him privately. Every moment was now seared into his brain, a vivid series of images he knew he'd take with him to his grave.

Calista had been his responsibility; he owed it to her to be there, if not in person, then in memory, during the last moments of her life. He'd actively pursued her—*not romantically,* he thought with a smile, running his hand up the gentle arch of Khela's spine and then back down to rest on the curve of her hip. Not like that. No one had ever captivated him the way his warrior woman had.

The smile fell away as his thoughts turned back to the day back on El Dorado when he'd heard of an ace pilot, a Space Force top gun who could fly any craft, ancient or modern. He'd known then that he had to convince Calista to come to Enfield Aerospace as its Chief Pilot once her tour of duty was up.

And she had. With Shannon, who at the time, had been Enfield's Chief Engineer, the two had been formidable. And then an unlikely set of circumstances set them on an intersect path with a covert operation that had irrevocably changed all of their lives.

For a brief moment, he bitterly regretted the events that had led to him accepting a role with Phantom Blade. But then—he glanced down at the sleeping form he held, and his grip tightened momentarily at the thought—this enigmatic and beautiful Marine would never have become a part of his life, never held a piece of his heart.

"Will he be okay, do you think?" Khela's quiet voice cut into the silence.

He should have known that she'd be aware of the direction his thoughts had taken.

"I don't know," he admitted honestly. "Maybe. Eventually." He sighed, bringing his other arm around her and rolling her on top of him. She stared down into his eyes, hers dark and unreadable. "He's suffered a lot, over the years."

Terrance's eyes shifted, his mind taking him back to a place and time light years away, where he'd stood, looking through the scope of a sniper's rifle, Jason's sister in his sights.

His eyes returned to meet Khela's. "Something happens to you when you experience that kind of pain, up close and personal. And it's happened to him more than once."

She stroked his chest rhythmically with her fingers as she contemplated what he'd told her.

"He's stronger, I think, than anyone truly realizes," she said after a moment.

Her hand stilled, and she cocked her head, her expression taking on a speculative look.

"What about Godel, will they be okay? So much food was lost when Barat took out those storage silos." Her gaze drifted inward, and he knew she was recalling her own brush with death.

He shrugged, the movement jostling her gently against him, and he ran his hands up and down her arms to steady her, and to offer comfort. After a moment, he spoke.

"I'd imagine they have some tough times ahead of them, but Edouard told me they'd feared Barat might try something like this. He said their secretary of agriculture advised farmers to retain a measure of their fall harvest on the farms against such an eventuality."

Terrance felt more than heard the relieved breath she blew out at the news.

"There was also a considerable amount of grain in transit, stored in maglev cars at the time," he continued. "And then…."

He drew the word out, pausing until she pinched him out of frustration.

"Okay, okay! Bloodthirsty wench," he growled, grinning as she scowled and slapped him lightly on the chest. "I offered to sell them Enfield's stealth tech, to help give them an edge and keep Barat at bay."

A slow, satisfied smile spread across her face. "Something tells me Barat is about to realize what happens when you stir a nest of angry hornets."

He responded with a grin of his own as he recalled Edouard's reaction.

"Good," Khela's voice held a note of finality. "I can think of no one more deserving. Speaking of deserving…."

Her voice lapsed into silence, and she turned her face up to his, eyes blazing with a focus that he felt more than saw in the dimness of the cabin.

"I think…we should agree to Edouard's proposal."

He cocked his head at her apparent non sequitur. "To check up on the rumors coming out of Sirius? About the atrocities there?"

She nodded. "It's on the way home, sort of. And going after them…." Her forehead wrinkled as she pursed her lips in thought. "It will give him a cause, something to focus on," she explained.

Abruptly, he understood.

"Jason you mean."

She nodded. "He has a need, almost ingrained in him, to rescue those in trouble." She smiled in gentle irony. "He plays at being the reluctant hero, but you can see it here," she tapped on his chest, "in his heart."

He smiled back at her. "I think you're right."

He took a deep breath in and brushed her hair out of her face, letting its silky strands slide through his fingers, enjoying the sensation as much now as the first time he'd seen her with her hair restored.

Pulling her face down to meet his, he whispered, "Why are you talking about another man when I'm laying right here?"

A wicked light glinted in her eyes, and with a swift move only a Marine could manage, Terrance found himself in a very…interesting position.

"Wait," she said suddenly, lifting her head, her eyes narrowing. "Where's Beck?"

Over the Link, they heard the sound of a throat clearing.

<Not to worry,> Kodi sent. *<He's down on Godel with Charley.>* There was an awkward pause, followed by, *<Oh, uh, don't mind me. I was just leaving. I'll be sure to set your status on the net to Do Not Disturb while I'm at it.>*

Terrance grinned as Khela rolled her eyes.

<Thanks, pal,> he sent privately as he pulled her down toward him once again.

<No worries. I've been meaning to catch up on a bit of reading anyway….>

THE END

* * * * *

Jason and Terrance have one more mission to complete before their return to Alpha Centauri.

Reports from Sirius speak of atrocities by the Sirian Hegemony, committed against AI and human alike.

Don't miss the fifth and final installment in the Enfield Genesis series, where the crew of the *Avon Vale* fly once more into the breach to free the oppressed. Grab ***Sirius*** now!

THE BOOKS OF AEON 14

Keep up to date with what is releasing in Aeon 14 with the free Aeon 14 Reading Guide.

The Sentience Wars: Origins (Age of the Sentience Wars – w/James S. Aaron)
- Books 1-3 Omnibus: Lyssa's Rise

- Book 1: Lyssa's Dream
- Book 2: Lyssa's Run
- Book 3: Lyssa's Flight
- Book 4: Lyssa's Call
- Book 5: Lyssa's Flame

Legends of the Sentience Wars (Age of the Sentience Wars – w/James S. Aaron)
- Volume 1: The Proteus Bridge
- Volume 2: Vesta Burning

Enfield Genesis (Age of the Sentience Wars – w/Lisa Richman)
- Book 1: Alpha Centauri
- Book 2: Proxima Centauri
- Book 3: Tau Ceti
- Book 4: Epsilon Eridani
- Book 5: Sirius (April 2019)

Origins of Destiny (The Age of Terra)
- Prequel: Storming the Norse Wind
- Prequel: Angel's Rise: The Huntress (available on Patreon)
- Book 1: Tanis Richards: Shore Leave
- Book 2: Tanis Richards: Masquerade
- Book 3: Tanis Richards: Blackest Night
- Book 4: Tanis Richards: Kill Shot

The Intrepid Saga (The Age of Terra)
- Book 1: Outsystem

- Book 2: A Path in the Darkness
- Book 3: Building Victoria

- The Intrepid Saga Omnibus – *Also contains Destiny Lost, book 1 of the Orion War series*

- Destiny Rising – *Special Author's Extended Edition comprised of both Outsystem and A Path in the Darkness with over 100 pages of new content.*

The Warlord (Before the Age of the Orion War)
- Books 1-3 Omnibus: The Warlord of Midditerra

- Book 1: The Woman Without a World
- Book 2: The Woman Who Seized an Empire
- Book 3: The Woman Who Lost Everything

The Orion War
- Books 1-3 Omnibus (includes Ignite the Stars anthology)

- Book 1: Destiny Lost
- Book 2: New Canaan
- Book 3: Orion Rising
- Book 4: The Scipio Alliance
- Book 5: Attack on Thebes
- Book 6: War on a Thousand Fronts
- Book 7: Precipice of Darkness
- Book 8: Airtha Ascendancy
- Book 9: The Orion Front (2019)
- Book 10: Starfire (2019)
- Book 11: Race Across Spacetime (2019)
- Book 12: Return to Sol (2019)

Building New Canaan (Age of the Orion War – w/J.J. Green)
- Book 1: Carthage
- Book 2: Tyre
- Book 3: Troy
- Book 4: Athens

Tales of the Orion War
- Book 1: Set the Galaxy on Fire
- Book 2: Ignite the Stars
- Book 3: Burn the Galaxy to Ash (2019)

Perilous Alliance (Age of the Orion War – w/Chris J. Pike)
- Book 1-3 Omnibus: Crisis in Silstrand

- Book 1: Close Proximity
- Book 2: Strike Vector
- Book 3: Collision Course
- Book 4: Impact Imminent
- Book 5: Critical Inertia
- Book 6: Impulse Shock

Rika's Marauders (Age of the Orion War)
- Book 1-3 Omnibus: Rika Activated

- Prequel: Rika Mechanized
- Book 1: Rika Outcast
- Book 2: Rika Redeemed
- Book 3: Rika Triumphant
- Book 4: Rika Commander
- Book 5: Rika Infiltrator
- Book 6: Rika Unleashed
- Book 7: Rika Conqueror

Non-Aeon 14 Anthologies containing Rika stories
- Bob's Bar Volume 2
- Backblast Area Clear

The Genevian Queen (Age of the Orion War)
- Book 1: Rika Rising (2019)
- Book 2: Rika Coronated (2019)
- Book 3: Rika Reigns (2019)

Perseus Gate (Age of the Orion War)

Season 1: Orion Space
- Episode 1: The Gate at the Grey Wolf Star
- Episode 2: The World at the Edge of Space
- Episode 3: The Dance on the Moons of Serenity
- Episode 4: The Last Bastion of Star City
- Episode 5: The Toll Road Between the Stars
- Episode 6: The Final Stroll on Perseus's Arm
- Eps 1-3 Omnibus: The Trail Through the Stars
- Eps 4-6 Omnibus: The Path Amongst the Clouds

Season 2: Inner Stars
- Episode 1: A Meeting of Bodies and Minds
- Episode 2: A Deception and a Promise Kept
- Episode 3: A Surreptitious Rescue of Friends and Foes
- Episode 4: A Victory and a Crushing Defeat
- Episode 5: A Trial and the Tribulations (2019)
- Episode 6: A Deal and a True Story Told (2019)
- Episode 7: A New Empire and An Old Ally (2019)
- Eps 1-3 Omnibus: A Siege and a Salvation from Enemies

Hand's Assassin (Age of the Orion War – w/T.G. Ayer)
- Book 1: Death Dealer
- Book 2: Death Mark (2019)

Machete System Bounty Hunter (Age of the Orion War – w/Zen DiPietro)
- Book 1: Hired Gun
- Book 2: Gunning for Trouble
- Book 3: With Guns Blazing

Fennington Station Murder Mysteries (Age of the Orion War)
- Book 1: Whole Latte Death (w/Chris J. Pike)
- Book 2: Cocoa Crush (w/Chris J. Pike)

Vexa Legacy (Age of the FTL Wars – w/Andrew Gates)
- Book 1: Seas of the Red Star

The Empire (Age of the Orion War)

- Book 1: The Empress and the Ambassador (2019)
- Book 2: Consort of the Scorpion Empress (2019)
- Book 3: By the Empress's Command (2019)

The Sol Dissolution (The Age of Terra)
- Book 1: Venusian Uprising (2019)
- Book 2: Scattered Disk (2019)
- Book 3: Jovian Offensive (2019)
- Book 4: Fall of Terra (2019)

ABOUT THE AUTHORS

Lisa Richman lives in the great Midwest, with three cats, a physicist, and a Piper Cherokee. She met the physicist when she went back to get her master's in physics (she ended up marrying the physicist instead).
When she's not writing, her day job takes her behind the camera as a director/producer.

If she's not at her keyboard or on set, she can be found cruising at altitude. Or helping out the physics guy with his linear accelerator. Or feeding the cats. Or devouring the next SF book she finds.

* * * * *

Michael Cooper likes to think of himself as a jack-of-all-trades (and hopes to become master of a few). When not writing, he can be found writing software, working in his shop at his latest carpentry project, or likely reading a book.

He shares his home with a precocious young girl, his wonderful wife (who also writes), two cats, a never-ending list of things he would like to build, and ideas…

Find out what's coming next at www.aeon14.com

Made in the USA
Coppell, TX
28 December 2019

13844570R00162